I0780581

That's What Friends Are For

By Tabatha Shipley

eBook 979-8-9880129-9-3
Paperback 979-8-9880129-8-6

Tabatha Shipley Books

Because of the dynamic nature of the Internet, any web addresses or links contained in this book may have changed since publication and may no longer be valid.

For information, email tabatha@tabathashipleybooks.com

Also by Tabatha Shipley

Kingdom of Fraun Novels
Breaking Eselda
Redeeming Jordyn
Training Tutor
Empowering Sawchett
Tin's Tale and other stories of Fraun
Kingdom of Fraun (omnibus)

Stand Alone Novels
30 Days Without Wings
Projection
A Spark of Magic
Noises from the Other Side
How to Schedule a Death
In Trust We Fall
Darkest Fears

Welcome

The story you're about to enter into is like nothing I've ever written before. Nothing in this story is fantastical, magical, or paranormal. No one is trying to kill anyone. It reads like a true story. It takes place in the late 1990's on an ordinary high school campus somewhere in Arizona.

Wait, I hear some of you saying, you went to an ordinary Arizona high school in the late 1990's. Is this a true story?

No, it's not. This story is a work of fiction.

I'm sure there were kids named Becca, Kate, Scott, Brandon, or Frank in my high school. I even knew a few kids with names similar to those.

But these are not those kids. These are not their stories. I'm not Becca. Sure, there are shadows of all of us in these characters, but we're not them. These aren't our stories. This one is entirely made up. If it seems real, that just means I did my job.

So, buckle up, turn the page, and find yourself solidly in the past. In an Arizona high school in 1995 with Becca Griffiths, a freshman who is about to discover a lot about friendship.

Chapter 1

Standing on the precipice of her high school career, Becca Griffiths was sure she knew a little about a lot of things. She knew how to play the flute, she knew algebra, she knew how to write an essay that would please even her tough old language arts teacher, and she knew what it felt like to move across the country and restart her life in a new state. There were also things she thought she knew a bit about but couldn't quite put into words, like friendship and love. Those were the things Becca secretly hoped to learn more about in high school by living her best life. How many times had she seen high school depicted in movies or television shows? The way she figured, if high school was half as exciting as it had been made out to be, she was in for some excellent experiences.

Behind her, Kate shifted. Becca's arms floated up to maintain her balance. The two girls were propping each other up, back-to-back, and listening to the radio sing a new song. Becca closed her eyes, convincing herself the sounds of the country music were amplified that way. Country music was not something she had listened to much of when she lived back east. Kate had introduced her to the genre the first summer she lived here. That was back when Kate was a flat-chested, awkward, cowboy-hat-wearing tomboy just ready to enter fifth grade. Becca had loved her right away. Really, Kate was kind of like country music. She'd never heard of it before, but she couldn't help but be charmed by it quickly.

The song ended and Becca felt the pressure of Kate's back slowly pull away. She opened her eyes and turned to face her friend, who was reaching to turn down the dial on the old-fashioned radio in Becca's room. "I don't know, maybe I'm outgrowing Kenny," Kate said.

"It's only one song. Give the album a chance," Becca offered. Sure, the song wasn't great. But the radio DJs talked about Kenny Chesney like he was a legend to be admired. Maybe it was the kind of song you needed to listen to more than once before you totally fell in love with it. "Anyway, Frank gave me a tape he said we should listen to. It's not country music, but it's new." Becca reached under her bed for the black shoebox she kept loaded with cassette tapes. Right there on the top was the new one. White background, pink tinted image of a woman's face, and blue smoke wavering around her mouth. It was the coolest cassette cover Becca had ever seen.

She handed it to Kate, who was closer to the tape deck. Kate peered down at it, a small smile teasing the corners of her mouth. "Look at her perfect little nose. I want that nose." Kate put a hand up to her nose, which she was forever lamenting about. Becca didn't see a problem with Kate's nose. Of course, Becca didn't often see things the way Kate did, although she tried to.

Kate tilted her head in confusion. "Alanis? What does that mean?"

Becca leaned closer, looking at the tape upside down. "That's her name. The album is called Jagged Little Pill." She tapped the words in the bottom corner.

Kate shrugged. "Let's give it a try." She slipped the tape out of the plastic cover and into the tape deck. Then she hit play, closed her eyes, and let the music ring out. By the end of the song, both girls had wide eyes. "That's intense," Kate said. She turned the knob to the left, reducing the noise. "All I really want," she said, stealing the lines from the first song on the tape, "is to figure out the perfect outfit for the first day of school."

Becca laughed and crossed to her closet, pulling the white

panel back to reveal the contents. "Are you borrowing something from me?"

Kate moved to stand next to Becca, leaning her head on Becca's shoulder as they both peered at the small selection of shirts, shorts, and jeans on display. Becca owned three dresses, but all of them were stored on the other side of the closet. Were dresses good "first day of school" fodder? Becca wondered.

Kate picked her head up and pulled her hair off her neck. She frowned at Becca. "I wish we had something more to work with for the first day," she said.

"We could always hit up the thrift store," Becca offered. "I can ask my Mom to take us tonight."

"No, that's not what I mean. I wish I had more to work with. More than ..." Kate pulled on a clump of her brown hair. "Brown hair of average length, boring brown eyes ..." She rolled her eyes as if to emphasize them. Then she tugged on the shirt hanging from her thin frame. "... not enough chest for a decent bra ..." She waved her hand down the rest of her body. "... hand-me-down size five jeans, and ..." She propped her hand on her hip. "... absolutely no butt."

Becca shook her head immediately. "Kate, that's ridiculous." She grabbed Kate's shoulders, spun her around to face the mirror, and quickly closed the closet door. She swallowed hard, fighting the urge to look at her own reflection. She knew what she'd see—too tall, too awkward, too much of everything. The very things she was trying to push away, just like Kate.

"You're beautiful," Becca said, trying to believe it. She caught Kate's eye in the mirror. "There's nothing wrong with you."

But Kate didn't look convinced. She turned away, fiddling with her hair again, her lips pursed in disappointment.

"Beauty is on the inside," Becca added, sounding like she was quoting a well-worn cliché. She wasn't sure if it worked, but it was something she thought people were supposed to say.

Kate didn't respond at first, but her eyes softened. "I know," she said quietly. Her voice cracked just a bit. "But maybe the outside can be better, too. You know?"

Becca felt a tightness in her chest. She nodded, though she couldn't say she agreed. Maybe Kate needed more than words, but Becca didn't know how to fix it, how to give her something more than just empty reassurance. She thought for a moment. "Your body will probably change this year anyway. In six months, you might not even recognize yourself."

In the mirror Becca watched Kate's brows shoot up. "That's true." Kate cupped her small breasts in her hands. "These should get bigger." She fingered the tips of her hair brushing her chin. "This could lighten in the sun." She smiled, evidently satisfied again.

Becca stepped back, feeling a small surge of relief as the tension between them lifted. Kate turned to face her. "You're the best, Beck," she said, a teasing grin on her lips. "Always there to remind me of what matters. You're my best friend for a reason."

Becca smiled faintly, the warmth of the compliment filling her chest. But something nagged at the back of her mind. It was the same feeling she'd had before, when Kate would talk about their appearance as if it was the only thing that mattered. Sometimes Becca worried she was the only thing keeping them grounded in the things that really mattered.

"We should dye our hair." Kate's said suddenly, cutting through Becca's musings.

"What? Why?" She didn't know if she was ready to go along with whatever idea Kate had next. She had barely come to terms with the idea of changing something as simple as her clothes.

Kate gave her an exaggerated sigh, her tone filled with playful impatience. "It's like I said. We're going to change this year, right? Might as well speed it up."

Becca felt trapped, a small thrill of unease creeping into her stomach. "I don't think —"

"It's either hair dye or we stuff our bras, Beck." Kate tilted her head, giving off an air of patience as if she would wait all day for this decision. Then she contrasted that by tapping her toe on the carpet.

Becca felt trapped. Part of her knew this gauntlet was figurative. Kate didn't need her to do these wild things. She was perfectly capable of doing them all on her own. Kate wasn't really asking for her approval. She was challenging her to keep up, to be part of her world, no matter how wild it was.

But Becca was curious, too. Would she be more... seen if she changed something, even something small? "Maybe I could try going one shade lighter," she said, testing the waters, her voice barely above a whisper.

Kate squealed, throwing her arms around Becca. "You're the best! I knew you'd come around!" She pulled back, eyes shining with excitement. "Promise you'll ask your mom? Promise?"

Becca didn't necessarily believe that her hair color would make a difference. It wasn't like she hoped she would suddenly be a beauty worth putting on the cover of a magazine if her hair were more honey-colored than walnut. It was just that this seemed like one thing she could control, one thing that she could get just the way she wanted before school started.

She smiled at Kate. "I promise," she said. She held out her pinkie and Kate wrapped it up with her own.

"This is going to be the best year ever," Kate squealed.

Becca smiled, but her heart wasn't fully in it. She hoped Kate was right.

Chapter 2

The idea of starting high school terrified Becca. Junior high had been hard enough, with the school dances that were supposed to be fun and the cliques that were supposed to be cool. Becca never really had a desire to be a part of those groups. She liked her band friends who were perfectly content to talk about music, old and new. She liked the friends from her neighborhood who were as likely to show up at her door unannounced to play basketball as they were to call her up and invite her to come over and watch a movie. She didn't feel like she was missing out on anything. Kate, however, seemed to feel like they were. Kate was always telling Becca that there was more to life, things that other kids were experiencing without them. Kate insisted that high school would be the perfect time to start over and fit in right from the beginning. "First impressions are everything," had sort of become Kate's motto.

That's why, as Becca stood on the sidewalk outside the enormous building labeled *Auditorium*, waiting for freshman orientation to begin, she felt like she was going to be sick. She wasn't the only kid her age standing around on the edge of campus, but Becca wasn't paying attention to anyone else. She was doing everything she could to avoid looking at any one person for too long. As if by not looking, she could somehow erase the feeling of being out of place.

Instead, she focused on her knockoff skater shoes, purchased from the local discount store this summer. She hoped no one else would notice they were *not* name-brand. Actually, Becca supposed she should be glad Kate had declared she was too cool for orientation. Kate would be the first person to make fun of the sneakers. Sure, she'd be "only teasing" or "just saying" but she'd say it loud enough for others to hear. Maybe others who wouldn't only be teasing when they picked up on the jokes.

Kate lived about two hundred feet from Becca's house, directly across the street. She was the first person Becca met when her family moved to Arizona the summer before fifth grade. Kate had wandered right up to the front door and introduced herself before the boxes were even unpacked. She'd stayed all day, helped find homes for things, and the girls had made fast friends. She'd even had dinner with them that night before helping to hook up the television and VCR so she could join all of them on the floor to watch a movie in the new house. They laughed at all the jokes together and shared large bowls of popcorn between the four of them. It was a core memory and Becca had a soft spot for Kate because of it. Kate was the friend who showed up when Becca most needed one, and she'd never left.

Becca risked a look at the assembled students, one just long enough to see if anyone looked as nervous as she felt. She worried she would be the only one who didn't know where anything was at the new school. She had clear visions of being the only student wandering this large campus on the first day, hopelessly lost among classroom numbers that didn't make sense. Of course, that was ridiculous. All of the students gathered here must be in the same situation. They were all here to learn the campus to avoid being lost on the first day of school. Surely every freshman didn't find themselves in Kate's situation, with two older siblings who had already attended the school. Surely any students who were in that situation would've chosen, like Kate, to stay home and enjoy an extra day of summer. Becca assured herself that the students waiting for the Auditorium to open must be more like her than Kate, at least as far as their comfort on a new campus must be concerned.

"You must be nervous."

Becca's head jerked up at the sound of the voice. She recognized it immediately.

Frank's familiar grin spread across his face as he took a few steps closer. His dirty blonde hair was pushed back from his face like he'd run his fingers through it after sleeping and decided that was "good enough." His brown eyes, always sparkling as if he were ready to laugh, crinkled at the corners when he smiled. Without thinking, Becca's lips tugged into a smile too.

"I didn't know you were coming today," she said, almost a little too relieved.

Frank shrugged, casual as ever. "Of course. You think I want to be wandering around this place on the first day of school trying to find my locker? If I do that, I may as well have a sign around my neck that says *freshman*." He winked. "Plus, I hear this is a good time to sign up for next week's freshman band camp."

Becca blinked at him, then laughed, feeling a small wave of relief. "Band camp, huh? Guess I should've thought of that. It's not like I want to look like I have no idea what I'm doing."

Frank snorted. "Right? That's how you get lost before school even starts. Gotta look like you belong." He bumped her shoulder lightly, and she couldn't help but feel a little bit better.

Frank and Becca had met in their junior high school band. Although he played a brass instrument, trombone, and she a woodwind, flute, they had become friends quickly. Both had auditioned before the band director of the high school already and earned spots in both marching and concert bands. Becca received a letter in the mail last week telling her that she had been placed into the intermediate band instead of advanced. It was something she hoped was an error. She also hoped it wouldn't be difficult to correct. Band was something she took pride in being good at. Plus, as the first chair flute player of her junior high band, she had expected to be in the advanced class. It kind of stung that she wasn't. She wondered if Frank was in the same predicament but decided she didn't feel like talking about it.

"How did you get here?" Becca asked, hoping to avoid the discussion about which band class she'd been scheduled for. She craned her neck to see the parking lot behind Frank, looking for a glimpse of the battered pickup truck his mother drove.

"Walked." Frank shrugged.

Becca's eyes widened. Frank lived just down the street from Kate and Becca, in the kind of apartments her parents told her to avoid going to at night. According to Frank, that was the right attitude. You simply didn't go there unless you had a reason to be there and, even then, you avoided going outside alone. She turned her attention away from the parking lot and back to her friend's face. "We live a mile away from here. How long did it take you?" Technically, he would be a little closer to the school than Becca's house. Still, it was a long enough distance for Becca to think walking every day seemed unreasonable.

"It's not too bad, actually." Frank bumped her shoulder with his. "You're probably going to have to walk it with me, you know."

It was true that when school resumed it would be awkward for her parents to get her to campus in the morning since they both worked in the opposite direction. It was also true that Becca hadn't considered this. "You're planning on walking every day?" she asked.

"Twice a day. I have to get home, you know." He pointed back in the direction of her house. "It honestly wasn't bad. Let me sell you on it." He held up his hand, ticking off the reasons on his fingers. "One: it's good practice for marching band. Two: I have to walk anyway and you can keep me company. Three: it'll seem faster with someone to talk to. Four ..." He bunched up his nose. "Shoot, I don't actually have a fourth reason. Did I convince you with three?"

Becca laughed. "Tell you what, we'll both sign up for freshman band camp and I'll test out walking with you in this heat for those days."

"Deal." Frank offered his hand like he was extending a contract.

Becca hesitated for only a heartbeat before signaling her agreement by shaking his hand even as she rolled her eyes at his exuberance.

Frank moved to stand shoulder-to-shoulder with Becca, looking at the Auditorium. He checked his watch. "We still have three minutes. Do you think this is everyone?" He leaned back a little and checked out the crowd around them.

Becca let her gaze drift over the others waiting around them. With Frank beside her, the nervous energy in her stomach settled a little bit. She found it easier to look at everyone around them, sizing them up. She'd never felt comfortable in a big crowd before, but Frank made it easier. It didn't hurt that she already knew Frank was "cool." He'd had friends from junior high, he was always invited to things, and his presence here at orientation only reassured her that it wasn't some kind of uncool move to show up. "Kate's sister said there are three hundred kids in her graduating class. This cannot be everyone."

"How is Miss Kate today?" Frank asked. "Why isn't she here? She is going to this school with us, yes?"

Becca bit her lip, trying to decide how best to answer that. Frank was like an older brother to Becca and Kate was Becca's best friend. So it made things difficult for Becca when they judged each other, which they seemed to always be doing. In the beginning, she had tried to get them to talk to each other and make friends. That proved to be futile so now she usually just avoided talking about them as much as possible in front of each other. "She's fine. She's been here enough times for her sister's events. She felt like she knew her way around."

Frank nodded his understanding. But Becca could tell his jaw was clenched around something he wasn't saying. Really she had two choices. Encourage him to say whatever was on his mind, which was probably something negative about Kate, or change the topic and let him get over it.

Becca was prepared to select option two and change the subject. Instead, she watched him relax his shoulders and put his smile back on. "Hey, what's with the new hair color? It's changed, right?"

Becca smiled. Her mother had allowed the change on two conditions: it had to be done at home with over-the-counter box hair dye and it had to be a natural shade that wasn't too different from her previous color. Against Kate's suggestions, which were based solely on magazine models, Becca opted for something a few shades darker. "You can tell?" Becca asked.

"It's darker, right?"

"A little." Becca shrugged. "Kate's is a lot lighter. Everyone will notice." She cleared her throat. "Hey, have you ever been here before? Like, on campus?"

"Nope." He tipped his head back to look at the sky for a brief second. "That's why we're here, right? Let's get our first glimpse of this massive campus together."

"Let's do it," Becca agreed.

As if the universe had been waiting for that cue, the doors to the Auditorium swung open and three people stepped out onto the top step. The tallest of the three, a male wearing a polo shirt with the mascot of the school emblazoned on his chest, spoke up loud enough to be heard by all the assembled students. "Welcome to high school. Who wants a tour?"

Chapter 3

The night before the first day of high school was Becca's mother's night to make dinner. In their family of three, they rotated this chore. Becca had been a solid part of the rotation since she entered junior high and started showing an interest in cooking. The first year she solely cooked supervised meals that required boxed or jarred ingredients. Then she graduated to use of the "kid's cookbook" her mother found at a yard sale. By now she was allowed free reign in the kitchen.

Becca consulted the calendar hanging beside the garbage can in the kitchen again, hoping that maybe she had remembered incorrectly. The little square had her mother's careful handwriting in bright blue pen denoting that it was MOM who would be cooking tonight. Becca hadn't remembered wrong. That meant Becca would have to find other ways to occupy her brain to keep from overthinking everything about tomorrow. She picked up her favorite paperback book and settled into a chair, hoping to completely immerse herself in the world of shapeshifting panthers. The book worked its magic and Becca lost track of time, having to be tapped back into reality by her father when dinner was ready.

Dinner provided a good distraction from thinking about school for a few minutes as everyone got their first bites of fresh vegetables and pasta. Then, it was mentioned. "Are you excited about school tomorrow?" her mother asked.

Becca nodded. "Yeah, sure."

"Have you met anyone at the freshman things this week?" her dad asked.

Freshman band camp had introduced her to a lot of people. Most of them were other band members—freshmen and upperclassmen alike. Becca felt a little better about tomorrow after the few days of practice, but she wasn't sure if she was ready for the real thing. Still, she figured she'd at least look like she belonged.

"A few," she said, taking another bite of her pasta. "I met the band director, the drum majors, and some of the other first-year woodwinds. Everyone seems nice. We learned some of the marching techniques, so I won't look like a complete idiot tomorrow."

Her mom shot her dad a look—one of those silent exchanges that Becca had learned to ignore. It wasn't just the "she's being strange" look; there was something deeper in it, something that always made Becca uncomfortable. The way her mom looked at her like she was an alien a little outside of the orbit she was supposed to be in.

Becca swallowed the bite in her mouth. She didn't want them to ask more questions. She could already feel them circling. She needed to offer more information. "The high school pulls from three different junior high schools, so there are a lot of people I didn't know before. But yeah, everyone seems okay. I mean, I haven't met *everyone*, but at least the band people are welcoming."

Her dad nodded. "Sounds like you've got a good start."

Her mom smiled faintly, but her eyes stayed distant.

To avoid the silence, Becca jumped up to clear the table, eager to keep moving. According to the schedule, it was her turn to wash the dishes anyway.

The kitchen and dining room were one big room in their small ranch-style house, with a counter separating the two areas. Becca could hear her parents talking softly as she washed. The sound of their voices was like background noise, a lullaby she half-listened to while she scrubbed the plates. Her dad grabbed the drying towel from the rack and joined her, his movements automatic.

"Looks like you're almost out of space there," he said, his hands brushing past her to grab a dish and start drying just as Becca reached for the last of the pans. She stepped back to give him room. He liked to help, and she was grateful for it. But sometimes, his attempts to make things easier felt like he was taking control of things she'd already handled.

She finished the last of the dishes, wiped the counter down, and hung the rag back on the faucet.

"Wanna shoot some hoops?" he asked.

Basketball was not Becca's favorite game. Really, sports weren't Becca's style. But her father had played as a teenager and it was absolutely his favorite game. Add that to the fact that Becca's height, at a little over five feet and nine inches, was unusual for girls and you realize why basketball was mentioned around her a lot. When the family moved to Arizona, her father had installed a hoop over their garage and promptly began teaching Becca how to shoot. He was never pushy and they always had fun with it. So, even though Becca never intended to play for a team, she was always up for shooting hoops with her dad. "I'll get the ball," she answered.

They dribbled around, taking practice shots and cheering each other on for about ten minutes before Kate showed up. "Two on one?" Kate asked as she jogged up the driveway, holding her hands out for the ball.

Becca's dad bounced the ball to her and held his hands up in the guarding stance he'd tried to teach the girls. "Bring it on," he said.

It wasn't long before the score was four to one in favor of her father. Becca was pretty confident he'd let them score their single point. He'd let Becca dribble right past him, a skill she was sure she didn't possess. Then he'd pretended to have trouble getting to her before she took a shot he probably thought she would miss.

Despite that one point, this was not going well. The girls needed reinforcements if they had any hope of winning tonight.

As Kate dribbled up toward the hoop, Becca checked her watch. 6:48. Usually they could count on Frank to walk by any time now, checking to see if there was a game going on in her driveway. Ignoring the game for a second, she turned around to check. Sure enough, she could see a person walking up the street toward her house.

"Frank's on his way," she called.

Her father blocked Kate's shot, grabbed the ball, and headed back toward Becca to clear it at the end of the driveway. "Good, he can be on my team."

"What?" Kate yelled. "No way, we're getting killed here. He's on our team." She leaned over, putting her hands on her knees and gasping for breath. "Becca, you cover your Dad. I need a break." She moved to the grass in the front yard, beside the driveway, and flopped down.

Becca scrunched her eyes in confusion. "Why would you need a break already? We just ..." she trailed off, realizing one reason Kate may be thinking of taking a break. Joe. The boy Kate declared was "adorable" who lived at the end of the street. Sometimes he would come by when they were playing basketball and join in on the game. Last year after a game he'd referred to Kate as a "tomboy". She hadn't wanted to play in front of him since. "Boys will never see a tomboy as a viable dating option," was her explanation.

Becca took a defensive stance in front of her Dad. He tried to dribble around her and she stepped into his path. She was pretty sure he was moving slowly to let her stop him. She reached for the ball, knocking it loose. When she grabbed it, she wrapped her arms around it and held on. "Let's wait for Frank and Joe and redo the teams," she said.

"I'm getting water," her dad said. He walked to the side of the house, turned on the hose, and took a big drink from the end. "Anyone else?" he called, holding up the hose so the water ran in the dirt on that side of the driveway.

Becca rolled her eyes and shook her head. She never understood why the boys couldn't be bothered to go inside and get a glass like civilized people. Frank, noticing the game was paused, jogged to close the gap. "Whose team am I on?" he asked.

"Mine," Dad called.

"We hadn't decided," Becca said at the same time. She bounced the ball to Frank. "I don't care as long as it's not all of you boys against me."

"What about Kate?" Frank asked. He looked down at Kate, flopped on the lawn Becca's father spent so much time and effort maintaining in the desert sun. "Aren't you playing?"

"No, I think I'll just be a cheerleader tonight."

As if that was his cue, which Becca supposed it sort of was, Joe jogged up. "Got room for one more?" he asked.

"The more, the merrier," Dad answered.

The teams were divided, Becca and Frank would take on Joe and Dad.

Despite Frank's best efforts, their team still lost ten to seven.

As the boys lined up at the hose to rehydrate, Becca flopped down beside Kate. She let herself fall all the way back so she could look up at the stars. Of course, in the overly-populated and smog-infested valley, there weren't too many stars to see. Becca had to let her eyes adjust before even the major ones came into focus.

"You're all sweaty," Kate whined.

Becca reached over and moved her ponytail off Kate's arm. "Sorry," she said. "That comes with the physical exertion of getting my butt kicked, I suppose."

"It was closer than it would've been if I played," Kate said.

Becca heard footsteps and tilted her head up to see who had crossed the driveway. Joe was looking down on them. "Hi Kate," he said like he had just noticed she was here.

"Hi," she turned up her full-wattage smile. Becca rolled her eyes and dropped her head back down into the grass. "Are you excited about starting school tomorrow?" Kate asked. "High school classes are supposed to give you more of an academic challenge. Plus, the girls should be cuter."

This, Becca knew, was Kate pushing. Joe was interested in higher-level academics, he talked about school all the time. He seemed to enjoy learning. His favorite class, apparently, was math. But when Kate mentioned girls, she was fishing for a compliment. With some boys, this worked. With Joe, it never did. Becca braced herself for a damaging blow to Kate's ego.

"I guess. I'm excited about the advanced algebra. I made it into the 1-4 course, so I'll be on track to get college credit before I graduate if I can just keep a good grade."

Becca picked her head up. "I'm in that class too."

"Yeah? Right on." Joe smiled at her.

Becca quickly dropped her head back to the ground before she had to give too much thought to that smile. The smile was cute. The smile made her heart flutter, just a little. But even that little was more than she could let it flutter because Kate had dibs on Joe.

She really hoped Kate hadn't seen that smile.

Chapter 4

So far, the first day of school had gone surprisingly well. Becca and Frank had walked to school early enough for the morning marching band practice where she'd met her entire squad. Most of them seemed nice enough. Then, because she was one of the few people who were in intermediate band later in the day instead of in the first period advanced class, Becca had changed quickly and practically ran out the door to her own first period.

So far she had survived beginning Spanish, physical education, and the first fifty-eight minutes of honors English. She'd had exactly one class with Kate, PE. So far, that was the only class that housed anyone she knew from junior high at all. There were people she recognized and a few names called during roll that sounded familiar. But none of the face and name combinations did anything for her memory. She was going to have to make new friends, like it or not.

The bell rang to signal the start of lunch. Becca was shocked to realize she was actually hungry. When she'd first opened the schedule that was mailed to her house this summer, she hadn't expected an 11:05 lunch to be reasonable. After an entire summer of eating no earlier than 12:15, 11:05 seemed like it was too early to be a real lunch but entirely too late to be breakfast. Of course, the early morning marching band practice probably helped.

Becca quickly zipped her carefully labeled notebooks into

her backpack and joined the crowd already pushing out the door of the classroom. Her eyes caught on Frank emerging from the class immediately next door. She shouted his name and waved. She felt slightly foolish when a few kids laughed. Frank ignored the sniggers and stopped in the middle of the walkway. "Hey there, stranger. How's the morning?"

"Good so far." As soon as she drew up next to Frank he fell into step beside her and together they headed in the direction of the cafeteria. It was strange to Becca how the foot traffic almost seemed to go in all directions at once in high school. In junior high school, although you changed classes frequently, there was always a steady stream of kids moving in the same relative direction especially when you were going to or from lunch. In high school, it turned out, there were always just bodies everywhere and somehow very few people actually seemed to be traveling in the same direction as Becca.

"I can already tell band is going to be my favorite," Frank said. "Hey, speaking of which, how did you end up in a different band class? I thought we'd all be in the same first-period class."

Becca sighed, she should've known she wouldn't be able to avoid this conversation forever. "Um, I'm not sure. He didn't say anything after my audition but intermediate band was on my schedule when it arrived."

"You didn't ask him about it?"

Becca pulled her head back in shock. "Does that sound like something I would do?" she asked.

Frank laughed. "Not really. But you're really good. Maybe it's a mistake."

Becca had been hoping the same thing. In fact, after hearing that the girl who played second chair in their junior high had made advanced band, she had been imagining some crazy scenario where the band director had mixed up the little index card of notes he carefully took while they auditioned this summer. Maybe he thought he had put Becca in the advanced class and her second chair in intermediate. She was, secretly, hoping this would all be cleared up when he saw who sauntered into his intermediate class. That's not what she admitted to Frank, however. "I probably just have a lot of things to learn before I'm ready for that level. I'll learn them and move up." She smiled at him. "It'll be fine."

The two of them turned the corner at the end of the building and the cafeteria came into sight. The cafeteria had been one of the buildings on the freshman orientation tour. They'd been shown the large interior area with carts for food, the patio seating outside, and what can only be described as a concrete bowl set into the ground where the teachers claimed many students chose to eat. But on the day of orientation, the surrounding area contained only the touring freshman and looked staggeringly large. On this first lunch period of the new school year, there were students everywhere and it was the noise that was staggering. Becca blinked back her shock. Every step of the concrete inset area they had made fun of had students sitting, some with lunches and some with open books. The teachers were right. Students voluntarily sat on the ground during lunch.

Inside the cafeteria, the lines for food were long, and the noise seemed to drown everything out. Becca could barely hear Frank when he nodded toward the sandwich line. "I'm going over there."

She followed without a word, not particularly picky about lunch, just glad to have something to eat. The chaos of the cafeteria had her feeling overwhelmed, her eyes darting from one thing to the next.

When Becca finally reached the sandwich counter, she had to shout to be heard. "Turkey, please!" she yelled.

"With everything?" the woman behind the counter yelled back.

"Uh, sure?" Becca said, not having a clue what "everything" entailed but figuring it was easier to agree than to keep shouting.

At the register, she swapped her mom's cash for the

sandwich and turned to see Frank waiting by the door. "Outside?" he yelled.

Becca nodded, grateful to escape the madness. The noise was even louder inside than it had been in the hallway, and she was starting to understand the appeal of the concrete bowl.

Outside they found a couple of round tables with umbrellas on the patio area. Kate was seated at one with an older girl Becca recognized from her PE class that morning. "There's Kate," Becca pointed. "Let's sit there."

Frank didn't argue and they wound their way through the crowd until they were seated beside Kate. "How was your morning?" Kate asked.

"Good so far." Becca unwrapped her sandwich and pulled the sub roll open to see what "everything" had resulted in. She noted lettuce, tomato, pickle, onion, and what was likely mayonnaise. She made a mental note to ask for no mayo tomorrow, put the sandwich back together, and took a bite.

"This is Michelle," Kate said, gesturing to the girl beside her. "She's a sophomore."

Becca swallowed her bite. "I think she's in our PE class." She reached her hand out to Michelle. "It's nice to formally meet you. I'm Becca."

Michelle shook her hand. "I failed PE last year so I'm taking it again. I'll make sure you know how to get through the class."

Becca stopped herself from asking how someone who failed last year would know how to get through the class successfully. That just seemed rude. Instead, she smiled. "Thanks."

Kate beamed. "I already asked her about Joe and Ernie." Her eyebrows danced as she waggled them.

Becca froze with her sandwich halfway to her mouth, her eyes narrowing at Kate. "Ernie? Who's Ernie?" Sure, Kate was always chasing boys. But this seemed like information her best friend should have before anyone else. Suddenly this Michelle person, whom they just met that day, was the first to hear this name? Becca was insulted.

"He's new. He's in my History class." Kate snapped her fingers. "Actually, you probably do know him. He's in all advanced classes, like you."

History. The one advanced class Becca wasn't a part of. Becca swallowed what suddenly felt like an insult to her intelligence, knowing this wasn't about her right now. "What does he look like?"

"He's really hot." Again, Kate's eyebrows waggled. "Hotter than Joe."

Frank, who was already a quarter of the way through his sandwich, cleared his throat. "Is this the Ernie with blonde hair? The one who is friends with Brandon from band?"

Kate smacked her palm on the table between them causing Becca to jump at the sudden noise. "Yes, that's him. Isn't he just the absolute cutest?"

Frank snorted. "Not really my type," he offered. He turned his eyes to Becca. "We met him and Brandon at freshman orientation."

Becca thought back. Brandon had been the trumpet player with brown eyes who was incredibly nice to her. He was the one with an older sibling who went to the school before him. He'd chosen to attend freshman orientation anyway because he wanted to make new friends. Becca had liked him instantly. Ernie, she reasoned, must have been the friend she didn't catch the name of.

"Yeah, I remember," Becca said.

"He's cute, right?" Kate asked.

Becca hesitated. Ernie definitely wasn't her type—too much muscle, too much... *everything* Kate liked. But she didn't want to hurt her best friend's feelings. "He's cute," Becca agreed, not quite meeting Kate's eyes.

Michelle, still watching the conversation with interest, grinned. "He's definitely the better catch, for sure."

Kate and Becca both turned to look at Michelle.

"What?" Becca asked, looking suspicious.

Michelle shrugged, a mischievous smile spreading across her face. "I just think Ernie's way cuter than Joe."

Kate had been all about Joe for as long as Becca had known her. Becca was pretty sure Kate had made it a point to walk her past Joe's house on only Becca's second day in Arizona to explain that he was the best prospect on the street. "I thought you liked Joe because he was nice, not just because he's cute."

Kate groaned. "Becca, you don't get it." She looked sideways at Michelle. "She doesn't get it."

Michelle shrugged. "Whatever."

"So, Becca," Kate started, "who are we going to hook you up with?"

This, apparently, was an interesting topic for Michelle who looked up from her lunch again. In fact, Michelle set her burrito down on the wrapper completely and leaned forward until her elbows were on the table. "What kind of guy do you like?"

Becca felt a slight chill. *Really?* This was what they were doing? She wasn't prepared for this conversation. She liked boys who were not on Kate's radar, because they were inherently safer, but she could've very well say that. "I don't know... smart guys, I guess," she said, uncomfortable.

"Smart is boring," Michelle said dismissively. "You gotta be more specific."

Before Becca could respond, Frank stood up. Becca was the only one who looked at him. He shoved the last of his sandwich into his mouth and audibly gulped it down. "I've got to meet my squad leader," he said. "Don't wanna be late."

"Okay, see you later!" Becca called.

As Frank walked away, Michelle turned her eyes to Becca. "Does he like you?" she asked, raising an eyebrow.

Becca's stomach dropped. "Frank? No. He's like a brother to me." She shrugged, trying to brush it off.

Michelle didn't seem convinced. "Alright. I believe you. What else besides smart since smart is so boring?"

Kate laughed. Becca didn't see the joke. Then Kate's laugh abruptly cut off like it was swallowed. The hairs on Becca's arms stood up. Michelle didn't look as though she thought anything was unusual but Becca knew this was Kate's fake laugh. Something was wrong. Something —

"What about Joe?" Kate asked.

Becca felt her blood run cold. Maybe Kate saw something last night at basketball. That smile did it, Becca knew it. Kate had seen Joe smile at Becca or she had seen on Becca's own face that she liked when he smiled at her. Either way, she was suspicious about Becca's feelings. That meant Becca had exactly two choices here: she could be honest or she could pretend not to know what Kate was hinting at.

She swallowed. "He's cute, I told you that before. I haven't seen him with Ernie, so I can't give you an opinion on who's cuter."

"He's also smart. He's in all those advanced classes, like you." Kate's voice had a strange edge to it, like a challenge.

"Yeah, I guess." Becca forced herself to take a bite of her sandwich, chew, and swallow. Act calm. Kate had dibs on Joe. Becca knew that. She'd known that since her second day in Arizona all those years ago. Nothing had changed. Becca was not, could not be, interested. "I don't get it, are we trying to help you decide?"

"I just want you to admit it," Kate said. "I want you to admit that you kind of like him."

Becca felt like she was trapped under a magnifying glass. She resisted the urge to squirm. Michelle was watching them both like they were a tennis match, looking quickly from one to the other. Becca blinked first and in that instant, she decided to attempt honesty. Her shoulders sagged. "He's cute, Kate. But I swear to you I'm not interested in being his girlfriend or whatever. I've never even thought about it, not really. I know you liked him first." She put her hand out, reaching for Kate, hoping that this wouldn't be the thing that broke them.

Time seemed to stretch out to infinity at that moment with her hand extended across the table as a peace offering. Her heartbeat raced in her chest and she felt like eating had been a huge mistake. Then, Kate smiled and put her hand in Becca's. "Thank you for being honest," Kate said.

Becca sighed with relief. She watched Kate dig into her lunch with what could only be described as excitement. But she pushed her own sandwich away. Somehow, it felt like that had been too close. Kate's temper was a bomb and Becca couldn't shake the feeling that she'd just lit the fuse.

Chapter 5

"Ladies and gentlemen, this project is not something to be taken lightly. It will be ten percent of your overall semester grade." Becca's math teacher walked to the far left-hand side of the room and gave a stack of packets to the person in the front row. Then she moved to the next row, her high heels clicking to announce the path. Again, she handed a stack of stapled packets to the first person in the row.

Becca watched her progress nervously. Those looked like big packets. That likely meant a large project with a lot of components. She could feel sweat breaking out on her upper lip. She needed to do well in this class. The first advanced class of a high school career could set the stage for the right track to the advanced diploma. She needed a good score. She turned her head a little to the side and the bright yellow stars hanging on the wall came into view. She needed one of those stars. Those stars were handed out for perfect scores on tests and major projects. You had to work hard to earn those. Becca wanted one of those stars.

"The project's components are all laid out in that packet, including a presentation and a group cooperation report. I expect you to work with other students for this project, there will be no solo acts for this one. Find yourself at least one other human who you can get along with for the duration of this week-long project." She stopped after handing packets to the final row. Kids in the front were quickly taking their own packets and passing back the stack. The math teacher cleared her throat. "What are we waiting for?" she asked. "Find your partners."

When she clapped her hands the entire class came to life. Becca jumped to her feet but stalled right there. Kate was not in this Algebra class. Everyone else she could think of was in another advanced class period or was not in the advanced course at all. Who was she supposed to work with?

"Hey, partners?"

Becca turned to the voice to find a brunette she recognized from a few of her classes smiling at her. She thought her name was Ellie, but she wasn't entirely sure. "What?"

"Sorry, I didn't mean to startle you. I don't know anyone else in this class and you seem cool. Wanna be partners?"

"Yeah, sure. Totally," Becca replied quickly, trying not to sound too relieved. She held out her hand. "I'm Becca Griffiths."

"Ellie Mackenzie," the girl said, shaking Becca's hand. Then she pulled her desk next to Becca's, flipping open her packet. "This looks... kind of intense," Ellie remarked, scanning the first few lines of the project details.

Becca glanced down at her own packet. It was long, but it didn't look impossible—solve a few problems, do some research, and put everything into a clear visual format. It was detailed, yes, but manageable.

"Yeah, it's pretty detailed," Becca agreed, trying to mask her nerves. She could do this. They could do this. Together.

Suddenly, Ellie looked up from her packet, eyes narrowing slightly. "Hey, quick question—who is Frank?"

Becca froze. Frank. She hadn't really expected anyone to ask about him, especially not so directly. But Ellie wasn't backing down, her gaze still on Becca. "Uh, sorry, what?" Becca's voice caught, and she felt a knot in her stomach.

"Frank," Ellie repeated, a little sheepish. "I was just wondering. You two seem pretty close."

Becca's mind raced. Ellie had asked about Frank. She was probably just curious, but it still made Becca feel a little uneasy. Was this some kind of test? Was Ellie fishing for something?

Ellie frowned. "Sorry, that's not relevant. I'm focused on the project, I swear. Let's start."

Part of Becca wanted to jump back into that conversation. This felt like Ellie trying to reach out, maybe strike up a friendship. Ellie seemed nice and Becca wanted to get along with her.

But, on the other hand, she really needed this project to go well. This was the first major project in an advanced class. She needed a good first impression here. "Yeah, let's focus on this for now. We can come back to that," Becca offered. "I just really need a good grade on this."

"Right. Me too." Ellie pulled a pencil out of her bag and flipped the page in her packet. "I think we start here."

They focused on the project, heads together and pencils flying, until the teacher clapped her hands together to bring everyone's attention to the front of the room. "That's our time for today. Exchange home numbers to complete work at home and pack up your belongings. Due dates are non-negotiable so don't even ask"

Ellie moved her desk back to its original location an aisle over from Becca. Becca began packing her stuff up. Guilt flared in her chest. It must have taken a lot for Ellie to get up the courage to ask her about Frank. Ellie and Becca, although sitting beside each other for a few weeks and seeing each other in some classes, were not friends.

"Hey, Ellie," Becca called, leaning across the aisle. Ellie turned, surprised. "I just wanted to clear that up. Frank's a friend. We've known each other for years. He's like a brother to me, honestly. He's a great guy."

Ellie blinked, then smiled. "I was just curious. No big deal."

Becca smiled back, feeling a weight lift from her shoulders. "Well, if you're ever curious about anything else, feel free to ask. I'm an open book."

Ellie's grin widened. "Thanks. Friends?"

"Friends," Becca agreed, holding out her hand again. She was starting to feel a little better about this whole "partner" thing.

As Becca watched Ellie head for the door, her mind wandered. She hadn't expected this today—not a new partner, not a new connection. But maybe this was a step in the right direction. Ellie seemed like someone she could get along with, and that felt... okay.

Chapter 6

Kate, Becca, and Michelle stood outside the cafeteria in the long line of people dressed in nicer clothes than usual and wearing uncomfortable shoes. The lights above the sunken pit area were all on, casting a yellow glow on everything. The color made the night feel special and somehow different. It changed the entire appearance of the school they had been attending for almost two months. This was the first school dance of the year and the excitement in the air was palpable.

Becca shifted uncomfortably on her heels and tugged at the skirt she had borrowed from Kate. It was too short for her, likely because Kate was about three inches shorter than she was. "Leave it alone," Kate said. She smacked at Becca's hand. "You can't see your butt. You only think you can."

"It's just shorter than I'm used to."

Kate rolled her eyes. "You have great legs. We're using our assets."

Kate's own outfit was not as short. In fact, her skirt reached almost all the way to her knees. Her top, however, was the part of her outfit Becca wouldn't have dared to wear in public. It was really low-cut. Kate was obviously aware her assets were on a completely different part of her body.

Michelle stood beside them in jeans and a long-sleeved shirt.

"Why couldn't I just wear jeans?" Becca asked, tipping her chin at the older girl.

"She has a boyfriend and no one to impress," Kate pointed out.

"Do you have a boyfriend?" Michelle snapped.

Becca shook her head. No, she didn't. They knew that.

The first few weeks of high school had been interesting so far. Becca had found that she enjoyed the challenge of her advanced classes and marching band. She had already proven herself in intermediate band, earning first chair. The director had even told her she was a shoo-in for advanced band next year. She'd made friends with Brandon and walked home with Frank every day. But still, Kate was her best friend. Kate could be counted on when things, like going to the dance without a date, got weird. Becca reached out and hooked elbows with Kate. "Thanks for helping me get ready."

"I'd do anything for you, bestie," Kate said. She winked at her. "Besides, this way my date looks hot with her new hair color." She reached up and fingered a stray lock of hair up near Becca's face.

Becca laughed and slapped Kate's hand away playfully. "Please, it's the same color. I swear I only see a difference in the sunlight and only because I'm looking for it."

"Whatever." Kate rolled her eyes. "You still look hot." She drew out the final word, making Becca laugh again.

Ahead of them, the doors to the cafeteria opened. The girls snapped into line behind Michelle to filter into their first school dance experience. Becca felt the magic instantly and a smile popped onto her face. There was a DJ at the front of the room and music was bumping through speakers set up on stands at intervals around the edges of the cleared room. She could feel the vibrations on the floor. Around the room, the lights had been turned down and bright flashy bulbs were set to bring pops of color. The younger girls squealed with delight and headed immediately for the middle of the floor to dance, their arms and legs moving to the music as they had so many times in Becca's bedroom. Michelle shook her head and wandered off, presumably to find more mature friends.

For the first hour of the dance, the girls remained right there as the crowd of students grew around them. They declared every song their "favorite" and paid little attention to anyone else in the room. They likely would've stayed there all night if it hadn't been for the DJ calling out "Let's slow it down," and turning on something that was only appropriate for a slow dance in the arms of a boy. A boy neither of them brought along.

Becca's eyes widened. "What now?" she asked.

Kate hooked her elbow through Becca's again and steered her friend to the outskirts of the crowded dance floor. The temperature out here was significantly lower. "Let's get a drink," Kate suggested.

The mere idea of liquid made Becca's mouth water. She let herself be led down the little hallway past the bathrooms and into the small vestibule behind the cafeteria. Here, in this room that was usually closed off to students, the girls found a snack table and a photographer. Both booths had long lines. Kate steered Becca into the line for the snack table.

"We absolutely have to find boys to dance at least one of these slow songs with," Kate said as they stepped into the back of the line.

Becca nodded, an absentminded gesture. She actually wasn't paying attention to this conversation. She was scanning the construction paper sign with handwritten prices. She was debating between getting a can of soda or a pouch of juice, both of which were likely to be the healthier options the school offered as opposed to something one might buy out of a vending machine off campus. She turned her head to look at the photo booth. "I didn't know they had photographers here," she said.

Kate turned to look as well. "Let's get pictures."

"How much are they?" Becca remembered that the junior high used to have a teacher with a Polaroid camera take photos for a dollar. She was pretty sure this elaborate setup, with a professional-looking backdrop, lights, and a real photographer, was going to cost her more than that. Her mother had slipped her a ten-dollar bill before she left the house tonight, but that was all the money she had.

"Stay here, I'll go ask." Kate didn't wait for a response before skipping out of line and across the little room. She spent a minute whispering with the lady at the little table beside the photo booth before skipping back, a huge smile on her face. "The standard picture package is ten dollars. I'll go halfsies with you."

"Perfect." The people in front of them took their food from the snack table and stepped out of the way. It was their turn. They stepped up and ordered: a grape-flavored soda for Becca and the closest thing they had to a cola for Kate. They crossed back to the photo table, paid their money, and filled out a little information card with their names and homerooms. Then they set their soda cans, both about half empty, down on the table while they took their pictures.

The photographer took three shots, promising to put the best two poses in the package. For the first one, the girls were back to back with their arms crossed in front of them and sassy looks on their faces. For the second, they were side by side with their opposite hips cocked, hands resting at their waist, and elbows out. For the final, they were cheek to cheek as if caught in a hug.

Both girls headed back to the dance floor without discussion as if the music were pulling on both of their souls, taking them back. Halfway down the hallway, a large trashcan stood waiting for the garbage discarded from the snack bar. Becca and Kate upended their drinks, finishing the last drops, and tossed the aluminum into the garbage. By the time they made their way back into the dark dance room, the faster music was filling the room again and the girls happily took up their places amongst the revelry.

When another slow number was announced, Becca and Kate wandered to the edge of the crowd and stood up against the wall.

Here the air moved a little more. Becca pulled her hair off the back of her neck to feel the temperature difference. "We really need to find people to dance with," Kate whined.

Becca shrugged. "It's not that big of a deal."

Kate's eyes were already moving around the room. "Have you seen Joe, Ernie, or even Frank?" she asked.

Honestly, Becca hadn't even thought about looking for them. This dance had been the most fun she'd had in a long time. The DJ was wonderful, the music was all a fun choice, and the crowd was fired up. The entire floor felt alive out there as if they were all connected by the need to dance. She hadn't once bothered to take stock of who else was here or what they were doing. She was getting lost in the music. She shrugged. "No." Feeling slightly guilty for not thinking of her friends, Becca began looking around for them.

Kate, who was looking in the opposite direction from Becca, made an excited sort of noise. "There's Ernie," she pointed off toward the back of the cafeteria. Becca followed the outstretched finger and found Ernie and Brandon standing together, whispering. It made her smile when she realized that was probably exactly what she and Kate looked like. "Do you think he'd dance with me?" Kate asked. She reached out and grabbed Becca's arm above the elbow. "Oh my gosh, you have to go ask Brandon. You're friends with Brandon, right?"

"I guess," Becca admitted. "We talk at band and stuff. He's nice."

"Right, and Brandon is friends with Ernie. So you have to go ask Brandon to ask Ernie if he will dance with me on the next slow song." She squeezed her hand a little tighter around Becca's arm. "But you absolutely cannot tell him that I told you to ask."

Becca's head whirled around the plan. She didn't really want to go up to the boys. She definitely didn't want to try and convince someone else to dance with Kate. Then again, this seemed like a small thing. Kate wasn't asking for much. "Do you think that will even work?"

"It's the best idea I have." Kate let go of Becca's arm and moved her hand to Becca's upper back. She pushed lightly. "Go do it right now. I'll stand here and act like I have no idea what you're doing."

Becca felt her feet begin moving before she even realized she had agreed to this plan. She wasn't a particularly outgoing person. She normally spoke to the people she had to speak to and that was about it. It took a lot for her to step outside her comfort zone and initiate conversation, even with a friend. She was tempted to turn back around and come up with a better plan.

The boys noticed her when she was about ten steps away. Brandon waved. Ernie leaned in to whisper something. In her head, Becca figured he was probably asking who she was. After all, they'd really only met one time. Brandon leaned down to whisper back. Becca tried to smile.

Then the gap was closed and she was standing in front of them. No turning back now. "Hi," she said. She felt awkward. She was sure she looked awkward. They were probably wondering why she was here. Why hadn't she planned how she would start this conversation?

"Hey Becca," Brandon said. "This is Ernie." He tapped his friend on the shoulder.

Ernie shot a hand out. "Hi."

Becca shook his hand, a gesture which did nothing to make her feel less awkward. Everyone put their hands down and then the three of them just stood there in a weird triangle, all wondering what to say next.

Becca swallowed. "So, um, do you guys know my friend Kate?" She pointed back to Kate who was still standing on the side of the dance floor exactly where Becca had left her. Both boys looked in that direction before snapping their eyes back to Becca as if wondering where this was going.

"Yeah, we've met," Ernie answered.

Becca smiled and felt a swell of excitement in her chest.

Kate would love knowing that Ernie knew who she was. This was good. "Cool. So we're not here with dates and she really likes dancing. I was kind of thinking it might be nice if someone were to ask her to slow dance on the next slow song." She looked pointedly at Ernie. "Maybe one of you could do that?"

The boys exchanged a glance. Becca tried to read their expressions for a clue to what they were communicating. She was so good at reading the little subtleties to Kate's expressions, but she didn't know either of these boys well enough to apply that here. She hoped it was positive.

"Yeah, that's a good idea," Ernie said. "Do you think ..." he shuffled his feet a little and looked down at the floor. Becca knew that one. Ernie was nervous. "Do you think she'd mind dancing with me?" he asked.

Becca smiled really wide. She reached out and laid a reassuring hand on his arm, right above his wrist. Her touch was light and friendly. "I know she would love that." She pulled her hand back and smiled at the boys. "I'll just go back so she doesn't suspect anything. Bye."

She ran back to Kate and relayed the good news, breathlessly. "He absolutely knew who you were. He also looked a little nervous, like maybe he secretly likes you too. He agreed it was a good idea. I think he's gonna do it," she said.

Kate tried to squelch her excitement in case they were watching, but she made a squeaking noise that gave her away. The slow song playing over the speakers came to an end. To Kate's utter delight, another one immediately started. "Oh my gosh, oh my gosh, oh my gosh ..." Kate mumbled.

Becca turned around to look and found Ernie crossing the floor in their direction. "Relax," she whispered to Kate. "It's just a dance. You got this."

Ernie stepped up to them and Becca noticed a blush on both of his cheeks. "Hi, Kate. Would you like to dance?" he asked.

Becca smiled as Kate laid her hand on his arm and the pair

faced each other right there on the very edge of the crowd. She watched a few steps before deciding this was a good chance for her to duck into the bathroom and see just how much damage her dancing and sweating had done to her hair.

By the time Becca had used the restroom, washed her face, fixed her hair, and returned to the dance floor the slow song was over and the fast stuff had returned. At first, she couldn't find Kate. But she decided not to let that bother her. Instead, Becca joined the flow of kids dancing. It wasn't long before she felt Kate at her elbow.

Toward the end of the evening, the DJ announced the final slow song of the evening. Becca moved to the edge of the floor, to the same spot they had been in previously. She started up a search for Ernie, wondering if he would extend the offer to Kate again.

Instead, she came face to face with Joe. He looked irritated, somehow. "Becca, do you want to dance?" he asked. The question didn't sound the same way it had when Ernie had asked Kate. Joe sounded angry.

"Sure," she said. Mostly she agreed out of a desire to find out what was wrong. She'd known him a long time and she'd never heard him this angry.

He led her onto the floor and put his hands on her hips. She put her hands on his shoulders, feeling a little strange. He slowly started moving them from side to side. It wasn't like any kind of formal dance Becca had seen before. Basically, it was just shifting her weight from one foot to the other and back again. "Are you OK?" Becca asked. "You seem tense."

"I'm fine," he snapped.

Becca frowned. This wasn't normal behavior for him, anyone could see that. "You don't seem fine," she said. "We don't have to dance if you don't want to."

"It's fine." He sighed. "This was Kate's idea anyway. This should make her shut up."

Becca's heart skipped a beat. "What?"

Joe's eyes snapped to her face. "Like you don't know."

Becca dropped her hand from his shoulders and took a little step back. Joe's fingers were barely on her hips now. "Honestly, Joe, I have no idea what you're talking about."

"Kate came to me a little while ago and told me I had better ask you to dance. She told me it was important." He shook his head. "It's not that I didn't want to dance with you or whatever, it's just that I'd already told another girl I was saving a dance for her and this is the last one. You heard the DJ."

Becca felt like her stomach was in her shoes. She shook her head. "No. That wasn't supposed to happen. I didn't ask her to. Did you tell her you already had a dance partner?"

"I told her. Then she threatened to show people that picture of me in the dress from that pool party. Do you remember that?"

Becca did remember. Last summer they'd had a party at Kate's. As a joke, Joe had put a sundress of Kate's over his swim trunks. He didn't have it on long, but it was long enough for Kate to snap a picture. She'd hoarded it over him ever since, but usually as a joke. This, clearly, wasn't a joke. Becca nodded weakly.

"Her sister is on the newspaper staff. I'm not saying Kate would give her that picture, but I couldn't risk it. So," he pulled Becca a little closer, angrily. "We're dancing, whatever. Forget about it."

Before Becca could think about what she was doing, she pushed Joe away, hands rising instinctively between them. "I didn't ask her to do that," she repeated, her voice coming out softer than she'd meant. Her chest felt tight, like the air itself had become thicker. She swallowed hard, her throat tightening in an almost painful way. She felt tears start to gather at the corners of her eyes, uninvited. Not now, she told herself. Not here. She blinked the tears back, fighting the urge to fall apart. She wasn't the one who'd messed up. This was on Kate.

Becca gripped the edge of her sleeve, fingernails pressing into her arm, trying to steady herself. "I'll talk to Kate," she said, more forcefully now, even though the words tasted bitter on her tongue. She's the one who needs to fix this. "I'll get that picture from her. I'll straighten this out. Go dance with the girl you wanted to dance with." Her voice wavered at the end, and she hated that it did.

Joe looked at her as if he didn't quite understand why she was so upset. He didn't get it. Becca's eyes burned but she wasn't going to cry over Kate's stupid mistake. She knew she shouldn't be the one who had to fix this but it needed to be fixed.

Becca's mind flashed back to how Kate had practically shoved her into talking to Brandon, into arranging things for Kate without giving Becca a choice. Her stomach twisted. Kate always did things like this. She decided what everyone around her should do and no one, including Becca, ever questioned it.

Her thoughts collided with another, quieter, truth: she didn't want to be the backup. She wanted Joe to want to dance with her. She quickly shoved that thought down. That wasn't the point. This was about respect. This was about Kate screwing up and making things weird for everyone.

Her eyes flicked to Joe, who was already looking away, his attention searching for the other girl. A small pang twisted in her chest. "Good luck with the girl," Becca said, her voice tight. She could feel her breath catching in her throat. With every step she took away from him, her anger toward Kate grew. It felt like a hot knot curling tighter inside her. Each step, each beat of the music vibrating through the floor, turned her frustration into something sharper, more tangible.

It was Kate's fault she felt like this. Becca gritted her teeth. She wasn't going to cry, not for Joe, not for the way things had gone sideways, and certainly not for Kate's selfishness.

Becca had no idea how this would affect her friendship with Joe. She didn't even know what she'd say to him after this, if it ever came up again. But what she did know was that Kate had just ruined any chance she might've had of a real connection with him. Becca could feel the sting of that. It was like a small, hidden crush she'd never voiced, suddenly gone—shattered by Kate's impulsive, reckless need to control everything.

She felt a wave of guilt mix with the anger. She didn't want to be mad at Kate, but it was too late for that. Kate had pushed her too far.

This was Kate's fault. This is all on her.

Chapter 7

The entire ride home, the girls were silent statues each curled into themselves with their eyes fixed out a different window. Becca's mother tried a few times to get them to open up. Each time she received a one-word answer, snapped at her from one girl or another. In the driveway of Becca's house, her mother turned off the car, flung her arm over the back of the bench seat, and faced the girls. "I think you two should stay in this car for a minute until you work out whatever is between you. I'm not sure what happened there, but you'd be surprised at the kind of problems you can solve with a little conversation."

When neither girl moved to get out of the car, she turned back around and grabbed the door handle. She sighed. "Do you need me to stay and mediate?" she asked in a quieter voice. She took the absence of an answer as a refusal of services and let herself out of the car.

The girls remained silent long enough for her to cross to the front door and let herself into the house. Then Kate spoke, softly. "Obviously you're mad. Want to tell me what I did?" Her voice sounded hard, angry.

"What did you say to Joe?" Becca asked without moving her eyes away from the window. In contrast to Kate's knife blade tone, Becca's was soft as a flower petal. She was biting back tears.

"What?" Kate turned her body, putting her right knee up on

the center of the bench so she could fully face Becca. "This is about Joe? I did the same thing I told you to do. I went over and told him to ask you to dance. I did it while you were in the bathroom. I thought it would be a good way to repay you for asking Ernie for me."

Becca sniffled. "What exactly did you say to him?"

Kate scrunched up her nose as if trying to recall. "I said you thought he was cute and told him to ask you to slow dance."

Becca closed her eyes as a wave of embarrassment at the thought of Kate telling Joe she thought he was cute threatened to drown her. She took a deep breath and loudly let it out of her nose. "Then what," she prompted. "What did you say after that?"

"He said he already told some girl he'd dance with her. He said if there was a second slow song after that he would ask."

Becca turned away from the window for the first time. "You told him that was great, right?" she asked, already knowing that, according to Joe, Kate didn't do that. "You told him he should dance with whomever he wants, right? Because I know you wouldn't be cruel enough to force someone to dance with me like some charity case, Kate." A tear slid out of her eye and down her cheek, she swiped at it with the back of her hand.

Kate reached out for her. "Oh my gosh, Beck. You are not a charity case. He's a bozo. Honest. I told him that if he needed to prioritize the two dances, he should give the first spot to you because you've been his friend for a while." Her hand connected with Kate's bare arm and she rubbed her thumb back and forth like you would distractedly pet a cat. "You don't understand. He wasn't going to make the right choice on his own. I was just trying to make things right for you. You know how much you mean to me, right?"

Becca sniffled again. She wanted to believe Kate. She wanted to believe that her friend's intentions were good, that she was only trying to help. But this had been so painful, so embarrassing. "Did you threaten him with that picture again?" Becca asked.

Kate's thumb stalled for just a beat like she had a rest placed between notes in her sheet music. "What picture?" she asked as her thumb resumed its motion.

Becca yanked her arm away. "Don't do that." She shook her head slowly side-to-side. "Don't pretend."

Kate's shoulders slumped, defeated. "I messed up, Becca." Her voice came out quiet, wounded. "I panicked. I wanted to do something nice for you, like you did for me. I wanted him to twirl you around and make you happy. I didn't care how I got it done. I knew it would mean so much to you. Because it meant so much to me that you talked to Ernie, that you got me that dance. I was just trying to return the favor." She turned her watery eyes on Becca. "I messed up. Please forgive me."

"It wasn't great," Becca snapped. "It wasn't magical. Joe didn't want to be dancing with me, he made that perfectly clear."

Kate sat up straighter and leaned closer to Becca. "What did he say? Was he rude to you?"

Becca blinked at the sudden change in Kate's tone. "I don't know." She tried to think back, remember exactly what was said. "No, I don't think so. He just didn't want to be there. He wanted to be dancing with that other girl, but you threatened him."

"I swear to you if he was rude—"

Becca waved her hand, and Kate bit back the rest of the sentence. "He wasn't rude. I just hated making him miserable." Tears fell from both eyes this time. "He obviously doesn't think I'm cute, Kate. He doesn't like me. Not like that."

Kate scooted over on the bench until her hip and Becca's hip were touching. Then she draped her arm across Becca's shoulders. Becca leaned into her and felt the tears increase. "Beck, I'm so sorry. I shouldn't have intervened. It'll be OK, you'll see." Kate continued to murmur little pleasantries while Becca sobbed into her shoulder.

Becca let herself cry until it didn't feel so bad. Until she felt like she could go to school on Monday and face Joe. Until she felt like she could, someday, put this behind her. Maybe.

Finally, out of tears, Becca picked up her head again. "Thanks, Kate."

"For what?" Kate asked. "For causing all this pain?"

Becca chuckled. "No, seriously. Thank you for listening. Thanks for trying to help me feel better. I don't think I was ever really mad at you. I was—" She took a breath, trying to think of a word.

"Hurt," Kate offered.

"—hurt," Becca agreed. "I guess I thought he would feel differently." She shook out her hands. "I don't want to talk about this anymore."

"Good, me neither. I'm going home to get some sleep. I'll see you tomorrow." Kate pushed open her door and stepped out of the car. Then she bent down so her head was in the frame. "Are we cool?" she asked.

Becca considered this. It was possible that Kate had been trying to help. Sure, it had been a huge disaster, but was that really Kate's fault? Besides, Kate was the one who sat right here with her and let her get it all out. She owed it to Kate to at least pretend to let this go, even if it still hurt. She forced herself to smile across the car at her friend. "We're cool."

Kate stood up, slammed the door, and practically skipped across the street in the time it took Becca to get out of the car and shut her own door. She stood in her driveway, waving at Kate's retreating form. Becca wasn't sure she could forget this. Part of her wasn't even sure she wanted to. But she had to try. She would go inside, take a shower, and try to forget this disaster of a night had ever happened.

Chapter 8

By Monday morning Becca had pushed the embarrassment of the dance out of her mind altogether. Saturday had been filled with family and a horse show that brought Becca more joy than she ever imagined one could get from watching stranger's horses compete in various events. Sunday she'd laid around her house with Kate, eating garbage and watching old movies. Her parents had been off running errands. By the time they got home for dinner, Kate and Becca had already whipped up some meatloaf and potatoes. The four of them ate and talked and basically just enjoyed a few good laughs. It was the perfect medicinal weekend for her heartbreak.

Marching band practice Monday morning was its own form of therapy. Becca couldn't exactly find the time to stress about the situation with Joe and who else may have heard of it while also counting her steps, remembering to roll her feet just right, and play the music she was supposed to have memorized. She was more focused on making sure no one noticed she had taped the small sheet music to her arm under her sleeve and took a few peeks at it when she forgot a note or a sequence.

After practice she hurried toward the restrooms with clean clothes in hand, eager to switch to her regular outfit for the day. She smiled quickly at Brandon, who was in the hallway outside the restrooms swapping his grass-covered practice shoes for cleaner sneakers. "Hey, Becca, how are you?" he asked.

Something about his tone made Becca stop her hurried pace. She turned to look at him. He was tilting his head to the side like you would when you addressed someone you feel sorry for. Panic gripped her. He knew. "Um, I'm fine," she said. "Why? How are you?"

"I'm good." He finished tying his right shoe and jumped to his feet, lithe and graceful. "I, um, heard about what happened with Kate and Joe on Friday." He dropped his voice to a whisper. "Are you OK?"

"What, exactly, did you hear?" she asked. Maybe there was something else that happened with Joe and Kate. Maybe Brandon saw her dancing with Joe and then Kate somehow had a free minute and used it to make out with Joe. Yeah, maybe that's what happened. Maybe he didn't hear about her utter embarrassment. Maybe—

"I heard she threatened him to get him to dance with you. Is that not what happened?"

Her face reddened. She felt the flames of the blush burning up her face. "I didn't know she was doing that," she said. She didn't want to be talking about this. Couldn't he tell that? Sure, they hadn't been friends for a long time, but couldn't he see this was painful?

"Oh, I know. I didn't think you would do that. No one thinks that."

Becca rubbed her eyes with the heels of her hands. "Who else knows?" She almost didn't want to know the answer. But she had to know. Was this how people would see her now?

"Just a few people, probably. Ernie and I were waiting for our rides after the dance and we ran into Joe. He told us. Honestly, I think he told us because he wants Ernie to know what kind of person Kate is."

Becca moved her hands so she could see Brandon's face. Did he look like he was telling the truth? "What did Ernie think?" She had firmly settled on the decision that this was not Kate's fault. Kate had been trying to help and she took it too far, she made a mistake. It was not Kate's fault that Joe didn't like Becca. It wasn't

Kate's fault that Joe was angry. Becca didn't want this to impede Kate's chances with Ernie. That wouldn't be fair. "He's not, like, mad at Kate, right?" she asked.

Brandon's eyes narrowed in confusion. "That wasn't a good thing she did, Becca. You know that, right?"

Becca resisted the urge to groan. Kate was trying to help, even if it felt awful. "She was just trying to help."

This time his eyes widened, like he was shocked. "Becca, it's one thing to ask someone to dance with a friend, like you did. She flat-out told him you like him and he was going to dance with you, no matter what." He reached out and laid his hand on Becca's shoulder in a comforting sort of gesture. It reminded Becca of Kate. "She threatened to tell embarrassing stories about him all over the school if he refused. That's not cool."

Becca felt the tears burning behind her eyes again. She turned toward the bathroom. "You don't understand," she said. "She wasn't expecting him to refuse. She was shocked. She just underestimated how completely unlikable I am. Don't judge her for this." She looked over her shoulder at Brandon. "Don't let Ernie judge her for this."

"Becca, wait..." Brandon called as she moved toward the bathroom. "I really don't think this was about you."

Becca could hear him even after she stepped into the bathroom, his voice echoing through the door that was closing painfully slowly. "You're not unlikeable," she thought he said. She shook her head and locked herself in an open bathroom stall. She had to have misheard him, she thought. Because that's what she learned on Friday at the dance. She was completely unlikeable and the only way Kate could even get someone like Joe to consider dancing with her was to do something unimaginable.

Becca changed out of her marching practice clothes, which resembled pajamas, and into jeans and a shirt for school. She pulled on her sneakers, tied them quickly, and ran her fingers through her hair. Then she checked her face in the mirror and splashed a little water on her cheeks to try and bring the red down. She took a deep breath and mentally promised herself she would get through this day without thinking about the incident again. If anyone brought it up, she would simply say "I'd rather not talk about this." She practiced the line in her head, her lips moving silently. She had to keep pretending like she was fine, that's how she would feel fine again.

Convinced she would be able to say it if she needed it, she slung her backpack over her shoulders and pushed her way out of the bathroom.

Brandon was still standing there. "Becca, I'm sorry. I shouldn't have said anything."

"I don't want to talk about this." She lobbed the practiced line at him and stepped to the side to get around him. He turned and followed her out of the little alcove and into the larger band room. "I have to get to Spanish class."

"Becca, you don't have to defend Kate. Hang on, please." His voice sounded so hurt that Becca felt her feet slowing without her permission. She didn't turn around. "I didn't mean for it to sound like I was attacking you, I wasn't. I wanted to just make sure you were OK." Brandon moved around her until he was right in front of her. Becca made a point to look down at the ground instead of at him.

"I don't want to talk about this," she said.

"I know. We aren't going to talk about it. I just wanted to say I'm sorry. I'm sorry Kate put you in that situation, I'm sorry you were hurt by the whole thing, and I'm sorry I brought it up." He bumped his fist into her shoulder. "Is there anything you need?"

Now she did look up at him. He was smiling a sort of half-smile, like a fish who got the corner of a lip caught on a hook. "Don't be mad at Kate, she made a mistake," Becca said.

He rolled his eyes. "Seriously? She pressured him in a way that's not normal and it's OK to be upset by that."

"It was a bad judgment call but she apologized and I forgave her."

Brandon nodded. "OK, cool. I can work with that. I'll talk to Ernie. Everything will be smoothed over, you'll see."

"Thanks, Brandon." The first bell rang. The one that signaled Becca, who didn't have advanced band and therefore was one of the few marching band students who had to get out of this room and across campus to her first period, had only three minutes to get to class. "I really have to go," she said as she moved around Brandon and practically started jogging.

All the way to class she continued to repeat one thing in her head: I'd rather not talk about it. Just in case she needed it again.

Chapter 9

It was officially November and school had been in session for a few months. The dance incident was sufficiently behind them, although Becca noted Joe no longer showed up for basketball games in her driveway. In fact, when her father had started a water fight in the street on an unseasonably warm Saturday Joe stayed only long enough to throw a water balloon at Kate before heading back to his own yard. It was fine with Becca that he was no longer coming around. She didn't need the reminder of what happened and she didn't need Kate wondering if Becca still thought Joe was cute. She was completely over him. It turned out that finding out someone never had any interest in you to begin with will successfully kill a crush.

Because Joe was no longer coming around daily, Kate had moved her obsession fully into the Ernie category. Becca knew more about this boy than she ever wanted to know, and then some. It seemed Brandon had been able to smooth things over and explain how sorry Kate was for what she did. Kate remained completely in the dark about Ernie ever judging her for her part in the Joe incident. As far as she knew it was between herself, Becca, and Joe. Becca decided it was better that way.

Becca walked out of her Spanish classroom and pulled her hoodie closed against the crisp air, zipping it up about halfway. She had PE second period, which usually meant she had plenty of time to get to class. She could probably stop and talk to a friend if she happened to see one crossing her path. Normally she would lazily lope across the campus. When the wind kicked up, she decided it wasn't worth it, and sped up her steps.

She reached the door to the locker room and noticed a white piece of paper standing out in sharp contrast to the blue-painted door. "What now?" she whined. She drew up close enough to read the paper. "Dress quickly and meet in the old gym," the note read. Becca's eyes widened. They'd been in school for three months now and the routine had been the same every single day: enter the locker room, change into your PE uniform, go to the gym, line up in your attendance line, silent when the bell rings. If you broke this expected pattern at all you risked losing some, or all, of your daily participation points. Then you ended up like Michelle, a Sophomore in a required Freshman course who didn't get enough points the first time around to pass the class. They had never met in another location. Becca wasn't even sure she knew where the old gym was. Was that on the orientation tour?

Michelle came up to stand beside Becca, who was effectively blocking the locker room door. "Oh, sweet. Do you know what this means?" Michelle asked, gesturing to the note.

"No," a voice answered. Becca swiveled her head to get a look at the speaker. Since earning themselves perfect scores on the math project, Ellie Mackenzie and Becca had become fast friends. It turned out they had quite a few of the same classes. According to everyone on campus, they looked too much alike to not be related. Both girls had slight waves to their long brown hair, brown eyes, and boring white girl complexions. Becca didn't see the similarities, especially since Ellie was curved in all the places she was not. "Hi Becca," Ellie added.

Becca waved in acknowledgement.

Michelle pulled the door to the locker room open and waited for Becca and Ellie to cross the threshold. "That note means it's time for square dancing," Michelle crowed. "The one time of the year when the PE teachers will put the boy's second-period PE classes with our PE classes. We'll get at least a week of this."

Becca slammed her backpack into an empty locker nearby and took out her PE uniform. She toed off her sneakers and pulled her jeans off. She was careful to keep her shirt low enough to cover her underwear, even though she was aware it was unlikely anyone would notice. She quickly pulled her regulation navy blue shorts on.

"Square dancing?" Ellie asked. "Like listen to country music and swing your partner round and round?"

"Yes," Michelle said. Her eyebrows danced up and down like they were the ones being graded on their dance moves. "With boys."

That sentence drew Kate from around the end of the row of lockers. "Did you say boys?" she asked.

Becca couldn't help it. She laughed. Kate had fully earned her reputation as the boy-crazy one in their circle and she loved reminding everyone of that.

"There's a lot to mess up in square dancing," Michelle went on. "But don't worry, I'll show you everything you need to know."

Becca turned to face her locker to change her shirt. The move served as a way to hide her massive eye roll. Should they really be taking advice from someone who failed PE last year? It seemed to Becca that someone like Michelle would actually have less understanding about what it takes to successfully complete this easy-A course than, say, anyone else in the sophomore class. Of course, they were fresh out of sophomores in here. She supposed, in the absence of any other choice, Michelle was the best they were going to get.

Becca threw her regular clothes into her locker, slammed the door, and spun the combination lock. "Let's go," Michelle barked. Even though her voice was taking on that high-and-mighty attitude again, the three freshmen hurried to follow her out of the door. "We'll want to get there quickly and get the right spot in line to make sure we aren't stuck with bad partners. Does anyone know any decent boys who have this PE class?"

"My friend Frank has this class," Becca offered.

"Is he the tall one that ate lunch with us when I first met you?" Michelle asked.

Kate nodded. "That's him. The almost cute one who needs a haircut."

Becca shook her head. She was used to the little digs at Frank, although he was usually here to defend himself. Of course, she supposed, he also wasn't here to hear the insult. She supposed that made it harmless.

"Brandon and Ernie have this class too," Ellie volunteered.

"Alright, that's three," Michelle said. "We'll need one more. I say we find them when we get into the gym and hope a decent guy is standing with them in line."

The girls arrived at the entrance to a smaller, disheveled-looking building that was on the edge of campus by the little-used tennis courts. Michelle pulled the door open and the freshman got their first glimpse at the aptly named old gym. This building, unlike the one they usually met in, seemed to be made of wood and smelled damp. The seats, which lined the entire outer edge of what was essentially a bowl, were an ugly orange shade that had to have gone out of style in the 70s.

At the center of the bowl, on the basketball court floor, there were already a few girls and a lot of boys forming parallel lines. "Where are they?" Michelle asked as the girls made their way down the stairs toward the floor. "We don't have time to mess around. We have to step in line quickly and hope we don't get stuck with people we don't like. The trick is to make it look like you're not counting. We need to know what number they are in line."

Becca started counting from the front of the boys' line. "Twenty-five for Frank," she said.

"Forty-seven and forty-eight for Brandon and Ernie, I think," Ellie added.

"That's not going to work," Michelle complained. "We need them to be together." Michelle flipped her ponytail over her shoulder. "Alright, executive decision. We'll make sure we are forty-five to forty-eight in line." She tapped Becca on the shoulder. "If you can get a signal to this Frank kid to move, go for it. Otherwise, I'm not sure what you're going to get."

They maneuvered their way down the stairs, counting girls who were already in line and a few who were making their way down another aisle. They stopped, pretending to wait for Michelle to tie her shoe, when they were almost to the floor. This effectively let three girls slip in front of them. Becca jogged after them because if her count was right that would make her forty-five, as planned.

She turned and smiled at the girl who stepped in behind her. "Can my friends cut in front of you?" she asked, gesturing to Michelle and the other freshman. "Please?"

"I'll just swap places with you," the girl offered.

How to proceed? Becca wondered. It seemed like such a nice gesture but it would mean they weren't the numbers Michelle had told them to be. Didn't Michelle say these numbers were important? She tried to remember why.

"Actually," Michelle interjected, saving Becca. "We'd prefer to all move up. I hate to do this, but can you please let us cut?"

Becca saw the girl's face register who was asking. There was something about Michelle being a Sophomore that tended to get her what she wanted in this class. Funny, because outside of this room she seemed to be content to fly under the radar like the invisible man. "Sure, I guess that's fine." The girl stepped to the side and let Becca's three friends take her spot. Then the girl popped herself back into line in position forty-nine.

Becca felt a surge of pride. They'd managed to do exactly what they set out to do. When the lines started moving she realized she should probably try to get that signal to Frank. She quickly counted out his line again and realized he was going to need to move back a lot. She waited until he looked in her direction and then waved. She pointed to her shoe. Frank squinted at her, confused. She tried to hold up her fingers, first in a four and then in a five. Then she pointed at Frank and showed a two and a five. She made a "come here" gesture with her hand and then repeated the forty-five signal.

Frank seemed to understand what she was getting at. He looked down at his shoe and backed out of line. Becca watched as he untied and then retied his sneaker, all the while keeping his eyes on the boys passing him.

She tried to count with him. She watched him stand up and talk to Brandon, signaling to cut in front of him. Brandon waved his hand and let Frank cut in front of him. Becca sighed. That would make him forty-six, she was pretty sure. She turned her eyes to the boy in front of Frank, wondering who that meant she was going to be paired up with. Her eyes fell on the boy who was going to be her partner and she felt a little jolt of surprise. She'd never seen this boy before but he was cute. Brown hair brushed his forehead and, if she wasn't mistaken, he was as nervous as she was.

Becca continued to watch him as she moved closer to the front of the line. She noticed that in addition to pairing one boy and one girl from each line, the teachers were then forming groups of eight. She realized Michelle must have known this because, she realized, forty-eight was divisible by four. They should be one group.

Michelle tapped her on the shoulder. "That guy is Scott, he's my boyfriend's little brother, actually. He's a nice guy."

Becca had never met Michelle's boyfriend. She hoped this Scott character was nice. He was certainly cute, she decided. He turned his head and looked in her direction, probably wondering who he would be partnered with. His startling blue eyes caught hers and she felt a little flutter in her heart. He was definitely cute. She decided this was something she would keep to herself, for now. No point in repeating that embarrassing encounter she'd had with Joe.

Chapter 10

As expected, the two groups met up near the teachers and were partnered off. Kate, who had either counted incorrectly or who wanted to play coy, either was possible, shook hands with Brandon. Becca reached her hand out in the direction of the cute boy Michelle had identified as Scott. "I'm Becca," she offered.

"Scott." They shook hands and he dropped hers quickly. The smile, however, lingered. He was even cuter up close, Becca decided. Immediately, she shook the thought away. They had to focus here. This was a class assignment.

Their group of eight was directed to a spot on the floor marked with masking tape. They quickly moved themselves onto the sides of a square, two to a side. Scott stood directly on Becca's left. To her right, forming the next side of the square, were Ellie and Frank. Across from her were Michelle and Ernie. Lastly, on Scott's left, were Kate and Brandon.

Becca noticed Kate's eyes darting toward Ernie as if to check on him repeatedly. She also noticed, with something like fear in her stomach, that Ernie was not returning the gesture. Becca knew Kate would notice that and it would really upset her.

The teachers finished the pairings and walked up the center of the old gym. As they walked they called out directions, playing off each other in a way only practiced partners can do, easily finishing each other's sentences. The directions were vague. On one hand they focused entirely on things Becca wouldn't have even considered, like no pausing to add your own dance moves or have any sort of hanky-panky. On the other hand, there seemed to be a serious lack of things she felt like she did need to know, like what the appropriate dance moves were.

Then, before Becca had time to really start getting nervous, they decided it was time to practice the basics.

"Circle left," the teacher called out, "is a simple move. All eight of you will join hands and circle in the direction we have indicated. Try it now."

Scott reached out for Becca's hand and she felt a little flutter as she placed her palm down on top of his. Then she reached beside her and took Frank's hand. Together, with only a little giggling, the group circled to the left. Eventually, they stopped at the same spots where they had started. "That was easy," Kate said with a laugh.

Becca had to agree. Nothing complicated about that move.

"No a do si do," the teacher called. "Watch me." The two teachers faced each other. Then they moved until they were back to back and continued until their position was the same as they began.

"Moon circling the planet," Ellie giggled.

"That actually helps," Becca said.

"Right?" Frank agreed. "Pretty smart."

"You all try," the teacher commanded.

Becca turned and faced Scott, her face instantly going red. "Hi," she said quietly. Sure, they'd already greeted each other, but something about facing him directly made her feel like they were meeting again for the first time.

He chuckled. "This is so weird," he said. "Square dancing? Is that supposed to be a sport or something?"

"Maybe it's just a nice way to get us to all hang out together?" Becca offered.

"Maybe."

They moved around each other in what Becca hoped was an

appropriate do si do.

"Not bad," the teacher called when it seemed like most of the partner pairs had completed the move. "Circle left."

The group didn't hesitate, which Becca supposed was the point. They all grabbed hands and immediately circled to the left until they were back at their starting positions. There was decidedly less giggling this time.

The teacher continued demonstrating basic moves, making the students practice, and then calling them out in random succession until Becca found many of them were memorized in her brain. She was surprised to find she had worked up quite a sweat, too.

"Alright, that's all for today. We'll try again tomorrow and see what everyone remembers. Head to your respective locker rooms and change quickly, we are short on time," the boy's teacher called. Then he clapped his hands and, around the room, bursts of movement started.

"Hey, thanks for being a good partner," Scott said. "It was nice to meet you."

"You as well," Becca said. She liked that he was taking the time to say anything at all. So many of the partners around the room seemed eager to jump apart and move in opposite directions. "See you tomorrow," she offered. Too late, she realized that might sound over-eager. Was she implying that she hoped he'd be her partner tomorrow? Did she mean to imply that? Did she want him to be her partner tomorrow?

"Absolutely," Scott said. "Tomorrow." He smiled at her and she felt her stomach somersault.

"Told you he was nice." Michelle's voice snapped Becca back to reality where all the girls were standing, watching her.

"You did say that," Becca agreed. Was he nice? Becca felt like she wasn't sure anymore. Sure, he hadn't embarrassed her publicly at a dance, but did that automatically mean that he was nice or where her standards too low? He seemed nice, but was it too soon to be thinking of him in this way?

"We better hurry," Ellie said, checking her watch. "It's later than usual. We have to change fast."

The girls hustled out of the door and toward the locker room. "Scott seemed friendly," Ellie said.

"Yeah, he did, right?" Becca agreed. "He made me laugh a few times too."

"That's good. This was actually more fun than I expected it to be. Square dancing, who knew?"

Kate reached out and tapped Michelle on the elbow. "Hey, how as Ernie as a dance partner?" she asked. Becca cringed. She hoped Michelle knew this was a test. She hoped even more that Michelle didn't fail it.

"Fine." Michelle shrugged. "He was decent and I don't have crushed toes, so that's a win. Tomorrow you should count right and find out for yourself."

Kate laughed and Becca was glad when it sounded like her real laugh. Maybe this square dancing thing would be fun.

Chapter 11

Becca found Frank exactly where she expected him to be after seventh period. He was leaning up against the bright red railing of the steps leading out of the auditorium, his ankles crossed in the perfect image of relaxation. He smiled and waved when he saw her coming. "How was your day?" he practically shouted when she was close enough to hear him.

"Uneventful," she answered with a smile. When she was practically next to him he pushed himself up to standing and fell into step beside her, hitching his backpack up so it rested on both shoulders comfortably for the walk home. "Yours?" she asked.

Frank shrugged. "About the same as always. I introduced myself to that new girl in English, the one I was telling you about. It turns out her name is Sarah and she does not play an instrument. She does, however, have decent taste in music." Frank had been in a relationship with the same girl for both years of junior high school. Becca knew he was seriously hurting from the breakup, more than even Frank would admit. She was relatively certain this new crush was a rebound, but she didn't want to discourage him from getting out there again. He seemed to be searching for the exact opposite of the monster ex-girlfriend. He wanted someone who didn't play an instrument since the monster was the best clarinet player in their junior high band. He also wanted someone tall. He kept claiming this was because of his own height, but Becca suspected it was more of a response to the fact that the monster fell on the shorter-than-average spectrum.

"That's great," she said, choosing to ignore any opportunity for a deeper analysis of the situation. "Did you turn in the poem we worked on?" Yesterday, on their walk home, they had brainstormed on a poem for Frank to turn in today. Poetry was something he usually struggled with.

"Yes, I did. I will let you know how we score once I get it back."

The crosswalk changed to the walking symbol and the pair fell into silence as they jogged across the normally busy street. With seniors trying to turn left out of the parking lot you could never be too careful, even when you had a clear crosswalk. On the other side of the street, Frank bumped Becca's shoulder with his own. "Speaking of romantic connections, how was square dancing with my pal today?"

Becca's heart fluttered just a little. She didn't put too much stock in Frank calling anyone pal. To Frank, everyone was a friend. He was easygoing and friendly, that was his biggest appeal. "Yeah, he seemed nice. I don't think I had ever met him before. His name is Scott, right?" She tried to sound casual like the name hadn't been the perfect name for that face. Like it hadn't been running through her head all day.

Frank chuckled. His full laugh was a signature calling card of his, one she could pick out of a crowd. This was more like he was trying not to laugh at her but found her ridiculous. She gave him a little side-eye. "Don't laugh at me," she scolded.

"I wasn't." He held up his left hand in surrender. "Yes, his name is Scott, which I suspect you knew. He's in my Science class, he's smart and practical." Becca counted fifteen steps, willing Frank to add more. She knew from experience that Frank would eventually fill any silence if you let it linger and drag.

"I noticed you signaled to me. That means you were picking

your partner," he said. His eyes twinkled mischievously. "Are you really going to pretend being partnered with Scott was an accident?" He turned his head a little to give Becca a look she imagined any big brother she had been born with would've given her when he meant business.

She rolled her eyes. "OK, so Michelle has taken PE before and she was trying to help us get paired up with decent partners so we wouldn't be miserable. Brandon, Ernie, and you were the targets. I actually tried to get you to move to forty-fifth, which would've made you my partner. Scott was just a lucky accident. Michelle actually knew him, it turns out. I guess his older brother is her boyfriend." Becca shrugged. Although she was technically telling the truth she felt like she was intentionally leaving out the part about the little flutter she'd felt when she noticed Scott. She was also pretending her heart hadn't skipped a beat when Scott had rested his hand on her hip while they were dancing.

Frank turned his head toward the street, looking behind him to see if the road was clear. Becca knew this was a sign he was preparing to jog across the street, readying himself to turn down in the direction of their houses. She turned her head in the same manner. Seeing the street was clear in both directions she picked up the pace and jogged across the road. Both teens hit the far curb at the same time and took a few steps in silence as they caught their breath. Then Becca noticed Frank looking over his shoulder back in her direction like he was analyzing something about her. "What?" she asked. "Why are you looking at me like that?"

"I was just thinking." He turned away from her in favor of looking forward.

Becca jogged until she was ahead of him and turned to walk backward, glaring at Frank. "Don't give me that garbage. What were you thinking about?" She poked him in the chest. "Spill it."

"I was just trying to picture you and Scott together. Like, on a date."

She froze in the middle of the sidewalk. Then, when Frank

was beside her, she turned around and kept walking shoulder-to-shoulder with her friend who she considered the older brother she wasn't lucky enough to be born with. "Really?"

He smiled at her. "Yeah, really."

She didn't want to ask but she found she couldn't help herself. A warm feeling had settled in her chest. "And?"

This time his laugh was real, reverberating off the apartment building on their right and making her chuckle. "You are obviously interested in him," Frank said as the laugh faded.

Becca rolled her eyes at being caught out. "But—" she hesitated, not wanting to sound like a fool. "He won't be interested, right?" She practically whispered it, feeling suddenly nervous.

"I don't know for sure." He bumped his shoulder up against hers again. "The better question, as far as I'm concerned, is would he treat you right."

Becca scrunched up her nose. "You sound like my Dad."

Frank pointed a finger at her. "Hey, your Dad is a good man. There are worse people to sound like." Frank's father had left him when he was too young to remember. He was raised by a mother who, as far as Becca was concerned, should be in the running for the strongest woman in the world. She never let anything get her down and she did a great job running her household and raising her son.

Frank had met Becca's parents for the first time at a band concert a few years ago. In typical Frank fashion, he'd walked right up and introduced himself to both of her parents and then tagged along for pizza after the concert. Becca honestly believed her father was the male role model Frank thought he needed. It's part of what made him a brother to her. "I know," she said.

Frank hit the crosswalk button beside him and the pair stopped to wait for the signal to change. Becca felt the burning in her calves that she only noticed when they stopped. This walk wasn't as difficult as she'd thought it would be before school started. Now that they did it twice a day, she actually found it pretty easy. But she could always feel that tingle in her legs.

Becca turned and looked behind her, noticing Kate was fast approaching. "Incoming," she warned. Frank didn't particularly trust Kate. He had pointed it out once, a long time ago. Since then, having said his peace, most people wouldn't notice any difference in the way he treated Kate when compared to how he treated everyone else. But Becca wasn't like most people. Becca noticed his real laugh and Kate couldn't coexist. She noticed he always kept a wary eye on Kate. She noticed he sometimes ground his teeth when Kate was being especially critical. Today she noticed the familiar clench in Frank's jaw signaling he had heard her warning. He didn't even have to look behind him to know what Becca meant.

The light changed and Becca heard the sound of Kate jogging to catch up and avoid missing the light, her sneakers slapping against the pavement. She felt a smack on her shoulder, too hard to be just to get her attention. "Ouch, Kate," she yelled.

"Sorry." The smack came again, a little lighter. "I was just trying to catch up. You two have such long legs."

Frank hit the sidewalk on the other side of the road first and immediately slowed his normal pace as if Kate had asked him to instead of just complaining about it. He might not like her but he couldn't help but be respectful. "How was your day?" he asked politely.

"Excellent," Kate's full smile lit up her entire face. Becca couldn't help but smile back. "Ernie saw me square dancing with Brandon and got totally jealous. He apparently asked Brandon about it." Kate wiggled her eyebrows. "I think he'll call me soon. I bet he'll even ask me to the next dance."

"When is the next dance?" Becca asked.

"The formal is coming up, stupid."

Frank's jaw clenched at the insult, but he kept his mouth shut. "Isn't that like a month away?" Becca asked.

"This kind of thing takes time, Beck." Kate put her hand on her hip. "You honestly don't know the first thing about boys and dating. It's like training a puppy not to pee in the house. I have to keep reminding you about every step."

"Who's Ernie again?" Frank asked. Becca considered pointing out that he already knew who Ernie was. He'd met him at freshman orientation, they had a few classes together, and he'd been part of their square dancing group today in PE. These clues led her to the conclusion that Frank was using this as a tactic to get Kate gushing about boys, her favorite subject, instead of picking on Becca, her favorite pastime.

"He's the absolutely dreamy blonde in Advanced History with me." When Kate said this sentence, she emphasized advanced. History was the only advanced class Kate was taking. It was also the only advanced class offered to freshmen that Becca wasn't taking. Somehow Kate was always able to make this feel like a huge failure. "He's absolutely the cutest freshman boy at school and I plan to make him my boyfriend before the year is over," Kate added.

Suddenly, Kate stopped walking, drawing in a breath like she was surprised. She laid her hand over her chest. Then, noticing the other two kept walking, barely glancing back at her theatrics, she jogged the few steps to close the gap. "Oh my gosh, I didn't mean to insult you." She reached up to lay a hand on Frank's shoulder. "You're a freshman boy too. You are pretty adorable. I just don't think of you like that," she said. She really leaned on him then, ducking her head until it was touching his bicep. "Don't be offended." She pouted.

They rounded the corner onto Becca and Kate's street. Frank looked quizzically at Kate, like being offended had never even occurred to him. "I'm not," he said, before rolling his eyes.

Kate bounced back up. "Good." She clapped her hands together. "So, what were you two talking about before I came along and brought some life into this walk home?"

Becca tried to wrack her brain for what they'd been talking about before Scott. There was no way she was bringing up Scott now. One, she didn't really trust Kate not to swoop in and tell him they'd been talking about him. Two, she didn't want to hear all the reasons she was stupid for having a crush on Scott, not right now. She convinced herself that once she sorted out how she was feeling, she'd tell Kate. But right now, it was her little secret. "English class," Becca said as she remembered. "Frank had a poem due and I was just asking how it went."

Becca could see Kate's house now, up on the right. "You were talking about classes? Good Lord, you're both such goody-two-shoes," Kate said. "Aren't you glad I came along?"

"Of course," Becca said with a smile. She noticed Frank had picked up the pace again as they drew closer to Kate's house. That was a good sign that he was annoyed. That thought made Becca feel a little better for what she felt inside. Because the truth was, for reasons she couldn't quite put her finger on, being around Kate always left Becca feeling hollow and worthless. What was wrong with her that she couldn't even have friends the right way? Why did she always feel as though she needed to be better for Kate? Why couldn't she find it in herself to actually be better? Really, she was a terrible person for thinking these things.

Wasn't she?

"Alright guys, try not to be boring without me. I'm going to take my phone off the hook so Ernie thinks I'm on the phone with someone else if he tries to call. Tootles." Kate waved at them as she jogged across her own front lawn toward her door.

Becca sighed. "I guess I'll see you tomorrow?" This was where they all split up. Her house was just across the street. Frank's was down the side road beside Kate's house. Becca wished they had more of the walk, just the two of them. She wanted to pick up the conversation where they'd left off. She wanted to hear what Frank really thought of Scott. She wanted to get that feeling that she was actually capable of being a good friend back, even if it was just for a second. Knowing that wasn't possible, she turned toward the street to check for traffic before she crossed.

"Hey, Becca," Frank said.

She turned back to him. "Yeah?"

"About Scott." Her heart fluttered. Frank gave her a thumbs-up. "He's good enough for you." He winked at her and walked off toward his street. Becca stood there, watching him go until he disappeared around the corner and out of sight.

Then she dashed across the road, a smile lighting up her entire face.

Chapter 12

Kate didn't walk to school with Becca the next day. By itself, that wasn't entirely unusual. Kate had been known to oversleep and get to school by other methods, once even including a cab. But when Kate also didn't show up for PE, Becca got nervous.

During their lunch period, Becca ducked down the hallway by the restrooms and slipped a quarter into the payphone to call Kate's house. She let the phone ring for about thirty seconds before dropping the receiver back onto the cradle. Hanging up before the answering machine could answer meant her quarter would come back out of the lower right corner of the machine. Becca retrieved it, slipped it back into the machine, and dialed again. The second time Becca let the phone ring for a full minute before slamming down the receiver and stalking back to her table.

"Did you get ahold of her?" Frank asked.

"No one answered."

"Maybe she's here and you just haven't seen her." It was a lame excuse and Becca suspected Frank knew it. Since she'd moved here in the fifth grade, Becca had never gone a full school day without seeing Kate. Actually, she wasn't sure she'd gone a full weekend or non-school day without seeing her either. Something was wrong.

All through sixth period, Becca made plans for how she was

going to check on Kate. The first thing she was going to do was head straight to Kate's house from school. If Kate wasn't there, she was going to go home and retrieve Kate's mother's work number from the Rolodex in the kitchen. She had never called there before and she didn't want to worry Ms. Tare, but if Kate was not at home maybe she needed to be worried. More likely, Becca figured, Ms. Tare would have some simple answer for her. She'd know exactly where Kate was.

Becca stepped out of her sixth period and into the large open quad area in the center of the school. This was a popular place to stop and hang out if you had enough time or distance between your classes. Becca only had to walk one aisle over, so she normally stopped to hang out there. But the nerves clenching her stomach made her want the day to be fast-forwarded. She kept her head down and moved quickly toward seventh period.

"Becca," she heard the shout over the voices of everyone in the quad and stopped, turning toward it. Kate? That sounded like Kate. Relief pulsed quickly through her veins at the sight of her friend. That relief was chased by a sudden cold because Kate was the picture of anger. Her hands were fixed on her hips, elbows jutting out to both sides. Her head was tilted just a little and her jaw was set. Also, although there were easily twenty kids and plenty of space between them, Kate wasn't moving to close the gap. She looked like a shooter at the O.K. Corral, waiting for her opponent to draw.

Becca moved closer, speaking in a normal volume and trying not to overreact. "Kate, where have you been?"

"I was late this morning because I didn't want to walk with you," she practically screamed the last word. Becca flinched at the tone. "I'm just so tired of it all, Becca," Kate continued.

Becca's eyes darted around the crowd, noting all the people who were watching this. She dropped her voice a little lower, jogging the rest of the way so she could face Kate directly and be heard. "What are you talking about? What happened?"

"Nothing happened. That's the problem, isn't it?" Kate was

still shouting, despite how close they were standing.

Becca had never been more confused in her life. When she saw Kate after school, she was heading into her house to take her phone off the hook, or some such nonsense. She hadn't spoken to her again all night. "Did something happen last night?" Becca whispered, leaning in close. "We can talk about it. Let's go over there," she pointed off away from the crowds. "We can talk about it." She reached out for Kate's arm, her fingers lightly brushing the long sleeves.

"No, get your hands off me," Kate shouted. She yanked her arm away from Becca. Now the crowd was starting to draw in closer and make noises. Becca felt the flame of embarrassment burning her cheeks. "I'm so tired of being such a good friend to you and getting nothing in return. I do things for you all the time. But when I ask you to do something for me, you can't be bothered. You're in your own head all the time. It's infuriating," Kate ranted.

Becca stood there in shock, staring at Kate. Her mouth was hanging open, but she felt frozen in place. She had absolutely no idea what Kate was going on about. Sure, she hadn't done anything specifically to help Kate lately, but she also didn't recall Kate asking. Obviously, Kate was going through something, maybe a better friend would've noticed. A better friend wouldn't wait to be asked. "Kate, I'm sorry. What can I do to help?"

"No, it's too late!" Kate screeched. "It's too late." She waved her hands dismissively between them. Her voice dropped to a more normal volume. "I don't want to talk to you right now. I want you to give me some space." Somehow, that volume hurt just as much.

Becca winced and reached out to Kate again. "Kate, honestly, I don't know what happened. But I want to help. Just tell me what you're mad about, please." This wasn't like Kate, not at all. Becca didn't like the public scene, but she knew something inside Kate must really be broken for her to act like this. "Is this about... " Becca looked around, checking faces to see who was nearby. She didn't want to cause more of a scene. She leaned in and whispered the name. "Ernie?"

Kate groaned in frustration. "No, it's not. Because he didn't call. Because even though I made sure the boy you were crushing on knew exactly how you felt so you had an honest answer one way or the other, like a good friend, you didn't do the same for me. He didn't call. He hasn't called since that dance because you must have done something wrong. You must have only told him I wanted to dance and not bothered to tell him how I felt. He didn't call."

Becca felt like she had been slapped, which she supposed she sort of was in a verbal sense. She was basically being word-slapped, right here in the quad in front of all these people. Her eyes stung and her throat felt tight. The warning bell rang for seventh period.

"And now you've made me late for class," Kate added.

A few kids watching started chanting, "Fight, fight." Becca felt her hands shaking and her heart racing. She had no idea what to do to make them go away.

Kate spun on her heel and glared at the chanters. They stopped. "I'm not fighting her, you idiots. Go to class!" Then Kate stomped off in their direction like she was going to chase them. When they turned a corner, she kept going straight until Becca watched her disappear into a classroom.

Becca stood there for a few more seconds, swallowing and blinking to come to terms with what she'd just heard. Then, not knowing what else to do, she turned and walked to her seventh period. The bell rang before she got to the door and the detention slip was in her hand before she could sit in her seat. She pulled out her notebook and her pencil and then stared off into space. She wasn't focused on the lesson or the teacher. Instead, she was processing everything she'd just heard.

Kate was right, in a sense. Becca hadn't told Ernie how Kate felt. She'd told him to ask her to dance. She'd told Brandon something, she remembered that. They'd talked about Ernie and Kate. But Becca couldn't remember if she'd told him how Kate felt. Was that really what Kate was mad about? Was it possible Kate was hurt because Ernie hadn't called and was just looking for someone to blame?

No matter the real reason, that entire situation was horrible. Becca had never been shouted at like that. Certainly not by Kate and certainly not in public. She was going to have to do some major damage control if she wanted Kate to be her friend again.

For a brief second, she allowed herself to imagine what high school would be like without Kate. Then she shook her head. No, Kate was hurting right now. She felt like Becca had let her down. Becca had to do better for her friend, she had to show Kate their friendship was important to her. Right after she healed from that verbal beating she just took.

She looked around the room, relieved to see she appeared to be the only person not focused on the lesson. With any luck this meant that their little argument wasn't overheard by too many of the people she interacted with daily. She didn't recall seeing any familiar faces in the crowd. Mostly it looked like upperclassmen who probably already viewed her as immature and ridiculous. They were just hoping for a fight.

A fight? Becca wondered. Is that really what they just had? She almost couldn't believe it. She had just had a fight with her best friend in the middle of the quad. A fight that all started because Becca wasn't being a good friend. Is that really what happened?

This question would bother Becca for the rest of her class, all of her walk home, a few hours of homework, and dinner that night.

Chapter 13

Becca had let her thoughts be consumed by the question of what kind of friend she truly was all through dinner, barely pushing food around on her plate. The phone rang as she was shuffling her way into the living room, intending to continue her pondering while she mindlessly watched something on television. Since the handset was just a few steps away, she retraced her steps to answer it. "Hello."

"Hi, is Becca there?"

She didn't immediately recognize the voice. It was deep, but not like adult deep. It sounded like a boy. It wasn't Frank. "This is Becca."

"Oh, hey. It's Scott." Her heartbeat fluttered away in her chest. "From square dancing."

"Right, yeah." She didn't say more because she was afraid she'd spill out all her personal thoughts, starting with "How could I ever forget who you are?"

"I hope you don't mind me calling. I got your number from Frank. I wanted to call and make sure you were alright."

She swallowed. "I'm fine, thanks."

"Great. I was worried after the way that Kate girl sort of attacked you before seventh period."

Becca sagged her shoulders. Evidently, Scott had seen the incident with Kate. That meant Scott had seen her be called out for being a terrible friend. Well, better he learn that now, she supposed. "Yeah, that was awful. I didn't know you were there."

"She was pretty fired up," Scott said. "What made her so mad?"

Becca sighed. "She asked me to talk to a boy about her, kind of lay the groundwork for him to ask her out or something. I didn't," she practically whispered the last two words.

Scott was quiet for a beat. Becca wondered what he was thinking. Was he judging her for being a bad friend? "That seems like an overreaction," Scott finally said. "Maybe there's also something else?"

"I don't know. I just know what she said. I haven't talked to her since," Becca admitted. The sentence brought a pang of regret behind it. Maybe she should've tried harder to call Kate. That's just another example of how she was being a terrible friend. "I should call her."

"Yeah, OK. Do you want me to let you go?"

Part of her really wanted to say no. But, that was the selfish part. The part that would rather spend all night talking to Scott than dealing with whatever was happening with Kate. The rational part of her knew she couldn't do that. Kate deserved better from her, more support. They'd been through a lot. "Yeah, I'm sorry. Can I call you back later?" she asked.

"Let me give you my phone number." He waited while Becca reached for the notebook and pencil her mother kept near the base of the phone then he rambled off seven digits and waited while she wrote them down. "You can call anytime, I have a phone in my room so it doesn't bother everyone else."

Becca looked longingly toward her own bedroom, where she'd have to drag this phone with its long cord if she wanted to talk in there. The door would still shut but everyone would know she was on the phone, the cord giving her instantly away. "That's really cool," she said. "I wish I had one of those. Or even a cordless phone. Kate has a cordless phone at her house so she can take it all over the place."

"We actually just got one of those," Scott admitted with a chuckle. "But my brother keeps forgetting to put it back on the charger so it dies pretty fast."

Becca laughed. "Hey, thanks for calling, I really appreciate you checking in on me."

"Absolutely," he said. "I just wanted to be a good friend." There was a beat of silence that somehow felt heavy. "I just think it's important to be there for your friends, even if it's messy."

The words had a heavy feel like Scott felt they were important. Becca was embarrassed to admit she didn't see the significance. Maybe it was a simple case of passing on some guilt for the way she handled things with Kate. "I'll call you back later," she said instead. "Bye for now."

"Bye, Becca."

Becca held down the little button on the receiver that would hang up the phone. She took a deep breath. It had never been this hard to call Kate before, what was she waiting for? She needed to dial the number and make things right.

She removed her finger from the button the dial tone sound filled her ears. Quickly, she dialed Kate's number from memory. After only three rings, someone answered. "Tare residence," they said. Becca smiled, despite the wiggling worms of fear in her stomach. Ms. Tare was always so formal when she answered the phone.

"Is Kate there?"

"Hold on one second, please." There was a muffled sound, presumably as Ms. Tare covered the end of the phone with her hand. Becca strained to hear something, but Kate's mother must be skilled at covering all of the speakers. She couldn't hear anything. "Who may I ask is calling?" the voice said, startling Becca.

"It's Becca." She didn't need to elaborate more than that, they knew her like family. In fact, she was a little insulted Ms. Tare even had to ask who she was. Didn't she know her voice as well as

Becca knew hers?

"Hold on, dear." Again, the noise was snuffed out by something.

Becca sighed. In her mind she imagined Ms. Tare approaching Kate, telling her who was on the phone. The Kate in her imagination planted a hand firmly on her hip and refused to take the handset. Becca hoped she was wrong. "Come on, Kate," she whispered. "Give me a chance."

"Becca," Ms Tare prompted.

"I'm here," Becca answered.

"It looks like she fell asleep, dear. Would you like me to wake her up?"

Becca didn't know how to answer that. On one hand, she worried Kate wasn't really asleep, just refusing to speak to her. On the other hand, if she was asleep, she may really need the sleep. Really it came down to this important question, would Ms. Tare lie to Becca? "No, that's alright. Will you just tell her I called, please?"

"Of course, dear." There was the sound of some movement, a door closing. "Becca, is everything alright? With Kate, I mean. She seemed really upset when I got home from work. She was in her room crying most of the evening. Of course, now she's asleep. She won't talk to me. I'm worried."

Becca felt tears prick her eyes. "We sort of had a little fight," she admitted.

"Oh, that's terrible." Becca heard the sound of a heavy sigh through the telephone receiver. "Hopefully it's the kind of thing you can work past. You two are such good friends."

"I'm trying," Becca admitted. "Please tell her I called, that will help."

"Alright, dear. Thank you for trying. I'll certainly give her the message. Have a good night."

"Thanks, Ms. Tare. You have a good night, too." Becca pushed the receiver button down just as her own mother crossed behind her, headed toward the living room.

"Who was on the phone?" her mother asked.

"Kate." Becca put the receiver down. "Actually, I was trying to call Kate. Her mom said she's asleep."

"That's strange, I thought I heard it ring."

"Oh, right." Becca tried to act casual, to make sure her mom didn't make a big deal out of this. "It was a friend from school. His name is Scott."

Her mom's eyes widened. "I haven't heard of a Scott before."

"Right. I just met him. He's in my PE class and we got partnered for square dancing."

Her mom made a noise like agreement, but her eyes were still wide. "He's just a friend?" she asked.

Becca knew her mom wasn't opposed to her having a boyfriend. That rule had gone out the window the second Becca turned twelve. She was asking out of a sense of curiosity, the same way she would ask Kate or Kate's older sister about their dating situations.

"Just a friend, Mom." She turned her back on her mother, mostly to end this conversation but also to hide the little blush that she could feel creeping up her cheeks. "A friend I should probably call back unless you need the phone."

"I don't need the phone. Go right ahead." Becca refused to turn around to see if that smile in her mother's voice was also on her face.

She dialed the number.

"Hello," the voice answered. It was Scott, Becca recognized the voice immediately.

"Hi, it's Becca."

"Hey, how did it go? Did she talk to you?"

"Her mom said she was asleep."

"You're afraid she was lying?"

Becca wondered how he knew that. "A little," she admitted. She stretched the cord of the phone, untangling it. Then she walked to her bedroom, pulled the cord to the bottom of the door, and shut the door with a click. She settled herself on the floor, her back holding the door shut. "She's so mad. I just need to find a way to fix it."

"Do you want to talk about it? Maybe bounce some ideas off of me?" Scott offered.

Becca had done nothing but think about this all afternoon. Suddenly, she found that she didn't want to think about it right this second. "Actually, can you just change the subject?"

Scott chuckled. "Sure. What kind of music do you like?" he asked.

Chapter 14

The next morning, when Frank swung by on his way to school and Becca dropped into step beside him, Kate was nowhere to be found. They didn't see her until they were halfway to school. She was walking fast on the other side of the street, arms crossed over her chest and the hood of her sweatshirt pulled up to hide her face. Becca pointed across the road at her. "I suppose you heard she's mad at me?"

Frank shrugged. "She's emotional. You got caught in her outburst. I bet she'll be fine within twenty-four hours."

Becca stared at him in shock. "Are you serious?" She shook her head. "Why do you do that? Can't you just admit that she's mad? That I messed up? I'm not perfect, you know."

Frank nodded. "Oh, I know." He winked at her. "No one is perfect, Becca. What, exactly, did you do to Kate? You tell me, in your words."

She hung her head, embarrassed. "She asked me to talk to Ernie and I didn't. I messed it up."

"When did she ask you to do that?"

"At the dance."

"I thought you did talk to him at the dance."

Becca let out a frustrated puff of air. "I did. I told him to ask her to dance."

Frank pushed her shoulder. "Look, the way I see it, Kate is

just mad Ernie didn't call, or whatever. You would have every right to still be mad at her for what happened with Joe."

Becca's eyes widened in shock.

"Yes, I heard about that," Frank said, rolling his eyes. "She was way out of line. But you forgave her. That's what friends do." He gestured across the street toward Kate. "If you actually messed up, which I'm not admitting I agree with, she'll forgive you. Otherwise, she wasn't that great of a friend to begin with."

Becca had to admit, he was on to something. It gave her hope. How much of the responsibility for this friendship fell on Becca? Surely she wasn't less deserving of forgiveness than Kate was. She could make this right.

As they crossed the street, Becca noticed someone standing on the sidewalk who looked like he was waiting for someone. Her heart pitter-pattered away in her chest. She had to wonder if, maybe, he was waiting for her. She chastised herself for the useless hope. If she wasn't careful, she'd turn into a hopeless, boy-crazy teenager. Wouldn't want that.

"Is that Scott?" Frank asked, waving.

"Maybe," Becca answered, although she knew full well that's exactly who it was.

Scott started walking in their direction and met them on the sidewalk. "Good morning," he greeted. Becca noticed the words were followed by a full smile that made the butterflies that seemed to live in her stomach lately flutter their wings. "How are things?"

"Things are good," Frank answered. The two boys exchanged a high-five. Not the complicated kind Becca had seen so many boys do before. More like a handshake that didn't involve the actual grasp of hands. "I should run to band," Frank said. "We didn't have practice this morning, but I still have to check in with my squad leader."

Becca narrowed her eyes at him. He didn't need to do that, she was pretty sure. His squad leader, a senior, didn't particularly care about him one way or the other. That was an excuse if she'd ever heard one. What was he playing at?

"See you later," Scott said, cordially. Then he fixed his startling blue eyes on Becca. "How are you?"

"I'm fine." She shrugged.

"Yeah? Awesome. What's your first-period class?"

"Spanish," she answered.

"Oh cool, I'm going that way. Mind if I walk with you?"

Her heart fluttered at the seemingly innocent question. Because it wasn't innocent, or at least it didn't feel that way. It also wasn't her idea. That meant Scott, a boy, came up with this seemingly innocent but not innocent idea all on his own. "Yeah, cool," she mumbled. At least she hoped that was what she mumbled.

She started walking in the direction of Spanish, Scott beside her. "So you and Frank, are you like twins, or how does that work?"

Becca turned a confused expression on him. "What?"

"He's your brother, right?"

"Oh, no. Not really." Scott looked genuinely confused, Becca noted. She hurried on with some sort of explanation. "He lives down the street and we're friends. He comes around a lot and plays basketball with my dad and stuff. So, he's like a brother. But he's not actually a brother." She pursed her lips. "I'm not explaining this very well."

"No, it makes sense." Scott smiled. "Your sibling act is just very convincing."

Becca smiled back. "I guess."

"But Kate is your best friend, right? Not Frank?"

This forced Becca to think. What made one more of a friend than the other, really? She remembered Kate had been the first one there for her, the first person to infuse herself into Becca's new life here. "Kate kind of chose me," she explained. "She was the first person I met when my family moved to Arizona and she's just always been there for me." She thought of the way Kate had supported her after the last dance when she was crying in the car. "She does her best to help me when I'm feeling down."

As if the words themselves had slapped her across the face, Becca stopped in the middle of the walkway. A few steps later, Scott also stopped, turning to look back at her with confusion. But Becca had figured something out. She had to do what Kate had done. She had to take action and do her best to help Kate when she was down.

"Can I walk with you some other time?" she asked. "I just realized something I need to do."

"Absolutely," Scott said. "Is everything OK?"

Becca smiled. "It will be."

She changed direction, picked up speed, and headed for the quad. She searched the faces, looking for one with a shock of blond hair among the gathered crowd. She spotted him, sitting on a bench beside Brandon, looking through a package of pictures. Before she could let her nerves stop her from something she was suddenly sure was important, she confidently crossed to the pair. "Ernie, can I talk to you for a second?" she asked.

Ernie startled before wiping his confusion off his face and offering her a smile. "Sure." He handed the picture packet to Brandon and stood up. "Should we step over there?" He pointed to a more private location, just a few steps away. Becca turned and headed that way.

"So here's the thing," she said. "I don't think I made this clear at the dance. Kate really likes you." Ernie nodded, but his eyes were wide. "I guess what I'm wondering is, do you think that's something you are interested in pursuing?" She gulped. "I only ask because I want to kind of help Kate know what her next move should be."

Ernie pursed his lips and narrowed his eyes, a move that automatically labeled him the thinker in her mind. "I hadn't really thought about it," he answered after a beat. "Kate can be kind of, like, rude. Can't she?"

Becca drew in a deep breath, nodding. "She's a little intense."

She let out the breath. "But she means well."

"She's your friend. You think she's a good person." They weren't questions. Becca didn't attempt to answer, just smiled. "Look, I don't really know her so I don't know what I think yet. But I like that you're sticking up for her. Here's what I can do. I can think about this a little more and give her a chance."

"That's awesome, thanks."

Ernie reached out his hand, offering a handshake. Becca eyed it suspiciously for just a second before accepting and shaking it. "Thanks for letting me know," he said.

Becca nodded once and dropped her hand from his. "Alright, I'm off to class. Thanks for being cool about this"

"No problem." He gave her a little wink. "Cool is something I'm good at."

Becca turned away and headed off toward Spanish. She took a moment to bask in the feeling of accomplishment that was washing over her. She felt like a good friend or a better one at least. She had taken the time to put Kate's interests before her own and help her out. That, she told herself, was what good friends did.

Chapter 15

As seventh period drew to a close, Becca decided not to disappoint herself by looking for Kate. The girl from across the street had been missing again during lunch, although Becca suspected she was only sitting in another spot altogether. Frank sat with Becca, telling her again that Kate would come around. She told him about her conversation with Ernie. Out loud he gave her his approval. But Becca noticed there was something else in his expression, something she couldn't quite put a name to.

She crossed the campus after the final bell and, again, found Frank waiting where he was always waiting. Ankles crossed, head back, sunglasses on, the picture of relaxation. "Mr. Dependable," she called.

Frank lowered his head and smiled. "I suppose that's me?"

"You're always right here where I expect you to be." She didn't add that this was especially appreciated right now because Kate seemed to be abandoning her.

"That's what friends are for," he said.

The two fell into their normal, fast pace for the walk home. Despite herself, Becca kept looking over her shoulder expecting to see the straight brown hair and stylish clothes following them home. She never caught sight of her.

She unlocked her front door and let herself into the house. It smelled like home. Not a smell that she could place or one that she could name, but one she recognized nonetheless. It just smelled comforting and familiar.

No one was home, except the dogs. She dropped her backpack next to the front door and made her way straight back through the kitchen to the door into the backyard. She barely got a crack in the door before her Bullmastiff, Honey, shoved the door open enough to allow himself entry. Becca tried to pet him on the way by but the zoomies had obviously grabbed hold and Honey was off, racing around the kitchen table like a Nascar driver. Marcia, the family's calmer and older dog, waltzed through the door and stopped to receive her pets. "Is he always this crazy?" Becca asked the German Shepherd as she scratched her ears. Marcia sighed as if the answer itself exhausted her.

The green wall-mounted phone beside the back door rang. Becca pushed the door closed with her foot and timed her move to the phone to avoid Honey's next lap. "Hello."

"Hey, it's Scott."

"Oh, hi. How are you?" Her heartbeat fluttered. She looked longingly at the closest kitchen chair. Normally she'd drop herself down there to sit and chat on the phone. But with Honey running her laps, that was unsafe at best. She scrunched her nose, brain working to find a solution. "Hey, can I put you on hold for a second? I need to give my dog a treat so he'll calm down. He's got the zoomies real bad."

A chuckle that was like an adrenaline boost for Becca's fluttering nerves sounded through the phone line. That was an adorable laugh. "Yeah, of course."

Becca set the handset face down on the table and headed for the cabinet that held the dog's treats. Marcia was already there, sitting demurely and waiting. Becca opened the cabinet, pulled out the red box, and popped it open. Honey raced in their direction. "Honey, sit," Becca commanded. The larger dog dropped to the floor, his bottom hovering as if it was taking all his willpower to even hold this still. Becca tossed him a treat. He caught it as he was standing back up and he retreated into the living room, no doubt to settle into the chair he was fond of sitting in even though Becca's mother insisted dogs weren't allowed on the furniture.

Becca turned her attention to Marcia. "You're such a good girl," she cooed. Marcia, as if to show off her agreement, raised one paw. Becca laughed and put her hand underneath it. "You want to shake? Good girl." She held out a treat and Marcia delicately took it from between her fingers. Then the older dog sprawled herself across the tile floor with a soft sigh. Becca scratched her ears and returned to the phone.

She dropped into her preferred chair near the kitchen table, stretching the short phone cord to bring the handset back to her ear. "I'm back," she said.

"Awesome. What kind of dog do you have?"

"We have two, actually. A Bullmastiff and a German Shepherd." She smiled at Marcia. "One just happens to be more calm than the other."

"We only have one," Scott said. "She's a big Rottweiler though so she probably counts as two."

Becca smiled. "I bet." She settled back in the chair, hooking her foot along the support under the table. A loud noise filled the receiver, something coming from Scott's end. Becca closed her eyes in an attempt to fine-tune her hearing. "What was that?"

There was a shuffling noise and then the sound of a door shutting. "Oh, nothing. Just... my family." Becca heard music start up mid-song as if Scott had just flipped on the radio. Immediately her mind flashed to afternoons at Kate's house, the two girls blaring music behind a closed bedroom door to drown out the sound of Kate's parents fighting about something. A sadness flooded her.

"Do you want to talk about it?" she asked, tentatively. She didn't want to encroach on a subject Scott didn't want to talk about, but he had called her for a reason.

"Not really. Not everyone around here gets along all the time. I'd rather you take my mind off it."

Becca ran her free hand through her hair, wondering what she could bring up that would erase the thoughts of people in his house screaming at each other. "Um, I tried to do something for Kate today. Sort of a goodwill gesture."

"Yeah?" Scott's voice sounded forced, eager. "Tell me about that."

Becca smiled. "I talked to the guy she's crushing on. I told him she likes him. He genuinely didn't know."

"Do I know this clueless guy?" Scott asked.

"I don't know. His name is Ernie. He's in your PE class."

"Oh yeah," he dragged out the words. "I don't know much about him."

"Me neither." For some reason, this made her laugh. "Other than that Kate likes him."

Scott laughed now too. It was such a warm sound. Becca felt more of her stress fade away. When his laughter faded, he cleared his throat before talking. "Michelle makes Kate sound a little boy-crazy like it wouldn't be difficult to find someone Kate likes."

Becca scrunched her nose up, considering. She felt an instinct to protect Kate, but then nothing he was saying wasn't something she had thought of herself. "Maybe a little," she conceded.

"I asked Michelle about you guys today when I got home, actually. She says Kate's a little intense and sort of rude."

Becca resisted the urge to ask what Michelle said about her by closing her eyes and forcing herself to take a deep breath. Once that was out of the way, the urge to defend Kate reared up behind it. This time, she didn't hold back. "She's intense because she's passionate and she's not rude." Her voice was sharp.

"Hey," Scott said in a soft tone. "I don't know her. I'm sorry. I shouldn't repeat what other people say."

"She's a good friend."

"Usually," Scott added.

Becca bristled again. "What is that supposed to mean?"

"I'm just saying maybe she's not being the best friend right now. She yelled at you in the middle of the quad the other day."

"I deserved that," Becca said.

"Agree to disagree?" Scott asked.

But Becca didn't want to do that. Becca didn't want all the blame for this fight falling on Kate. She hadn't done her part and Kate was just reacting. When Kate forgave her, she didn't want her other friends to hold this against Kate and she really wanted to be able to count Scott among her friends. She sighed. "Not in this case. You're wrong. Kate was angry. Like I said, she's a passionate person. Maybe a public venue wasn't the best and it's not what I would've chosen, but it was the first time she'd seen me all day and she just needed to get it out."

"OK."

Becca was a little taken aback by the ease with which Scott caved. She gave a shocked look to the phone. "You believe me?"

"I can tell that you believe it and I believe in your judgment. I'll try to get to know Kate for myself before I judge her."

Becca's smile lit up her entire face. "Thank you, that's all I ask."

The two stayed on the phone for another hour or so. They talked about movies, books, music, and dogs. They talked about school projects and homework they should be doing. It turned out Scott was in the other section of Advanced Math, with Joe. Becca was proud of herself for steering the conversation in another direction when that came up, in case Scott knew about the dance fiasco.

Time passed too quickly and before Becca realized it, it was time to hang up and make dinner. "I just noticed the time," she said, her voice suddenly urgent.

"Yeah, I guess it's getting kind of late."

"I really need to go make dinner before my mom gets home from work, it's my turn to cook." She remembered the noises in the background, her assumption about why he had called. "Are you going to be alright?" she asked.

"Me? Yeah, I'm great. Thanks for distracting me." He didn't say it like it was a bad thing. In fact, in his voice, it sounded like flirting. It gave Becca warm fuzzy feelings in her core.

"Any time," she answered.

She was still smiling when she hung up the phone. She smiled while she cooked dinner. She smiled at her mom when she walked in the door. Her mom noticed the change and, when Becca wasn't looking, she gave a knowing sort of smile of her own.

Chapter 16

For the first morning in a while, Becca got herself ready without agonizing over thoughts about Kate and every way she'd let her friend down. Instead, as she showered, brushed her teeth, picked out the perfect outfit, had breakfast, and made sure everything was in her backpack, she was thinking about Scott. She thought about the conversation they'd had last night, she thought about his favorite music, and she thought about those dazzling blue eyes that always looked like they were enjoying every moment.

Becca dropped her meticulously packed backpack onto a nearby chair and stepped into the backyard. She called Honey and Marcia. The younger dog flew out with his normal gusto, almost knocking Becca over. She laughed and scratched his ears. Marcia stood in the doorway, looking wary. "Yes, you have to come out here," Becca said. "I filled your water bowl. I know you don't want to be out here. But Honey can't be inside all day." She sighed. "Please, Marcia. You have shade, water, and blankets." Marcia knew exactly what was happening. This may be the way Becca's parents had decided to solve the Honey-chews-on-everything problem, but Marcia was not happy about having to be banished to the backyard. Becca grabbed a tennis ball off the ground and threw it for Honey. He didn't hesitate before dashing off after it across the wide yard. Then she pulled her secret weapon out of her pocket, a bone-shaped dog treat. "For you," she offered. "He didn't get one."

Marcia took the bait, as she always did. She crossed the yard quickly and took the treat. Becca noticed she snapped a little harder than she normally did, communicating her frustration with Becca and the situation. "I'm sorry, girl. Really, I am."

Becca slipped past the dog, shut, and locked the back door. Then she headed immediately for the front door, checking the clock on the VCR on her way by. She was right on time, as always.

She stepped out the front door and turned to slip her key into the lock. "Morning, sunshine," a voice called.

Becca jumped and spun around. Kate was leaning up against the chainlink fence bordering the lawn. "What are you doing here?" Kate was dressed for school and wearing a light jacket, her arms were crossed over her chest and she had a smile affixed to her face. If Becca didn't know about the last few days, she would certainly not be able to read any clues of their fight in Kate's facial expression.

"Picking you up for school, obviously." Kate pushed herself off the fence and crossed to the driveway. "I can't believe I was ready for school before you." She froze, her eyes wide as if something had scared her. "You don't think I'm turning into a goody-two-shoes because of all the time we spend together, do you?" she asked.

Becca stood there, her keys still in her hand, her front door still unlocked, blinking and staring at Kate. Were they really about to pretend like nothing had happened? Like everything was perfectly fine?

"Don't you need to lock your door?" Kate asked, gesturing toward the house. "We should go."

"Yeah, right." Becca snapped out of her freeze and shook her head. She turned around to lock the door, trying to focus on resetting herself. This was a good thing, she told herself. Kate obviously was ready to forgive her, just like Frank predicted. This was a good thing. So why was she feeling like this was a test? Was she ready to forgive Kate so quickly? Of course she was, what was she even thinking?

She turned around with a smile affixed to her face. "Ready," she said.

"Awesome." Kate led the way out of the driveway and down the street. She turned her head and called over her shoulder. "Do we need to wait for Frank?"

Becca looked down the street that led to his apartments. She could see a figure in a black jacket coming their way. It was probably Frank. "He's right there, I think. Just walk slow, he'll catch up."

"How is Frankie?" Kate asked. "I haven't seen him in days."

"You haven't seen me in days," Becca wanted to say. Something told her to keep that observation to herself. Instead, she shrugged. Then, since Kate was about three steps in front of her and not turning around, she realized she had to answer verbally. "He's fine."

"Good."

They walked in silence for a few steps. They passed five houses, then six, before Frank's sneakers could be heard jogging up behind them. Becca turned and felt relief at seeing him. Then she felt guilty for feeling relieved. Kate was talking to her again, she shouldn't be thinking about how awkward this was. She shouldn't be feeling like she needed a third person to help make this less awkward. She was such an awful friend, she noticed with a pang.

"Morning, ladies," Frank said. He eyed Becca and raised his eyebrows in an unspoken question.

Becca's answering smile was forced, strained. "Morning."

"Frank," Kate yelled with entirely too much excitement. "How the heck have you been?"

"Fine, thanks. Are you girls good?" he asked. He spoke loud enough for Kate to hear but he was looking at Becca, who he'd drawn up beside.

"We're great," Kate answered.

Frank bumped into Becca's shoulder, entirely on purpose as a way of repeating the question without having to ask. Becca nodded. They were fine, at least she thought they were.

"Hey, I almost forgot," Kate said. She stopped to wait for Becca and Frank to catch up with her. Then fell into step beside them before she explained what it was that she had forgotten. "I tried to call you yesterday. Your phone was busy for hours. Did Honey knock it off the receiver again?"

Becca felt a blush creep up her neck. "Um, no. I was on the phone."

Kate's reaction was exactly what Becca had anticipated. Her eyes widened as if the shock of Becca having someone else to talk on the phone to was too much to bear. As if Becca would've been completely alone for these days when Kate was refusing to speak to her. Becca felt a shock of annoyance travel up her spine. She shook it away before it could show on her face. Then Kate grabbed Becca's arm as if to anchor them back together. "Who were you on the phone with?" Her voice sounded cheery enough, but to Becca, it felt like an accusation.

"Um, just Scott. He called because he was going through something and he wanted—" she stopped herself. This line of conversation was going to invite questions about what they talked about and what he may have been going through. Those details were Scott's to share, not Becca's. "He just wanted to talk. We talked about, like, music and stuff."

"For two hours?" Kate asked.

Becca wondered how Kate knew that number. Did she really try to call for two hours? Were they really on the phone for that long? She wasn't sure, but she figured it was probably pretty accurate. "I don't know, maybe." Then she edited her answer, shrugging, downplaying what felt like a perfectly amazing conversation last night. "Maybe not. I might not have put the phone down on the receiver all the way after the call."

"That's probably it," Kate agreed. "I love you and even I can't spend that long on the phone with you before you get bored and space out on me." She was the only one who laughed. "Anyway, I was calling you last night to tell you Ernie called me."

For the first time since they left the house, Becca felt a genuine smile fill her cheeks. This was the reason for Kate's good mood. Nothing nefarious, just happiness. "That's awesome, Kate. What did you talk about?"

"Well, not much. He couldn't talk long. He has an older brother, I guess, who's in college. Anyway, the brother was down for the night to have dinner or whatever. Ernie didn't have long before he had to go." She flipped her hair over her shoulder. "He just wanted to call me and say hi. Make sure I had his number." She fluttered her eyelashes at Becca. "Isn't that just the sweetest thing you've ever heard?"

Becca smiled. "It's very sweet."

"I wonder what made him decide to call," Frank said.

Becca spun her head around to glare at him. She obviously hadn't told Kate about talking to Ernie and she really didn't want to have that conversation right now. Kate was excited he called, she didn't want to make this about her. "Maybe he just finally had a minute. He seems like he's pretty busy," Becca said.

"Yeah, probably." Frank shook his head. He put his pointer finger along his upper lip and his thumb along the bottom and moved them, miming a zipper closing. Becca nodded, agreeing with the you-want-me-to-keep-my-mouth-shut gesture. Frank shrugged a reluctant agreement.

The rest of the walk passed in the same way, with Kate ahead of the other pair with a bounce in her step, a smile on her face, and a look that betrayed the fact that she had not a care in the world. Becca and Frank, easily ten steps back, were walking in silence. Frank continued to steal glances at Becca, worried about the dark shadows that had fallen over her expression this morning. It didn't take a genius to figure out the cause of the unrest in his friend was Kate but he didn't know how to go about patching this up. More importantly, he didn't know if he wanted to help fix this for them.

Chapter 17

After seventh period, Becca rushed to get to the band room. The morning practice had been cancelled but this meant the squad leaders were expected to run marching drills on their own. Her squad leader had put it directly after school.

She shoved her backpack into her instrument locker, pushing her small flute to the very back of the long locker. Then she grabbed her marching sneakers, still covered in grass from the last morning session, and shoved her stocking-clad feet into them.

"Hey, Becca, how's it going?" Brandon asked, sauntering up in his own socks.

"Going fine. You have marching practice too?"

"That's what I've been told." He ducked into the smelly room where the band kept their marching sneakers and emerged again quickly holding a pair of ratty-looking, grass-covered, but still name-brand shoes. He dropped onto the ground next to her and put the shoes on.

Becca finished lacing the second shoe but stayed there on the ground. "I heard Ernie called Kate last night," she said. She tried to drop the fact calmly, hoping to bait him into offering information about Ernie and his feelings.

Brandon's head shot up like Becca had said something surprising. "Are you and Kate talking again? I'd heard you weren't."

"We are." She smiled. "We're cool. It's all good." She stopped herself from adding a fourth version of the same statement. Surely that would start to indicate the exact opposite.

"So you forgave her for that whole fiasco? You're recovering?" He looked back down, focusing on tying his laces.

"Fiasco?" Not only was it an impressive word, it was not the one Becca would've chosen. They had a fight. People fight all the time.

"Yeah, the dance fiasco. It's big of you to forgive her." He finished with his second shoe and pushed himself up to a crouch. "You're a good friend."

Becca tipped her head back, slowly, in realization. "Oh, no. That's not what we were fighting about. That's old news."

"Really? Awesome." He stood up. "Where is your practice today?" he asked.

Becca pushed herself up off the floor and pointed with her left hand toward the field. "On the big field. You?"

"Same." As if reaching an unspoken agreement to walk together, the two fell into step beside each other to cross the band room in the direction of the football field. "Can I ask your advice on something?" Brandon asked.

Becca shrugged. She reached the door to the band room first and stood with it open so he could pass by. "Sure," she said.

Brandon ran a hand through his dark hair. "My girlfriend wants to go to this art show thing in the park next week. I'm not a big fan of art." He held out his hand in front of him, a stop gesture. "Don't get me wrong, I'm going to go with her. But, like, how do I keep from sounding like an idiot when we're at the show? Do you know anything about art?"

Becca considered this. "First, it's good you know you should go anyway because it's important to her. Second, I don't think she would be expecting you to be an art expert." Becca didn't actually know who Brandon's girlfriend was. She was drawing from experience. "If she knows you at all, she's noticed you never talk about art, right?"

Brandon shrugged.

"Right, so just let her talk about it." She thought about the conversation she had on the phone with Scott last night, although he was not her boyfriend and, therefore, it was not the same thing. They'd talked about things he liked that she knew nothing about. But she loved his excitement. It had been contagious. "Maybe just ask her questions about things that she's looking at or likes, does that make sense?"

"That seems simple. It's a good idea. You don't think I should do some research and find out what artists will be there ahead of time? Maybe learn something about them?" They reached the gate for the field, which wasn't supposed to be kept open. Brandon pulled it open and waited while Becca stepped through. Then Becca stood on the grass, thinking about his question and waiting, while he pulled the gate shut again.

"I think researching would be cool, actually. But not to trick her into thinking you knew it all ahead of time. Just sort of as a way to show you're excited. Like, I'd never heard of this band Scott mentioned on the phone yesterday but I plan to go out and get their tape sometime. I want to listen to them myself, hear what he likes in them. It's not to trick him into thinking I always listened to it, it's just because I'm interested. Does that make sense?"

Becca turned her head to look at Brandon, who was nodding. "It does. Also, can we backtrack a bit?" He smiled. "On the phone with Scott?"

Becca rolled her eyes. "We're friends."

Brandon gestured between the two of them with his pointer finger. "We're friends. We don't talk on the phone."

Becca shrugged. "He called me. I'd talk to you if you called me."

"Alright, fair." Brandon pointed off toward the left side of the field where a group of trumpet players were gathered. "I'm this way." He tipped his head a little, reminding Becca of Honey. "Hey, thanks for the advice. It was pretty cool they way you were so honest. That's nice." He jogged off before Becca could even think of calling out an answer. Not willing to be left standing alone in the middle of the field, she jogged off toward the right side of the field and her own waiting squad.

"Hey Becca," Ellie called, waving. Becca smiled and waved back. Ellie was not in her squad for marching band. She was, in fact, a clarinet player instead of a flute player. For this reason, although Becca was happy to see the friendly face, she must have also looked confused. "I can't be here after school tomorrow for my makeup session so I got permission to join another squad," Ellie explained to the confused expression.

"That's awesome," Becca said.

"Hey, are you going to the formal in a few weeks?" Ellie asked.

Becca shrugged. "I hadn't really thought about it. Why?"

"Just curious." Becca's squad leader clapped her hands, interrupting any further explanation Ellie may have been preparing. She instructed them to line up in formation. Ellie, since she was usually in another squad, jogged herself over two yard lines and set up.

They marched the first number for the show to the beat the squad leader tapped out on her leg. Becca concentrated on rolling her toes, landing on the right marks, and making sure her steps were exactly the right size to fit eight steps inside ten yards. The practice wasn't perfect, but it was better than yesterday.

"Get a drink if you need it and then we run the second number," the squad leader called. Becca jogged across the field to the water fountain. After getting a deep drink she noticed Ellie was behind her. She waited while her friend grabbed a drink. They fell in step beside each other for the walk back to the field.

"Back in junior high my friends and I used to get together before the dances at my house. We had dinner and got ready together. It was sort of a pre-dance ritual." Ellie frowned. "None of them go to this school so I was kind of wondering... "she trailed off.

The pain on Ellie's face was raw. Becca felt a pang in her chest at the sadness exposed by that frown. An idea formed in her mind and Becca smiled. "That sounds like fun. Do you think we could keep that idea alive this year?" she asked.

Ellie looked relieved. "That's what I was going to ask." She smiled. "Maybe you could come by my house before the formal and we could do the same thing?"

"Great idea," Becca said. "Should I invite Kate too?"

"Definitely. The more, the merrier." Ellie smiled.

Becca was glad she could help. "Cool, I'll let you know what she says tomorrow in PE." The wheels in Becca's mind were already whirring. She would have to come up with a way to make this their new tradition, make it just a little different from what Ellie had done in junior high. Otherwise, whatever that sadness was that had invaded her smile would surely make a comeback. She didn't want that. She resolved to ask Kate about it later. Kate was always good for ideas.

The rehearsal for the second song went well. Becca was starting to be confident in every move of her feet on the field and the routine was becoming second nature. On the walk back to the band room, Ellie snagged her arm. "One more thing," Ellie said as if they had never been interrupted.

"Sure, what's up?"

Ellie's cheeks flushed pink. "Your friend, Frank. Does he have a girlfriend?" Ellie seemed intensely focused on the rock she had just kicked, watching it skitter across the dirt.

Becca smiled. "No." She bumped Ellie's shoulder. "Do you like Frank?"

Ellie pulled her hair back into a ponytail, the act looked like an excuse to keep nervous hands busy. "Maybe a little," she admitted.

"I'll see what I can find out." Over Ellie's shoulder, Becca could see a group of boys walking their way. "That may be him right now. We walk home together. No promises, but I'll put some feelers out." She smiled at Ellie, who blushed even deeper.

"Thanks, Becca." Ellie pulled open the door to the band room and ducked inside just as the wave of brass players closed in.

Chapter 18

Becca followed the throng of boys into the band room, changed into her regular shoes, and retrieved the backpack she had buried in the locker. When she emerged from the locker room hallway back into the main building, she found Frank standing by the door. "Why are you always so much faster than I am?" she asked, sauntering up to stand beside him.

Frank smiled. "I guess you just dilly-dally more."

Becca rolled her eyes and pushed the band room door open. "Did you really just say 'dilly-dally'? That's seriously old school. We need to work on your vocabulary."

Frank laughed at the good-natured teasing. The two friends fell into an easy rhythm as they made their way across campus toward their normal route home. The afternoon was cool despite the sun beating down on them. The empty campus was quieter than usual. These times, when the only students on campus were band students and faculty, were Becca's favorite times to be on campus. It felt more private as if the campus really did belong to her. She was seeing the campus at its most vulnerable and bare. She loved it.

The peace of the quiet campus was broken as they emerged from the central corridor of the open hallways and came face-to-face with the busy street that ran in front of the school. Becca assumed it wouldn't be as busy at this time of day because students were not trying to drive out of the campus. She was wrong. The street was still bustling. All four lanes were loaded up with cars zooming in both directions.

She hit the crosswalk sign and turned to face her friend. "So, how's it going with that girl you liked in English?" she asked. In her mind, she was thinking about how to open the door to talking about Ellie. But she felt like she couldn't just come out with that. She needed to lean into it, be smart.

"It's not really going anywhere," Frank admitted. He raked his hand through his hair. "She's friendly but I'm not sure I need more than a friend."

Becca frowned. "At all or from her?"

"Are you hitting on me, Beck?" Frank teased. The little symbol indicating they should walk illuminated and the annoying chirp of the crosswalk blared. They crossed the street. "No," Frank continued. "I just don't know right now. I was talking to her after class the other day and I realized something didn't feel right." He stared off into the distance for a few steps, then shook his head clear and faced Becca with his full smile. "Guess I'm still looking for the right girl."

Becca brought her hands around to the front of her body and cracked her knuckles. It was a terrible habit, one that she normally tried not to do. Kate had told her repeatedly that it would make her fingers brittle or give her misshapen joints. Becca was relatively sure that was all garbage, but she still tried to stop doing it. She pulled her hands apart and shoved them into the pockets of her light hooded sweatshirt. "What if there was a girl I knew about that had a crush on you? Would you want to know?"

Frank squinted at her, his mouth cocking up on only one side. "Seriously, are you hitting on me? You're being weird."

"No," Becca snorted air through her nose in a sort of half laugh. "A friend mentioned a crush. I just wondered if that is the sort of thing you'd be interested in."

Frank bobbed his head a few times. Then his eyes widened and he stopped suddenly on the sidewalk. "It's not Kate, is it?"

"What? No."

Frank breathed a sigh of relief and continued walking. "I don't think I could handle what that would do to our dynamic if Kate decided to sink her claws into me." He started looking both ways, his signal for readying to cross the street. Becca let their focus be on not getting hit by cars, staying silent until they crossed the street.

"So, you'd want to know?" She pushed.

"Sure." He nodded. "Yeah. Tell me."

Becca smiled. She considered how to tell him, exactly. Should she just come right out with her name or should she give him a little information, sell him on the idea of her? She liked Ellie, she decided. She wanted Frank to like Ellie.

"She's in the band. She plays clarinet." Beside her, Frank gave a thumbs up. "She's very caring and she likes being around people, instead of being alone." This was something Becca had never really understood. Personally, she adored being alone. She saw nothing wrong with it. But, she assumed, you'd want a girlfriend to be someone who enjoyed actually leaving the house to do things with you. "She's also very pretty." Becca wiggled her eyebrows at Frank, who chuckled. "Brown hair, brown eyes, thin, tall," she listed Ellie's characteristics.

"I'm glad you led with clarinet so I didn't think it was secretly you," Frank said.

Becca rolled her eyes. "I like being alone." Why did he continue to think she was talking about herself? She laid her hand on his arm. "Seriously, we're friends. Is there something you need to tell me?"

Frank laughed. His real, full laugh. "No, sorry. I guess you have me worried you are going to change this whole friendship we have. I like us like this, Becca. Honest."

"Good, me too." She slipped her hand back into her pocket. "But I like Ellie for you, Frank. I think you should ask her to the formal."

Frank turned his head, pinched his lips together, and nodded. "Ellie Mackenzie?"

"The one and only."

When Frank turned his head forward again, Becca let the silence linger. She imagined thoughts of Ellie were flooding his brain at that moment, drowning him in good memories of the times they'd interacted. She felt proud of herself for how this had gone down. "I'll give it some thought," Frank said.

Becca's shoulders sagged. "I suppose that's good enough."

"What did you expect? Did you want me to run to her house and propose marriage?" he teased, a laugh tickling the edge of his words.

Becca stuck her tongue out at him and rolled her eyes.

"Speaking of matchmaking," Frank poked her in the shoulder, in case she hadn't been aware he was calling her the matchmaker. "Why didn't you tell Kate it was your idea for Ernie to call her?"

"I don't know." Becca drew out each word making the sentence more of a groan. "That whole situation was so awkward this morning, wasn't it?" Frank nodded. "She just showed up and acted like nothing happened. I didn't really know how to act or what to say."

Frank cleared his throat as if he was preparing for something important. "Do you want to be friends with Kate?" Frank asked, delicately.

"Yes, absolutely. I know you don't like her, but she's been there for me a lot. I'm not saying we're not friends. I hope we are. I'm glad things felt almost normal this morning, that's what I want."

"I'm not sure that normal with Kate is the same as normal with everyone else, but you'd know better than me. If this morning was what you want, then what's the problem?"

Becca pulled her hands down her face. "I don't know," she repeated in the same tortured groan. "Me, I guess."

Becca watched Frank's sweatshirt swell as he took a deep

breath. Then she watched it fall in slow motion as he audibly blew it all out. She had the thought that it was preparing for something, like maybe he was going to yell at her. Except that didn't make sense. If he was going to yell, he would've started on the inhale. Maybe he was trying to be patient with her. Maybe she was irritating him.

"Is this conversation awkward?" he asked. He didn't sound angry. He didn't sound disappointed. He sounded plain, like vanilla yogurt.

"No." Except that she didn't know what point he was making.

"So it can't be you, Becca. That's not how it works. It's something between you and Kate. The two of you together. Honestly, I've been thinking for awhile that the way you two interact is strange. You let her say things to you that are really hurtful. It bothers me some times."

"She doesn't mean—" Becca started.

"Please don't defend her right now. That's not what I was saying. I just had to put that out there so that you think about it a little. Maybe I'm wrong, I don't know. It's not you. That was my point. It's the two of you together, your dynamic or whatever."

Becca sighed. "So I need to figure this out with Kate, is what you're saying."

They reached the second stoplight and Frank pushed the walk button. "I'm saying if you want to be friends with Kate then, yes, you need to have a heart-to-heart or whatever with Kate. Until then I have a feeling it's going to be awkward."

He pointed off to the right. "I'm gonna go this way today because it's getting late. My mom drives this way home from work. If I go this way she might stop and pick me up when she passes. Is that cool?"

Becca nodded. "Of course." She looked to the right, down the street that would come up on the back side of Frank's apartments. The street where there were, sometimes, unsavory characters standing in the shadows. Where further up a little ways shoes were hanging from telephone wires. "Be careful, OK?"

"Always. Call me when you get home?"

"Sure."

They parted ways when the crosswalk signal changed and Becca jogged across the road and hurried toward her own house. She felt like the conversation she had just had with Frank was deep but she didn't feel guilty about it. In fact, she was feeling pretty good. She wondered why her conversations with Kate never had the same effect. Then, she decided, this was not something she was going to figure out on her own. She needed to have a conversation with Kate.

Chapter 19

Becca checked the dinner chart on her way to retrieve the treats for the dogs from the cabinet. It was her father's turn to cook tonight, meaning Becca had time to work on an Algebra assignment before dinner. If it had been her night things may have been different. She tossed Honey her treat and gently handed Marcia hers. The cabinet was clicking shut beneath her fingers when the phone trilled. "Who could that be?" she asked Marcia, who tipped her head to the side as if to ask "How would I know?"

"Hello."

"Are you coming over here or what?" Kate asked.

Becca knew she had a lot of homework to do. But she also knew she should probably try to talk to Kate. She decided to compromise, she wouldn't leave but Kate could come here. "I've been home for two minutes. The dogs are barely inside. You should just come over here."

"Be there in three." The phone clicked in Becca's ear and she hung up. She grabbed a glass, filled it with water from the jug in the fridge, and headed to the living room. Honey was already there, curled up in his favorite armchair. Becca shook her head at him. "I'm not supposed to let you sit there." She scratched his ears as she passed. "Don't shed on it and move your butt if you hear Dad's car."

Her jeans barely touched the fabric of the couch before the

front door flew open and Kate blew in like a hurricane. The door slammed against the wall behind it and Honey lifted his head, preparing to bark. "Oopsie," Kate said. Honey dropped his head back down. Kate threw the door shut again, dashed across the room, and flopped onto the other end of the couch.

"Where's your backpack?" Becca asked.

Kate rolled her eyes. "At home. Where else would it be?"

"Don't you have homework?" That was, after all, the logical reason for Kate to need her after school.

Kate waved her hand dismissively. "Yeah, I'll do it later. This is more important." She used her foot to push Becca's backpack away from the couch. "Remember the boy from junior high who wrote for the newspaper? The geeky one with the cool last name?"

Becca had also written for the junior high newspaper. She was actually the editor for the last quarter of eighth grade, a fact that Kate normally remembered because it meant Becca had inside information on a lot of people and stories. Kate also liked to throw this fact around because, in her opinion, it proved she was perfectly capable of being friends with a geek. Becca could only assume Kate was referring to Carl, who happened to share a common last name with someone Kate believed was worthy of drooling over during their time in junior high. "Carl Johnson?" she clarified.

Kate snapped her fingers. "Yes, that's it. I knew you'd remember." She reached out and tapped her forefinger on Becca's forehead. "You're so smart."

"What about Carl?"

"He's transferring to our school."

The school district was large, hosting multiple schools for each grade level. Carl had started the year at the rival high school, along with about half of the population of their junior high. "OK," Becca said. Her voice was hesitant, questioning. She hadn't yet grasped what any of this had to do with her or what made it more important than the homework assignment she needed to get done. She reached her hand out and pulled her backpack closer to her again.

Kate scoffed. "Becca, he liked you." She rolled her eyes. "Like-liked you."

Nothing in the memories of Carl that Becca had matched up with this information and yet she found herself shyly smiling. Had she missed something? "Did he say that?"

Kate shook her ponytail back and force with the force of her head shake. "God, no. If he said it then I'd think he was up to something. He was always staring at you during class and stuff when you weren't looking." She tilted her head to the right and batted her eyelashes like she was the one dreamily ogling Becca. Becca giggled and Kate returned to her normal posture. "I think you should ask him out," she finished.

It was Becca's turn to roll her eyes. "That's not going to happen." She reached down and retrieved her math textbook, paper, and a pencil from their designated spots in her backpack. She settled the book on her lap, flipped it open to a random page, and set the paper on top. "I have homework to do. Go get your backpack." She started writing her name at the top of the paper.

"I'm serious." Kate watched Becca writing, waiting for Becca's eyes to come back to her. When Becca instead continued writing, adding the date under her name, Kate reached out and stopped the pencil. "You don't exactly have a bunch of hot guys breaking down your door to take you out on dates. This one is interested. You shouldn't let that get away."

"Ouch, Kate," Becca said. This was the kind of hurtful thing Frank had been talking about, wasn't it? "Why do you have to say things like that?"

"Like what?" Kate asked. "Oh my God, Beck, I'm just saying. You shouldn't let a guy who wants to be with you get away so easily."

Becca sighed. "I'm not asking him out —"

Kate scoffed.

"— but I will talk to him."

Kate hopped up, clapping her hands. "Perfect." She pointed

her finger sternly at Becca. "Promise me you'll even try flirting with him."

Becca laughed and used her finger to draw an X over her left breast. "Cross my heart and hope to die," she said.

Kate smiled. "Good. I'm going home to get my backpack. You start your smart people's math homework. I'll be back in ten."

Becca started her homework and managed to get through two problems before she was interrupted again. This time, it was the ringing telephone and not the front door that demanded her attention. She set the books beside her and reached across the couch, snapping the handset up before it could start its third ring and trigger the answering machine. "Hello."

"Becca?" Scott's voice filled her ears and tugged a smile onto her face. "It's Scott."

"Hi. Yeah, I recognized your voice." She sagged into the couch, relaxing her posture a little.

"Hey, who do you eat lunch with?" Scott asked.

Becca was suddenly very aware of her heartbeat. "Kate or Frank, usually. Why?" she choked out.

"Just wondering. Do you think, maybe, I could eat with you tomorrow? Just to chat about stuff?" He didn't sound at all like his normal self. He sounded like someone with a lot clouding up his mind.

"That would be great. Are you alright?"

"Yeah, I'm good. I'll see you tomorrow at lunch, OK?"

"That's all you needed?" Becca heard the front door open. She turned her head and saw that it was Kate. She waggled her fingers in a sort of wave. Had it not been for Kate, Becca realized she may have pushed this conversation. Maybe made sure Scott truly was all right, since he sounded distracted. But, for reasons she didn't feel like digging into right now, she didn't want to have that conversation in front of Kate. "Yeah, alright. Talk to you later. Bye."

She hung up the phone and pushed herself back up to a sitting position. "Was that Frank?" Kate asked.

"Oh no, Frank!" Becca grabbed the phone again. This time she punched out the seven numbers that would connect her to Frank.

"Hello," he answered. He sounded normal. Safe.

"Hi, it's Becca. I forgot to call you. I got home safely. I hope you weren't worried." Guilt propelled her voice out of her faster than it normally traveled. "I'm so sorry I didn't call you right away."

"It's OK, Beck," Frank said. Becca stopped talking and took a breath. "It's cool. Thanks for checking in. Glad you're safe."

"Thanks for not being mad," she said.

She heard the sound of Frank sighing through the phone. "Never over something that little, I promise. Goodnight." Then she heard the sound of the click and returned the phone to the cradle.

"What was that all about?" Kate asked.

Becca turned her head to see that Kate was standing directly beside the couch, looming over her and looking down on her. She tried not to see that as a metaphor for how good of a person Kate was, looking down on the lowly Becca. Why did Kate always make her feel that way?

She pushed herself up and Kate flopped onto the cushion beside her and dropped her backpack onto the floor. "We split up when we were walking home," Becca explained. "I was supposed to call him after I got here."

"That's cute," Kate said. Becca was surprised. This seemed like the kind of thing Kate would normally make fun of. Of course, any excuse to pick on Frank was normally something Kate would capitalize on. "Maybe you should ask Frank to the formal." She threw an accusatory glare at Becca. "Maybe that's why you didn't want to ask Carl."

Becca pulled her homework onto her lap and started on the next problem. "Nope. Frank is thinking about asking someone else, I don't like Frank, and we're just friends. Also, I said I'd think about Carl."

She didn't add anything about Scott, even when it was

burning in her chest to burst out. She wanted to give the thoughts a voice. She wanted to tell Kate about the phone calls. She wanted her friend to tell her the lunch date tomorrow could, possibly, be a chance for him to ask her to the dance. She wanted to hear all the right things.

But the fear of all the wrong things held her tongue.

What if Kate pointed out that Scott was too good for her? What if she knew another girl that Scott liked better? What if, and this was the one that made Becca feel guilty for even thinking thoughts like this, Kate decided she liked Scott too?

Chapter 20

The next night, after dinner had been cleaned up and the dogs walked, Becca and her parents were settled in the living room watching some comedy show on TV when the phone rang. Her Dad reached behind him for the phone, bringing the receiver to his ear as the last of his laugh lingered in the air. "Hello," he said cheerily.

He listened to something on the other end before politely asking, "Who may I say is calling?"

Then he held the receiver out toward Becca, the end pointing like an accusatory finger. "Someone named Scott," he said.

Becca felt herself blush even as she pushed herself out of Honey's favorite chair and crossed the room. "He's a friend from school," she said, although her father hadn't asked. "Probably asking about Algebra or something." She put the phone to her ear. "Hi, Scott."

"Hey, Becca. Is it OK that I'm calling?"

"Yeah, of course. Why wouldn't it be?" she asked. She glanced over her shoulder and saw that the show was on a commercial break. She had a bit before she risked annoying her parents by talking over the show.

"I'm just checking," Scott said. "It's not important or anything, I can let you go. I didn't really call to ask about Algebra."

Becca winced. He must have heard her give her father the

excuse. "No, I know that," she said.

"I just called to chat, nothing important. Do you want me to let you go?"

Becca considered this. The show was funny and her parents were cool, but she found she really would prefer to talk to Scott. "No, it's fine. Hang on just one quick second."

"Yeah, alright," Scott agreed.

Becca took the phone away from her ear. "I'm going to take this on the other phone, down in my room. Then I can help Scott with Algebra without bothering your show. Is that alright?" she asked.

Her father looked at her mother. Something passed between their faces, but Becca couldn't quite be sure what it was before it was gone again. Then her father looked at her. "Yes, that's alright. Hand me that. Go grab the other receiver. I'll hang this one up when you're done." Becca did exactly as he said, practically skipping to the other side of the room. She picked up the ugly green receiver. "Got it, you can hang up now," she said. She watched as her father did that and then she brought the new receiver up to her ear. "Are you still there?" she asked Scott.

"I'm here. Loaded with all my algebra questions," he joked. Becca smiled. "What are you up to tonight?" he asked.

Becca walked down the hallway and shut her bedroom door around the cord. Then she situated herself on the floor, her back to the door. "Nothing really. We had dinner and we were just watching something on TV. You?"

"Did homework, had some dinner, now my brother is out there playing some video game. I couldn't be bothered to sit and watch him."

"Do you play video games too?" Becca asked. At her house, they had an old Nintendo system with exactly one game, the one that came free with the console. They'd played it until they won, now it was rather boring. She knew all the tricks and cheat codes and somehow that made it less of a challenge. She supposed there were other games out there, but they'd never really bothered to get any of them.

"Sometimes," Scott answered. "Mostly my brother is the one who plays."

"You just have the one brother, right? Michelle's boyfriend."

"Yup. His name is Ron. He's a junior."

"How did he meet Michelle?" Becca asked. She didn't have a lot of interaction with older students. The only reason she knew Michelle was because of the failed credits in PE. Really, how common could that be?

"I think he met her at some club or something, I don't really know. But they've been dating for a while now."

"Michelle doesn't really seem like the club type," Becca said.

Scott laughed. "Neither is Ron, actually. Maybe I have the story wrong."

Becca laughed right along with him. "Maybe," she agreed.

Scott's laugh faded, sort of like someone was turning down the volume. "Hey, thanks for eating lunch with me today. Do you maybe want to do that again?"

Today had been easier than Becca expected. There was no strange confrontation with Kate where Becca was forced to come up with some reason why Scott was joining them. Kate had to stay back for tutoring in English so she could retake some test. Frank and Becca had simply eaten lunch with Scott. It was fun, carefree, easy. She'd enjoyed it. But somehow she expected Monday would be more complicated. What were the chances Kate would be missing from lunch twice?

"We can try, yeah. I'm not sure if Kate... " Becca trailed off because she didn't know how to make this explanation. She hadn't told Kate about these phone calls, not really. So how to explain the desire to eat lunch with this boy she didn't talk about? More to the point, how did Becca plan to keep Kate and Scott apart if she drove them together at lunch?

"Yeah, Kate doesn't really like me too much. At least that's what I figured out," Scott said.

"You talked to Kate?" Shock clouded Becca's tone.

"No. That's sort of what I mean. I talked to Frank at lunch. I've chatted with Brandon, who by the way I didn't realize you were friends with. And, of course, Michelle mentioned you a time or two. But Kate seems to, sort of, avoid me."

"I'm sure it's an accident," Becca said. "I don't think she really knows much about you."

"Yeah, I'm sure." Scott didn't sound sure. He sounded hurt, actually. "Well, if you all want to eat lunch Monday that would be great. I like the company of all your friends. They're good people."

"Let's plan on it," Becca said. "How do you know Brandon?" she asked, changing the subject to something more comfortable than her rocky, recently healed relationship with Kate.

"He's in my English class and my Social Studies class, actually. I didn't know him before this year," Scott said. "But it turns out he also lives right up the road from me. I saw him after school today when I was outside getting some chores done. He said hi and came over. We talked for a bit. I didn't realize you knew him until he mentioned you."

"I hope he said something nice," Becca said. She closed her eyes tight, realizing that made her sound like she was fishing for a compliment, which she wasn't. Not really.

"Yeah, he said you were really helpful with some advice for dealing with some art show and his girlfriend." Scott sort of chuckled, the sound bubbling through the phone line and tugging a smile from Becca's lips. "He seemed to be telling me that to make it clear he has a girlfriend. I think he thought I'd come to the conclusion that you two were a thing otherwise."

"Oh," Becca said. She couldn't think of how else to say what she wanted to say. She wanted to ask if that would bother him, to hear that a boy was interested in her. She wanted to ask if he was interested in her. She wanted to tell him about the little burning sensation in her tummy right now. The one that told her she was highly interested in him. But she couldn't bring herself to do any of that, so she stuck with the simple syllable.

"That was nice of you to offer him advice though. Are you usually good at advice?" he asked.

"I guess I can be," Becca answered. "I like giving advice. I think it's because I read a lot of books. So I often draw experience from stories, if that makes sense."

"Maybe you can give me some advice," Scott said.

Becca didn't know what to say here. Sure, she would love to. But the last advice she'd been asked for involved a girlfriend. She wasn't sure she could bring herself to listen to Scott talk about a girlfriend. She said a little prayer to a god she wasn't familiar with, a generic one, that he wouldn't mention another girl. "Sure," she said. "No problem."

"Really? Great. So there's this girl," he started.

Becca felt her shoulders sag. Of course there was a girl. He was cute and sweet. There had to be a girl. Why had she let herself think for even a second that there wasn't a girl?

"I like her, but I'm not sure if she feels the same way," he continued. "See, she has a lot of friends that happen to be boys. I think she may honestly think of me as just a friend. I'm not really sure if I should take the chance and tell her how I feel."

Becca didn't want to know which girl. She had this fear that the girl might be Kate. It was irrational. She didn't have any evidence for this, other than a bad feeling. She tried to swallow the fear, bury it underneath something else. She tried to pretend this was Frank or Brandon asking for advice, someone she wasn't emotionally invested in. What would she tell them? "You say she has lots of friends," Becca said.

"Yeah, some."

"Alright, so maybe start by talking to one of them? Friends always seem to know things about each other," she said. Thinking about Frank and Ellie, how she had been able to bridge that gap for them. "They can often feel people out, find out how they feel about someone else. Maybe one of her friends might be able to help you understand how she feels, or find out for you. That may be easier than talking to her if you're nervous about it."

Scott was quiet for a beat. Becca worried he was going to suddenly say, "Good idea, so how does Kate feel about me?" and laugh. She wasn't sure she could handle that. She decided if he said that, she'd say her dad was calling and that she had to get off the phone. She was ready, the excuse already forming her in mouth, ready to pop out.

"That's not a bad idea," Scott finally said. "I think I'll try that at school next week. Thanks, Becca."

She let out the breath she was holding, grateful she didn't have to spit out her excuse. But something else flew out her mouth without permission. "It's not Kate, right?" she asked. Her hand flew up to her lips, too late to hold back the question she didn't really want answered. She hung her head, completely embarrassed that she had let the question fly.

"What? No," Scott said. "No, definitely not. She's too—" he paused, considered. "—crass for me, I think."

Becca's burning desire to defend Kate and her utter relief at his answer battled inside her heart. Before she could decide which one would win, Scott spoke again. "Hey, I have to go. I'm sorry, my mom is home from the store and I can hear her shouting about chores we missed or something. She'll be knocking on my door any second now."

"Yeah, alright," Becca said. "Thanks for calling. I'll talk to you soon, at lunch."

"Count on it," Scott said.

Becca heard the soft click from his end and pushed the button on the receiver in her hand to hang up the phone before it could start with the dial tone in her ear. She smiled, thinking that she was glad Kate wasn't Scott's choice girl. She didn't even really care who it was, she decided, so long as it wasn't Kate. That thought lasted for only a beat before another one chased it away. This one was stronger and more violent. This one was the idea that Becca was being a terrible friend. Here she was being glad someone didn't have a crush on Kate. This terrible thought brought darkness to her entire evening because this one had visited before.

She was a terrible friend.

Chapter 21

Saturday morning brought a competition for the marching band. That meant, among other things, a bus ride to and from the competition with the full marching band. This particular ride would take close to an hour each way. Becca rode up to the competition with her squad on the first bus. The band earned the highest rating possible at the competition and the energy getting back on the bus was high and intense. Brandon waved at her on the way by. "Sit up here with me," he suggested.

"We aren't supposed to change seats," she said.

"No, we are expressly told not to change buses," he clarified, winking at her. "Besides, it's fine. No one sat next to me on the way down."

Becca shrugged. The girls in her squad were nice enough but no one was really a friend. They mostly talked to each other and seemed seriously obsessed with clothing and makeup, two things Becca didn't find particularly fascinating. "Let me just grab my stuff," she said. Quickly she scrambled back to her seat and pulled the items she'd left there into her arms. Then she darted back up to Brandon's seat and dropped in beside him, stuffing everything into her backpack in a hurry. She felt oddly guilty like she was committing some sort of crime. She wondered if she should hide. "Are you sure we won't get in trouble for moving?" she asked.

Brandon was already slouching in the seat, his backpack stored beneath him and his knees propped on the seat in front of him. "We won't get in trouble. Look around, Becca, hardly anyone is sitting in the same seat."

She turned in her chair so she could take in the length of the bus. He was right, the same people they rode down with appeared to be on the bus, but the seating chart was certainly more flexible than she'd been led to believe. She relaxed, adopting a posture almost identical to Brandon's. "How's the girlfriend?" she asked, not wishing to spend the entire bus ride in total silence.

"She's good." He smiled at her. "How's Scott?"

"Friendly," she answered, arching an eyebrow. "But it's not the same thing, we're not dating."

"So you've said." He chuckled at her. "Did you know he lives on my street?"

"Actually, I had heard that."

"Right, I should've guessed. So has he asked you to winter formal?" Brandon asked.

Becca's legs dropped to the floor, the slapping sound of her feet hitting the bottom of the bus a perfect compliment to her total shock. "What? Why would he do that?" she realized too late that her voice was coming out louder than she'd meant for it to. A few of the rows around them quieted. Becca felt her face flush. She consciously pulled her legs up onto the seat, crossing them underneath her, and lowered her voice. "Did he say something about winter formal to you?"

Brandon was watching her movements closely, seeming to catalog them all. Becca felt like a science experiment. She frowned at him. He rolled his eyes. "No, he didn't say anything. I was just curious." He bumped her with his elbow. "But clearly you'd say yes if he did. Want me to talk to him for you?"

Becca frowned. She definitely didn't want that. That reminded her too much of the whole Joe fiasco that she had barely put behind her. "I don't know. Kate thinks I should consider this guy

Carl from our junior high." She shrugged. "I don't really remember him that well." She sighed, the sound lost in the noise of the kids around them deep in the throes of their own chatter. "This is all pointless, you know. No one has actually asked me to go to the dance or mentioned having any interest in me at all. I'm not even sure why it's a conversation I keep having except that it's some kind of wishful thinking." She tilted her head in his direction, looking serious. "Change the subject."

Brandon scrunched his face up. "You aren't talking about Carl Johnson, are you?" he asked.

Becca blinked rapidly, annoyed that he was clearly refusing her request to change the subject. "Let me guess, you happen to know him."

"Actually," he chuckled, "I do."

Becca threw her hands up. "Oh, come on. What are the odds of that? He went to my junior high and he's been going to a different high school so far this year."

Brandon's laugh got deeper. "He goes to my church," he said as the laughter died down. "I've known him for years. He's a really nice guy. How do you know him?"

"I told you, we went to the same junior high."

"You and hundreds of other kids," Brandon pointed out. "How did you happen to know this one?"

"We were on the newspaper team together."

Something in Brandon's expression changed until it was almost curious like he was trying to solve a puzzle. "Why did Kate want you to take him to formal?"

"She's hoping to go with Ernie and she doesn't want to leave me going alone, would be my best guess," Becca answered.

"OK, but why Carl?"

Becca considered their conversation on Friday when Kate had first mentioned Carl. "I don't really know. She seemed to have it in her head that he might have liked me in junior high." She shook her head. "Whatever, didn't I ask you to change the subject?"

"I don't want to feed Kate's ego, believe me," Brandon said, "but there was a girl in newspaper he was always talking about."

Becca refused to let herself feel an ego boost. She rolled her eyes. "There were twelve of us that wrote for that newspaper and only three boys. Lots of options for this mystery girl."

"Yeah, you're probably right." Brandon shook his head and the curious look in his eyes vanished. "What are the odds that you're that girl and Kate's actually right about something, right? Besides, I'm pretty sure he mentioned she wasn't a writer. She was like an editor or something."

Becca's mouth fell open. She was the editor of their junior high newspaper. Technically, she wasn't the editor the entire time, but the person who'd been editor before her had been a boy. She was the only female editor in the two years they'd been in newspaper together. Something in her heart fluttered a little. Not because she felt the same way. In fact, she still didn't really remember Carl or her impressions of him at all. But because, for the first time, she felt like there was a possibility that someone had noticed her. Not like a sister, not like a friend, but as a potential girlfriend. She wasn't sure what she thought of that, but it felt pretty good. "Are you sure?" she asked, her voice quieter and somehow more breathless.

"I think so. Why, do you know who that girl was? Does she go to our school?"

Becca nodded, her head bobbing slowly up and down once, twice, three times.

"That's cool. Maybe I'll mention it to Carl tomorrow morning at church. I wonder if he still thinks she's cute, maybe this move to the new school will turn out to be good for him after all. He was pretty stressed out about it." Brandon stopped talking and seemed to notice Becca's expression had changed, her eyes were wider. She looked shocked, somehow. "Are you alright?" he asked, laying a hand on her elbow. She nodded again, slowly and deliberately. "Are you sure?" he pressed.

"I'm just confused, I guess," she answered. "Why didn't he ever tell this girl how he felt? How come he never called her or talked to her or anything? How is a girl supposed to know?" she was asking about Carl, but she was thinking about Scott. What were the signs you were supposed to look for? What told you when someone was interested in you?

"How do you know he didn't do those things?" Brandon asked, narrowing his eyes at her.

Becca smiled. "I was the editor of our junior high newspaper, Brandon."

Now it was Brandon's turn to drop his feet to the floor. He sat upright, turning his body to face Becca. "OK, I didn't know that. I probably shouldn't have mentioned the crush. I don't know much about it. I didn't know he didn't tell the girl. He's pretty shy, honestly. Were you, like, friends?"

Becca shook her head again. No, they weren't that. They were barely even acquaintances. Really, this was all kind of a shock.

"I feel like I shouldn't have told you," Brandon confessed.

"I feel like Carl should have," Becca said. "Sometime last year he should've mentioned it, maybe called me or something." She shrugged. "Seriously, how are girls supposed to know how guys feel when they won't say anything?"

Brandon pointed a finger right in her face, almost touching her nose. "That's not fair," he said. "You can't say that you girls are always honest about these things either."

"Maybe we are," Becca challenged, swatting his hand away. "You don't know. Who said they liked who first, you or your girlfriend?" Brandon looked sheepish for a second. Becca grinned in triumph. "Ha, see. She did, didn't she?"

The sheepish look faded, replaced with a dangerous-looking and somehow challenging expression. "Does Scott know how you feel?" he asked.

"That's not the same thing. I don't even know how I feel about him. I certainly don't run around to my church group talking about how much I like him."

"Neither did Carl, not really. We were just friends, we talked about girls sometimes." Brandon shrugged. "Whatever, I bet it wasn't really that big of a crush. He would've told you if it was." He turned himself forward in the seat again, propping his knees back up. "Besides, would you have even been interested if he did tell you?"

Becca sighed. "I don't know," she whispered. She flopped her head back on the seat and turned her eyes to the aisle. She let the silence wrap around them, deciding she didn't really want to talk about this anymore. Maybe she should've just stayed in her original seat.

Chapter 22

Monday morning Becca and Frank lucked out of having to walk to before school band practice in the dark by getting a ride from Becca's mother on her way to work. Band practice was productive, but required all of Becca's attention. In fact, her squad stayed to practice one more thing briefly after they were dismissed to change, meaning Becca had to really hurry to change her clothes and get herself to her first period. All this meant that when she ran into Kate on her way to second period it was the first time she had seen her friend all morning.

"Oh my god, there you are. Guess what?" Kate trilled. She snagged Becca's elbow and pulled her away from the crowd surging down the center of the sidewalk

"What's up?" Becca asked. Kate didn't look like she was angry or upset, she looked excited. Her eyes were wide and her cheeks were flushed. Becca saw Ellie over Kate's shoulder and waved at her. Ellie crossed over to them.

"I ran into Scott at the grocery store this weekend," Kate said.

Becca froze, her hands wrapped around the straps of her backpack. Scott was not a subject she spoke about in front of Kate. Her brain tried to think of a question she could ask, something she should say. But the seconds slipped by in silence. Kate was likely waiting for her to probe the subject and show her interest. But Becca couldn't think of a single thing to ask. It was as if her brain had been dropped into a bucket of ice water and was no longer functioning.

"Scott from PE?" Ellie asked. "He's a nice guy."

"Very nice," Kate agreed. She turned her eyes back on Becca. She had an impish sort of smile on her face like she was up to something. "We had a quick conversation right there in the cereal aisle. Nothing too serious."

"Wh-wha-what did you talk about?" Becca stuttered out the question, unsure until it was out of her mouth what the question was going to be. Her brain was still not processing things at normal speed. Was Kate angry that she hadn't mentioned her nightly phone calls with Scott? Did they talk about her at all? Was this Kate's way of telling her that she was now interested in Scott? And the biggest fear, was this related to his questions? Was Kate the mystery girl? Had Becca been filling in the role of "friend he reaches out to for advice"? He said it wasn't Kate but what if he was just embarrassed? Her fears had her heart slamming away at her ribcage as if it was trying to escape her body and run away.

"Not much. We didn't have long." Kate let out short, barking laugh. "Anyway, he mentioned he was going to eat lunch with us today, isn't that sweet?"

"That is nice," Ellie said, her tone of voice indicating she didn't fully understand this line of conversation and was quickly losing interest. She threw her long ponytail over her shoulder. "Anyway, we should probably get to class." She pointed over toward the locker room, which the girls had been headed toward before Becca's feet betrayed her by freezing.

"Right, yes." Becca used this as a thing for her to focus on. One foot at a time, head to PE. It was just a conversation. A short conversation in a grocery store. It meant absolutely nothing. Kate was just sharing because she knew Becca was friends with Scott. She found her feet taking on a faster rhythm as her thoughts calmed her racing heart. She was overreacting, she convinced herself. This was not a big deal.

Kate reached the locker room first and pulled the heavy door open. Ellie disappeared inside and Becca stepped to follow. "Becca," a voice at her back stopped her. She closed her eyes. Oh no, was that—

She turned around and came face-to-face with a jogging Scott. "Hey, hang on a second."

She was aware of Kate behind her, coaxing Ellie back out of the locker room. Her eyes caught on Brandon who was behind Scott, almost looking as if they may have been walking together before Scott jogged off. Becca stepped out of the way of the locker room. "What's up?" she asked. Behind her, Kate and Ellie stepped to the side as well, not even attempting to hide their eavesdropping. Brandon didn't step any closer, just maintained his distance, somehow looking serious.

"I don't really have time for a conversation right now," Scott said, checking his watch. "Can we, maybe, chat for a second before lunch?" His eyes darted over her shoulder in the direction of Ellie and Kate. "Just the two of us?"

He almost sounded sad, for some reason. Becca had an urge to reach out and comfort him, which was silly. She didn't know why he would need comforting. She gave him a reassuring smile, reminding herself that this was Scott. Her friend. She could trust him, couldn't she? "Absolutely," she agreed.

Scott nodded in acceptance of the agreement but didn't look relieved. In fact, as she watched him step away toward the boy's locker room, she thought he looked more stressed than ever. Ellie and Kate came up behind her and she felt Kate's hand on her shoulder. "That was weird timing," she said. "We were just talking about him."

Becca nodded and turned to Kate. "Did you say something to him about me?" she asked, quietly.

Kate scrunched up her nose, making a big show of thinking.

"I don't really remember. We talked a little about friendship and stuff, nothing really big. I think you're name came up, but I don't remember anything specific." She shrugged. "I guess you'll just have to wait for lunch to see what it's all about." Then, frustratingly calm, she turned and sauntered back into the locker room like this was any other day and boys requesting lunchtime meetings was perfectly normal.

Ellie looped her elbow through Becca's. "It's probably nothing."

"Right, yeah," Becca said. Except id didn't feel like nothing. She allowed herself to be led into the locker room and over to the locker bank she regularly used. She suddenly felt like she was going to explode if she didn't share everything with someone. She unhooked her elbow from Ellie's and dropped her backpack into her locker. "It's just that he mentioned something about liking a girl on the phone the other night."

She found herself needing to get this all out. Ellie, she was sure, would be able to tell her it was nothing. Ellie would tell her truthfully if she thought the girl was Kate, which was what Becca found herself truly worried about. "He said she had a lot of male friends and he was afraid that's how she saw him. I told him he should talk to her friends and find out from them."

Ellie, who had been hiding in her locker and changing her shirt, popped her head out from behind the metal. She had a huge grin on her face. "And the next thing he did was talk to Kate at a grocery store?" she asked, her voice an octave higher with excitement.

"Right, so what if I was the friend and I gave him the go-ahead for Kate?" Becca said, her shoulders sagging.

Ellie stepped out of the locker, tugging down on the sides of her t-shirt. "Becca, what if you were the girl?"

Becca's carefully calculated movements, pulling her shorts up over her bottom quickly to avoid showing anyone her underwear, slowed for a beat. "What?"

Ellie laughed at her shock and repeated the question, slowly emphasizing each word. "What if you were the girl?" She raised her eyebrows, letting the question sink in.

Becca's eyes unfocused, staring at the floor. She thought about the conversation. What, exactly, had made her think of Kate? What had he said? Something about friends that were males, she had those. Something about her being his friend, she was that.

Her eyes snapped back into focus on Ellie's face. "Oh my gosh," she said. The possibility unfurled inside her like a flower blooming in sudden sunlight. She felt excited, alive. What if she was the girl Scott had a crush on? As if the idea itself could call up a video, her mind remembered square dancing with him. Her hand in his, his blue eyes laughing at something.

"Maybe," Ellie said, drawing Becca back to reality. "He's going to ask you to formal at lunch."

Becca quickly tied her shoe and slammed her locker. Suddenly she was very eager to get on with her day and get to lunch.

Chapter 23

Time crept by, as it only seems to do when you're waiting for something that could change everything. Becca watched the clock in each class period move as if the hands were special effects in a movie, slowed down to add a dramatic pause. Finally, when there were only five minutes left until lunch, she allowed herself to feel the full excitement of the situation. She hadn't admitted it to anyone, but she really did like Scott. He was kind, funny, cute, and he seemed to like talking to her. Admitting it, even in her head, made it somehow real. It made her lightheaded and giddy. She had a crush on Scott.

Somehow it seemed as though Ellie's guess at what may be happening allowed Becca to imagine the scenario she had been blocking from her mind. She supposed, as she sat there in class watching the clock, her brain had already seen this possibility. After all, she was pretty smart. She was good at solving logic puzzles where the clues brought you to the correct answer. Surely she had imagined he may have been talking about her, at least for a second. But she hadn't allowed the thought to take over her mind because it had seemed so impossible. Boys didn't like her. That wasn't how it worked. They had to be forced to dance with her, threatened with terrible secrets. That's what boys did when Becca was concerned.

This thought deflated the happy balloon in her chest. Her

shoulders sagged and she sighed. Scott had never once treated her like Joe had that night. But the memory had the power to bring fear. Becca suddenly worried that getting her hopes up for this lunchtime meeting would be devastating. Scott had never given her any reason to think something terribly awful or wonderfully brilliant was happening today. This was just going to be a simple meeting between friends. Maybe something was going on with his brother and he needed advice. Maybe he just wanted to talk about homework. With one minute remaining until lunch, Becca forced herself to take a deep breath and calm down. "You're only going to get yourself all worked up over nothing and then be disappointed when it's nothing," she thought. "Calm down."

The bell rang and Becca sprang out of her chair, grabbed her backpack, and practically sprinted to the cafeteria. As far as she could see, she was the first of her friends to arrive in the large carved-out bowl outside the building. She stepped down onto the first step and sat on the curb, intending to wait. Her knee spang to action, bouncing out the fractions of seconds she waited.

When Scott came around the corner of the building nearest her, she saw him right away. He was shoulder-to-shoulder with Brandon, who still looked serious. Scott looked nervous, his hands shoved deep into the pocket of his jeans and his eyes nervously scanning the crowd. When his eyes found her, she looked away and took a deep breath. It was no good, she realized. Once you'd already let yourself admit you had a crush you saw him differently. She couldn't see her friend Scott anymore, not really. Now she saw the easy smile and the hair he'd been running his hands through. She heard the laugh, the friendly teasing, and the questions about her family and her dogs. She had to get this crush under control.

She looked up again and met eyes with Brandon. His mouth twitched a little, but not in a happy smile. Becca squinted in confusion. Brandon looked apologetic like he'd done something wrong. She didn't have much time to think about it before Scott's feet were next to her. "Can I sit?" he asked, gesturing to the concrete beside her.

She nodded. "Of course," she said. She watched as Brandon walked into the cafeteria, presumably to get some food. She could suggest she and Scott do the same, but then he may want to wait until they had food to talk. She wanted to hear what the message was that he had to deliver more than she wanted to eat. Actually, she realized, her stomach was too tangled up around itself to eat right now anyway. "What did you want to talk about?" she prompted, tired of waiting.

"Right, um... " Scott sat down beside her and dropped his backpack between his feet. He kept the loop at the back of the simple blue bag in his hand, fingering it. "There's something I sort of have to tell you."

"Sort of?" Becca raised an eyebrow.

"Brandon says it's the kind of thing you'd want to know." Scott shrugged. "I don't really know why it would be important, or anything. I mean, it doesn't seem like the kind of thing you'd care about. But Brandon said I had to tell you."

Becca gulped. She pulled up the sleeves of her sweatshirt to her elbows, suddenly feeling hot. She leaned forward a little, adjusting her posture. "So tell me," she said.

Scott sighed and turned to her. Becca had never been this close to him before. His left leg was pressed up against her right one. His blue eyes were close enough that Becca could see they were really more grey with a blue tint. Her heartbeat hammered away.

"On Sunday, at church, I invited a girl from my youth group to go with me to our winter formal," he said quietly.

Becca instructed her face to remain calm. Don't move, don't react, don't show surprise, she commanded herself. It was silly, really, how hurt she suddenly felt. Scott didn't know how she felt. Heck, before this morning, Becca hadn't known how she felt. This was perfectly fine. Good for him. Plus, he thought of her as a friend who should know. "That's great," she said, forcing a smile. "Really great." She hit him playfully on the arm, like she would probably do if this were Frank telling her about a date. Somehow, it felt wrong.

A smile sort of twitched Scott's mouth and then it was gone. "Thanks. Do you—" he shook his head, started again. "Do you have any idea why Brandon thought it would be important for you to know that?" he asked.

"No." She shrugged and looked toward the cafeteria. "I think I'm going to go get some food. Kate will be looking for me by now," Becca said. Her voice betrayed her, cracking just enough to make her cringe. She couldn't believe how much this was bothering her and she certainly would not be crying in front of this boy today. She turned back to him, a fake smile plastered on her face. "I'll talk to you later?" She didn't wait for a response before she pushed herself up and headed toward the building.

"Becca," Scott called. She stopped and turned her head a little so her ear was pointed in his direction. "This is OK, right? We're friends, you and I?"

She turned all the way around and gave him a more realistic smile. "Totally fine," she agreed. "We're friends." Then, because she wasn't sure she could control the tears if she waited too much longer, she hurried off into the cafeteria. As soon as her feet hit the temperature-controlled room, she felt a tear slip down her cheek. She headed immediately to the bathroom and shut herself in the stall. She bitterly remembered Ellie's excited question from earlier: *What if you were the girl?*

Yeah, what if?

The tears weren't overly dramatic. They were controlled quiet tears. She let them fall for thirty seconds or so before she took a deep breath and wiped her eyes. "Enough," she mentally told herself. Scott was her friend. She would be happy for her friend and his date. She was fine.

She opened the stall door to find Kate standing there with her arms open. Becca walked right into them and let herself be closed in the warm hug. "What happened?" Kate asked.

"It's stupid. He just wanted to tell me he asked a girl from his church to the winter formal." Becca's words were muffled by Kate's warm sweatshirt. She pulled her face away, and Kate let her arms fall back to her sides. Becca swiped at her face again. "It's so dumb that I'm even upset."

"I didn't know you liked him," Kate said, pushing a stray strand of hair behind Becca's ear.

Becca let a little bubble of laughter escape her sudden sadness. "I didn't either."

"Oh, honey." Kate hugged Becca again, briefly. Then she pushed her to arm length, her hands on Becca's shoulders. She stared into her friend's face. "Here's what you're going to do. You're going to go to that formal with Carl, you're going to look adorable, you're going to have fun. We're not going to worry about Scott anymore. He's not worth it."

Becca shook her head. "He's a friend, Kate. He's a good friend. He doesn't know about the crush and he doesn't need to. This is fine. Keep this to yourself." She pushed Kate's arm off her shoulder and held up her own pinkie. "Pinkie swear that you will keep all information relating to this crush to yourself. Right now."

Kate wrapped her own pinkie around Becca's. "If that's what you want, it's done already," she promised.

Chapter 24

By the time school ended, Becca was ready to put the entire weirdness of the day behind her and move on. She still had a crush on Scott, sure, but crushes came and went every day. She would get over it. She had no other choice. She smiled at Frank, waiting in his customary spot. "How was your day?" he greeted.

"Fine." She shrugged. Frank didn't know about the whole crush-turned-heartbreak saga and she wasn't ready to explain it yet. She could feel his eyes on her, probably assessing something she was projecting. He would be able to tell something was up and he would ask for details.

Just as she was preparing her thoughts about the topic that could be shared, Kate jogged up and rescued Becca from what likely would have been an uncomfortable conversation. Instead, the trio made it all the way home without ever talking about winter formal, Scott, or Becca's feelings.

That afternoon Becca was curled in Honey's favorite chair right in front of the window looking over her front yard. She had a book packed full of fictional characters on her lap. The kinds of characters who seemed to have bigger problems than who to take to a winter formal.

A noise broke through her imagination. Her attention was diverted away from the book and to the front yard. She frowned at the cause of her distraction. Frank was holding a hose and water was dripping off the glass of the window beside her.

She pushed herself up and opened the front door. "Are you crazy? It's cold out there."

"It's not cold," Frank hollered. "Come out here, I'll show you."

"If I come out there you'll just spray me with the hose."

There was a beat of silence and then Frank's laugh. "Yeah, probably."

"Why would I come out there then?"

"Because sometimes," Frank said, "you just need to act like a kid for five minutes. It's good for the soul."

Becca rolled her eyes and smiled. She couldn't actually think of a single reason why she shouldn't run outside and get in a water fight with Frank right now. That seemed like the most simplistic, brainless, kid-like thing she could choose to do. Suddenly, that was exactly the kind of thing Becca wanted. She tossed her book onto the chair and stepped out the door. Frank was kind enough to wait until the door closed before following through on his promise to soak her with the hose in his hand.

She dashed across the front of the house, water spraying up into the window, and lunged for the end of the hose. She wrenched the dial to turn the water off. "Cheater," Frank teased. Becca stood up and ran for the garage door while Frank ran for the dial. She pulled the door up and slipped under it, heading straight for the supply of water guns kept along the back wall. By the time she had managed to grab two, Frank had the water back on. She held up the spoils, "we should play fair," she yelled.

"Why would I agree to that," Frank laughed. "I'm winning."

Becca cocked her head to the side. "You can't spray inside this garage without my dad getting mad at you. I could just stay here and it ruins all your fun." She shook the water guns. "Or I can emerge from the depths of the garage, arm us both equally, and we can settle this."

Frank leaned down and turned the dial, ending the spray of water. "Deal," he called.

Becca walked to the edge of the garage and held out the two water guns. "Fill them both," she said.

Frank took them and knelt to do just that. Becca watched him carefully, concerned that he may try to pull a fast one on her. But he did exactly what she asked him to do. He filled both large tank water guns to the top, turned off the water, and handed her back one of the guns. "Five count to scatter?" he asked. Becca nodded and dashed off to the other side of the house, her laughter trailing behind her like the veil behind a runaway bride.

They sprayed water at each other from around the tree in the front yard, from around the corners of the house, or straight on when they got caught running. They refilled the water tanks and started the process all over again. On her third dash to refill her tank, Becca saw Frank coming close to do the same thing. She put her palm under the spigot and turned the water on full blast, using her fingers to guide the water in Frank's direction.

He threw his hands up. "Alright, you win, you win."

Becca turned off the water and dropped to the ground, her back up against the spigot in case Frank tried to change his mind. "I knew I'd win," she teased. She looked down at herself, every stitch of clothing she was wearing was soaked and clinging to her body. "Even if I look like a drowned rat."

Frank sat beside her in a similar state of soaking wet. "It was fun though, wasn't it?"

Becca smiled and wrung out her wet ponytail on his shoulder. "Thank you."

"Wanna tell me what was wrong earlier?"

"It's dumb." She shrugged. "I shouldn't even be upset."

Frank nodded. "But you are."

"I am," she agreed. "I sort of have a crush on Scott."

"No offense, but I already kind of knew that." He bumped his arm into hers. "Sorry it was news to you."

Becca smiled. "I guess I just hadn't really admitted it." She turned her head toward Frank but looked down at his t-shirt to avoid looking at him. It was a simple black t-shirt although it was dripping with water now. "It was bad timing, I guess. Right as I realized I liked him he was asking a girl from his church to go to our winter formal with him."

Frank sighed. "That is bad timing."

"But I shouldn't be upset. It's not like he knew how I felt or that I had any expectations that he felt the same way." Becca shook her head and looked out at the house across the street. "I really shouldn't have let myself think he maybe felt anything. That was my biggest mistake."

"You know there are guys out there that are going to have feelings for you, right?" Frank asked. "I mean, it's not unreasonable."

Becca rolled her eyes. "Whatever."

"Hey," Frank bumped her again with his elbow. "I would take you to the formal, you know. Just say the word."

Becca shook her head. "I'm not going to winter formal with my brother." She turned and trapped him with her best I-mean-business glare. "Take Ellie, we both know you want to."

"What are you going to do?" he asked.

Becca took a deep breath and smiled. "I am going to go alone. I am going to get ready at Ellie's house with Kate. I am going to dress nice and walk into that dance with my head held high because I don't need someone else to tell me I'm beautiful." It was all words, she didn't really believe any of it. But she knew if she delivered it with enough passion, he might believe it. She could act, she was good at that. She knew the lines she should say and the way they should be said. She stood up, pulling at her wet shirt. "I'm going inside to change and start dinner. I will see you tomorrow."

"Alright," Frank said. He stood up and handed Becca the water guns from the ground. "I'll see you tomorrow."

"Tomorrow it is." She winked at him.

Becca disappeared into the garage to put away the water

guns. She allowed her smile to fall away in the darkness of the space. Then she allowed herself a deep breath before affixing the smile back in its place. She emerged from the garage and pulled the door shut. When she straightened, Frank was still there. He was watching her, likely looking for signs that she wasn't as good as she was pretending to be. She widened her smile. "What's up?"

"Nothing," he said. "Goodnight."

"Goodnight." She turned and headed toward the front door. When she reached it, she turned around and again found him still standing there. "I'm fine, Frank. Honest." She waved her hands in front of her in a shooing gesture. "Get out of here before you catch pneumonia."

He nodded and she watched him saunter off in the direction of his own house. Then she let her smile fall and ducked into the front door.

Chapter 25

Kate was leaning on the fence around Becca's yard the next morning when Becca emerged from the house. "What are you doing here this early?" Becca asked. She had been intending to walk to marching practice with Frank, which took up an hour before school started. Kate wasn't in marching band, meaning this would be a wasted hour in which she could have been sleeping.

She pushed off the fence and pulled her jacket in closer around herself. "I wanted to walk with you because otherwise I wouldn't get to see you this morning and I have the best news." Kate's words came out in a breathless rush.

Becca started walking down the street, Kate at her side. "Alright, spill it," she said.

Kate clapped her hands together. "Ernie called last night." She squealed with delight. "He asked me to go to the winter formal with him."

Becca realized, with a jolt, that meant she was the only one of her friends going to this dance without a date assuming Frank was going to ask Ellie as planned. Immediately, she chastised herself for that thought. She was being a terrible friend, spinning this to be about her. This was about Kate and something Kate had wanted for a while. The smile she flashed her friend was genuine. "That's awesome, I'm so happy for you. Do you have a dress already?"

Kate and Becca both came from families that didn't exactly

have budgets that allowed for the purchase of new dresses. Because of this they often repurposed things they already owned, borrowed from Kate's sisters or each other, or shopped for adorable second-hand things at the thrift stores. "I have a few contenders. Will you come by sometime and help me pick something out?" she asked.

"Of course. I should pick something too. Maybe we can swap?" Becca asked.

"Yes. Great idea." Kate looped her elbow through Becca's. "Are you going to ask Carl to the formal?"

Becca had yet to see Carl on campus. So far she'd had conversations about this boy but had yet to actually speak to him. She had no desire to let herself develop another painfully unrequited crush on anyone. "No, I don't think so. I honestly think I'd rather just go alone." She realized that sounded sad. So she adopted a tone of voice she had only ever heard in cheesy romantic comedies. "I want to keep things flexible," she said. "No strings."

Kate squealed again. "That could be fun."

Frank popped up behind them, surprising Kate. Becca, who had heard his footsteps drawing closer, smiled. "Morning Frank," she called.

"What would be fun?" he asked.

"Becca was just telling me her plans for winter formal," Kate said, stepping closer to the street so Frank could walk between the girls. "She doesn't want to take a date. She wants to keep her options open so she can dance with all kinds of guys. She has her eye on a kid we used to go to junior high with, maybe she'll dance with him a few times."

Becca didn't know where to start with that claim. She hadn't actually said she was planning on dancing with anyone, she certainly hadn't agreed to dance with Carl. Plus, she noted with mild annoyance, Kate was acting like Frank wouldn't know Carl and didn't go to the exact same junior high school as them. She grunted in frustration. "I didn't say that. I said I was going without a date."

"Are you saying you wouldn't dance with Carl if he asked?"

Kate said.

Becca's heart skittered past a beat. "Don't ask him," she said, her voice suddenly dangerous and low. She pointed a finger at Kate. "Do not interfere."

Between them, Frank's eyes widened. "So you're just planning on hanging out with everyone and having fun, not worrying about dates and labels," he offered. Becca could tell by his tone of voice that he was trying to downplay what could potentially be an awkward situation. She didn't like to talk about what happened with Joe and the sad truth was this could turn into a hashing out of that situation. She and Kate had moved past what happened, they didn't need to bring it back up.

"That's exactly what I'm thinking," Becca agreed.

"That could be fun, too," Kate said. She offered a smile and she actually looked apologetic. "It's your life, Beck. We'll handle it however you want. I promise."

"Thank you," Becca agreed. "Frank, did you ask someone to the dance yet?" she asked. Of course she knew they had discussed Ellie, but she wasn't sure her friend had taken the opportunity to make it happen yet. Also, she wasn't sure how much Frank wanted Kate to know about his plans.

"I'm asking today unless you want me to try the solo thing with you. We could go as a group—"

"No," Becca cut him off with a wave of her hand. "I absolutely do not want you to do that. I want you to ask her and I want us all to have a great time."

"Alright, I'll let you know what she says."

"Do I get to know who this mystery girl is?" Kate asked, setting her hand on her hip and fixing them with a stern look.

"No," they said at the same time. Frank laughed. "Not until we have her answer, OK?"

"Whatever," Kate said, rolling her eyes.

Becca considered how the weekend would likely go. She, along with the rest of the band, would have to be in attendance at the football game on Friday. Then Saturday she was supposed to be helping her father with some yard work, but that was in the morning. She would have plenty of time to get ready for the formal. That reminded her. "We'll miss you at Ellie's getting ready for the dance party, Kate."

"What? I'll still be there," Kate said. "You're not getting rid of me that easily."

"I just thought, because of Ernie... " Becca trailed off.

"He's meeting me at the school, outside the gym." A little laugh bubbled out of her mouth. "He doesn't drive yet, so it didn't make sense to have him pick me up at her house when I can just meet him there."

"I guess that makes sense." Becca couldn't explain why that suddenly felt like a bad idea. Kate would be ecstatic about her date and they'd probably be treated to endless stories about how amazing Ernie was and everything they planned to do. She shook her head, disappointed to be catching herself being a bad friend again. Sure, those thoughts were only in her head but how long before they managed to find their way out of her mouth and offend Kate? It wasn't fair of her to be like that. Kate deserved complete truth from her friend. She should be looking forward to the dance. She should be glad she got to get ready for the dance with two of her friends, turning the event into a fun experience.

She forced a smile. "I guess it'll be fun," she said, her voice just a little flat. "Yeah, great."

"It will be great, you'll see." Kate waved her arms slowly from side to side like she was moving to some music only she could hear. "We're going to the dance and we'll be dancing the night away." She brought her hands up and used them to form a rectangle framing Becca's face. "We'll work our magic on you and by the time you walk into that dance you'll be a different person. People won't even recognize you."

Becca smiled, but the thought of being beautiful felt like a weight. Half of her was excited by the idea of someone else liking the vision in the mirror. The other half felt repulsed by the idea of changing who she was just to fit in. She hated the idea that she might be someone's project, needing to change things about herself before she would be accepted.

"Oh, I almost forgot to tell you," Kate said. "I also told Scott he could meet up with us outside the gym and we'd all hang out. We'll all sort of be hanging out in a group, right? That will be alright."

Becca's eyes widened. Frank whipped his head around, trying to read Becca's expression. He seemed to be communicating that he was concerned, he thought this was a bad idea. Becca refused to let this bother her. Instead, she smiled. "Totally fine," she said.

Frank squinted at her. "Are you sure—"

"I'm sure. He's a friend and we're hanging out with our friends at this dance." Her voice was hard-edged, challenging him to disagree with her. "He's a friend of ours, right? You aren't trying to tell me you aren't friends with Scott, are you?"

He shook his head, conceding. "He's a friend. Good idea, Kate." But he kept his eyes on Becca for a beat longer. Almost like he was waiting to see if the real feelings would be revealed in some last-minute expressions. Becca winked at him.

He turned forward again, watching the path ahead of them. "When did you talk to Scott about the dance?" he asked Kate, nonchalant.

"What?" she squinted at him. Becca wasn't sure why she was asking him what he meant, it was pretty obvious what he meant. Was Kate trying to stall for time? Trying to think of an answer? No, that would imply she was trying to make something up. She surely didn't have to lie about this. "Oh, when we were talking at the store. I mentioned we should all hang out at the dance together."

"Him and his date?" Frank asked.

"Well, at the time I didn't know he had another date." She glanced back at Becca, briefly. "That was back before I really knew anything about this guy." She shrugged. "It doesn't seem right to take back the offer now just because he asked another girl. If we're all friends and we're all cool, we should really keep that up. Right?"

"Right," Becca agreed. She was going to be perfectly fine with this because it was perfectly fine. She threw her shoulders back and raised her chin. "It's going to be fun," she declared.

Chapter 26

Becca spotted Scott immediately as she rounded the corner into the lunch area. He stood in the bowl, hands shoved into his hoodie pockets, looking like he was scanning the crowd for someone. The spot was so familiar—it was almost exactly where they'd sat when he'd casually told her about his date to the formal. She didn't know if he remembered that moment the same way she did, like it was burned into her eyelids. She couldn't stop the flush that rose to her cheeks.

"Hey," he greeted, once she had pulled up close enough to be heard. "How are you?"

"Hungry," she said, tipping her head toward the entrance to the cafeteria.

"Wanna get some food?" he asked.

Becca smiled. "Totally." She led the way into the cafeteria and immediately jumped into the line for a slice of pizza. Usually, she would ask whoever she was eating with what they were in the mood for. Today she decided she wanted pizza. If Scott wanted something else he was welcome to get in a different line. He didn't. He got in line right behind her. The volume in the cafeteria was still high, but she realized she was getting used to it. In fact, she was pretty sure she could probably have a conversation with Scott while they were in line. She turned herself to the side so he could see her profile. "How was your—" she started.

"You know I'm just friends with this girl," Scott said, cutting her off mid-sentence. His voice was awkward, and he quickly added, "Sorry, that was rude. What were you saying?"

He placed his hand on her shoulder, and Becca froze, feeling the warmth of his touch through her thin shirt. Her heart skipped, her words stalled. Was it possible for her to feel this much from just a touch? "Nothing." Becca shrugged. "I was just making conversation. So you know her from church? What's her name?"

"Yeah, we are in the same youth group. Her name is Sarah. I've known her family for years and we're just friends. She was upset on Sunday about not having anything to do, she had a pretty nasty breakup recently and now she feels sort of lost."

Becca thought of Frank and how he'd been after his breakup. "I get that," she said.

"Right, so I decided to go ahead and ask her."

The line moved and Becca stepped up to the counter and ordered a slice of pepperoni. She grabbed the offered plate and headed to the drink selection. She heard Scott's footsteps behind her. She paid for her lunch and settled at a table where Frank and Kate would know to look for her. Scott sat beside her, his own slice of pizza covered in sausage instead of pepperoni. "Anyway, I'm sorry if that blindsided you."

"No, it's cool. You don't owe me an explanation," Becca said.

"It sort of felt like I did owe you something. Or maybe I... " Scott took a bite of his pizza and took his time chewing. Becca's heart sped away, wondering what he was getting at. What endings to that sentence were possible? Could she see the multiple-choice options and choose her favorite? After what seemed like a year, he swallowed his bite. "Maybe I thought it would matter."

Becca felt like she'd just been swallowed by a whale who had emerged from beneath the dull, scratched tile on the cafeteria floor and taken her down in one gulp. She was in darkness now, fumbling for something to illuminate her world again. "You matter," she whispered.

Scott's eyes trailed slowly from his pizza toward her. She watched the subtle movements until the blue was suddenly locked in place. It was all she could see. "Thanks," he said.

Becca noticed his word sounded as soft and somehow as serious as her sentence had. Did this mean anything? It felt like it did. It felt electric. Her skin was humming, alive with the feelings flowing through her.

Scott's eyes snapped back to his food and, just like that, the moment was over. Becca sat watching him take another bite of his lunch and feeling her senses reawaken to the other students in the crowded room.

Frank arrived, dropping a burrito and some hot sauce packets down on the table before climbing onto the awkward stools attached to the round table. Becca took a bite of her own lunch to encourage her body to do something normal. Frank, oblivious to anything awkward Becca might have been feeling, dug into his burrito right away. He had a third of it down when Kate arrived, setting a salad on the table.

Becca, by this point, had shaken off whatever spell she'd been under. She used her pizza to point to Kate's lunch choice. "You aren't a salad person," she said.

"I am when I have a hot date this weekend," Kate answered. She opened the plastic lid and doused the vegetables inside with dressing.

"Salad won't do much for a healthy body in less than a week" Frank said.

Kate glared at him. "Shut up," she commanded. She speared a piece of lettuce with her fork and frowned at it. "I hate salad. It makes me cranky."

Becca tore her slice of pizza in half and held one piece out in Kate's direction. "I'll eat half of your salad if you'll help me finish this pizza," she offered.

Kate took the slice. Then she dropped the fork full of

untouched lettuce back into the container and pushed the salad toward Becca. "Deal," she said. She shoved the pizza into her mouth and chewed happily.

Scott pointed at Kate. "So, you're going to the formal with Ernie?" he asked. He held his finger there until she nodded and then he slid it over to Frank. "How about you?"

Frank swallowed his mouthful of burrito. "I just asked someone, actually." He smiled. "I'm taking Ellie."

Becca clapped. "This will be so much fun. I really do like Ellie for you."

Frank nodded. "I do too, I think."

Kate's eyes narrowed, her usual playful smirk faltering. She leaned forward, her tone sharp now. "You knew that's who he was asking?" It was more than a question—it felt like a challenge.

Becca shifted uncomfortably. Had Kate always been this competitive about relationships?

"I did," Becca said.

"You should've told me," Kate pushed. Her eyes were hard and cold.

Becca felt a war brewing inside herself. She wanted to calm Kate and stop this fight before it started. But she also didn't understand the sudden ire coming off her best friend in dangerous waves. "It wasn't my news to tell," she said. She shifted in her seat, suddenly uncomfortable.

Frank cleared his throat. "Kate, I told her not to say anything. I wasn't sure I was going to ask Ellie." He reached out and touched Kate's shoulder tentatively like he was an action star in a movie reaching for a bomb that needed to be diffused.

Kate twitched, pulling away from his touch. "You're not a matchmaker, Becca. Stop trying to control everyone else's happiness."

Becca flinched. Did Kate know about her conversation with Ernie? Is that what this was about? "OK, I can do that. No meddling." She held out her hands in surrender. "Sorry I meddled,

Frank."

Frank looked confused. "All good," he said.

Kate stood up. "Whatever, I have to go." She reached across Scott and snagged the last of Becca's pizza. "You don't need this, you have salad."

Becca stood too, reaching for Kate. "Don't walk away angry. What's really up?" she asked.

Kate frowned. "Nothing. I told you, salad makes me cranky." She shrugged, shoved the pizza in her mouth, and stomped off. Becca dropped back to her seat, embarrassment coloring her face.

"That was unnecessarily dramatic," Frank said, his tone lighter.

"Do you think she knows I talked to Ernie?" Becca asked. "She yelled at me for matchmaking. That didn't feel like it was about Ellie."

Frank sighed. "If she was aware of the conversation you had with Ernie, it could be bothering her. I don't know. She doesn't always make logical sense to me. Maybe you should ask her about it."

"That would require me to talk to her about Ernie. If she doesn't already know she'll be even more angry than she just was," Becca whined.

"Wait," Scott said, leaning in slightly, his eyes narrowing. "You talked to Ernie about Kate?"

"Yeah," Becca replied, her voice a little too tight. "Twice."

"And then... what? Ernie asked Kate to the dance?"

Becca's stomach tightened as Frank confirmed it with a casual, "Yup."

She looked at Scott, suddenly feeling exposed. This felt like it was spiraling out of control—something that had started as a simple conversation with Ernie was now being laid bare in front of her friends. She hadn't expected this. "Why would she be mad about that? Apparently, your matchmaking was effective," Scott said.

Becca shrugged. "I guess I'll have to work that out with her later." Her shoulders fell a little at the prospect of bringing that conversation up later. If this little preview was any indication, that would be a terrible tongue-lashing she was buying tickets to.

"Speaking of the dance," Scott pointed his finger at Becca, "who are you going with?"

Becca shook her head. "I think I'm going alone, actually."

"Maybe that's Kate's problem," Frank said. Becca threw him a confused look. "All her matchmaking attempts have failed epically and she's projecting her jealously about what a crappy matchmaker she is onto you." He took a huge bite of his burrito like he hadn't just dropped a bombshell.

Becca stared at him, blinking without speaking. In her mind, she had plenty to say. She wanted to tell him that her un-date-ability was absolutely not Kate's fault. She wanted to say that he was embarrassing her, bringing up her epic rejections in front of Scott. But she also staunchly refused to talk about this right now. She hoped all of that was in her expression and her silence.

Frank looked at Scott and swallowed his bite. "Kate sucks at matchmaking. She gets too aggressive with her approach and turns people off altogether. She's too emotional, I think. She takes it personally,"

"Yeah, I know." Scott shrugged. "I got the brunt of that at the grocery store."

Becca wanted to be somewhere else right at that moment. Anywhere else, actually. At another table, in another room, sick at home. She wished that ground whale would return and swallow her again.

"She was trying to push you and Beck together?" Frank asked.

Scott tossed a glance at Becca then turned right back to Frank. "Not exactly. She was just pushy. Wanted to know what I was doing for the dance. She wanted to make sure I wasn't planning on getting in the way of some other guy Becca had her eye on."

This snapped Becca back to reality. She put her hand on Scott's forearm. "What?" she said.

Scott turned to her. "Some guy from junior high?"

"Carl?" Frank asked.

Scott snapped his fingers. "Yes, that was his name. That's why I was surprised you didn't have a date already."

"She told you that I wanted to go to the dance with Carl and that you needed to let that happen?" Becca asked. "Those were her actual words?" Becca's sudden flash of anger burned her embarrassment out of her body completely.

"I don't know about the exact words, but that was the basic gist of the conversation, yeah."

Becca stood up, her hands shaking slightly. "I think I need to talk to Kate about this. But, just so you know, Carl and I? We haven't spoken in years. We were never really friends, and definitely nothing more. So whatever she's thinking... I'll straighten it out with her."

She walked away before either boy could even think of responding. Inside, she knew there had to be a logical explanation, something Kate misunderstood. But right now, she couldn't find that excuse. She could only find anger and disappointment.

Chapter 27

Becca had to bask in her anger and frustration for the entire afternoon. When the end of the school day came, Frank was in his normal spot. He pushed himself off the wall and sauntered over to her. "I'm walking in another direction today," he said. "I wanted to meet up with you and tell you that. You can walk with Kate and I think you should." He put his hand on her shoulder and winked at her. "You two have a lot to talk about."

Becca nodded. "Alright."

"You good?" Frank asked.

Again, Becca nodded. "I can handle Kate."

"Good." He smiled at her. "See you later. Call me if you need me."

He was halfway back down the long hallway that ran through the center of campus when he crossed paths with Kate. Becca watched them, noticing that neither of them bothered to acknowledge the other. She really was the glue that kept bringing those two together. If it wasn't for her, she mused, they would've been completely content to forget ever knowing each other. They would probably never speak to each other again, becoming a distant memory of some person you felt like you knew once upon a time.

Like Carl, she realized with a little pang of regret. Kate felt about Frank the way she felt about Carl. He was a guy she knew in junior high and had absolutely no feeling about one way or the other.

He was a guy she was perfectly fine forgetting about. Maybe that was what she needed to tell Kate.

She pushed off the wall as Kate drew closer. "You waited for me?" Kate asked. All traces of anger were gone from her voice.

"We need to talk," Becca said.

The girls headed off toward their houses. "Is this about lunch?" Kate asked. "I shouldn't have snapped at you like that. I'm sorry. I think I'm just nervous about the dance." She hung her head, the perfect picture of remorse. "My life has just been so crazy lately, I wasn't thinking."

Becca scoffed. "It's not about what you said at lunch, although that hurt me." She ran her hand down her face, trying to physically wipe away any cracks in her anger that had erupted at Kate's apparent sorrow. She reminded herself why she was upset. "What did you say to Scott when you spoke to him at the store?" she asked.

Kate picked up her head and replaced her deep pout with a confused scowl. "What? I told you, I don't remember."

"He remembers," Becca challenged.

"Oh," Kate had the decency to blush. "I may have mentioned you. What did he tell you?"

Becca shook her head, anger flickering to life in her chest. "No, I want to hear you say it, Kate. No lies. No excuses. What did you tell him? I know you remember."

"Look, I wasn't trying to be mean. I didn't know you liked Scott. You never told me that." Kate's voice rose in pitch and volume, she was getting angry. "I would've handled it differently if you had just told me. I didn't realize how you felt until I saw the way you reacted when I told you I talked to him. How was I supposed to know? You never tell me anything anymore. I was just trying to look out for you."

Becca's shoulders sagged. That was technically true. She had been keeping the stories about Scott from Kate. Why had she done that? She couldn't remember. She only remembered that she hadn't told Kate. But why did this feel like Kate was twisting it into something worse? "I didn't really know how I felt until after all this happened," Becca said. Her voice betrayed her sudden sadness.

Kate took a step toward the middle of the sidewalk and slipped her arm around her friend's shoulders. "I'm sorry you're upset," she said. "But this isn't my fault. This is what happens when you keep secrets from me. You should've told me you were talking to Scott so much. I could've protected you from this. I would've told you he was out of your league."

Becca felt tears burning the back of her throat. "You think he's out of my league?" she asked.

Kate squeezed a little, bringing Becca into a hug. "I'm sorry. That sounds so mean, doesn't it?" Becca nodded. It did sound mean. "I don't mean to hurt you. He is a really cute boy, he's smart, and he has a very cool older brother."

"I don't like him for his brother," Becca said.

"Honey, I know. But that's part of what makes him so cool. It's fine. Now you know exactly how he feels, no surprises anymore. We can start healing."

"I don't want to get hurt," Becca said. "But he is my friend and I like talking to him."

"I know, sweetie." Kate let her arm fall back to her side. She smiled. "Just don't let him take the best friend role anymore. That's how this whole mess got started. I'm your best friend. I'll always be your best friend."

Becca tried to smile back, but it was a little forced around the tears stinging at her throat. "I know," she said. "I'm sorry."

"I forgive you." Kate squeezed Becca's upper arm. "That's what friends do."

The girls walked for a bit in silence after that. Becca was lost in her own thoughts about how much she'd let Kate down. She hadn't told her friend about Scott. She was sure she had a reason for that at one point, but she couldn't remember what it was. As Kate had pointed out, that hadn't gone the way she'd planned. Instead, she'd ended up hurting Kate and breaking her trust. It hadn't exactly worked out with Scott, either, she realized. It wasn't like she had that crush to lean on, he'd obviously shut that down.

Becca heard the footsteps beside her quicken and realized, with a jolt, that Kate was running across the street. She looked and saw a car was coming. It wasn't going to hit Kate, but Becca would have to wait it out. She stopped walking, waited for the car, and then ran across the road. "What were you doing?" Kate chided, laughing.

"Daydreaming, I guess," Becca answered. "I'm sorry about not telling you."

"Stop apologizing," Kate said. "It's over. You apologized and I accepted. We're good."

"I will," Becca promised.

Again, they fell into silence. When they reached the light to cross again, Kate pushed it and then leaned on the pole, one leg bent up behind her. "He's a good friend, you said?" Kate asked.

Becca didn't have to ask who she was talking about. It would be easier, less uncomfortable, if Kate were talking about Frank. But Becca knew she wasn't. She was talking about Scott. The boy who had come between them. The boy Becca had lied about. "He is."

"How often do you guys talk on the phone?"

"A couple times a week," Becca answered. "Maybe three."

"Does he call you or do you call him?" The light changed and Kate pushed off the pole and started walking. Becca didn't have to hurry to keep up, but she noticed that Kate was walking faster than her normal pace. This was a good sign that, although she claimed she was fine, Kate was still angry.

Becca sighed, filled with guilt for the way this truth would make Kate feel. "He calls me, usually." She didn't want to hurt Kate. But it was obvious that Kate wanted these details. Becca decided she wouldn't lie to her, not again. She would tell the truth and deal with the consequences. "Sometimes he fights with his brother and he calls me when he doesn't feel like dealing with it."

"So you're safe," Kate said. "You're the person he can call who won't judge him for his reasons. You don't read into it."

"Isn't that what a friend is? Someone you can rely on?" Becca asked.

Kate sighed like Becca was stupid, like it was taking all her patience to explain this. "I suppose. But Becca, think about this. What do you get from the conversation?"

Becca let the silence linger for a few steps while she considered this. Do you have to get something out of every interaction with a friend? She supposed two people with a mutually beneficial relationship was the ultimate goal, but sometimes that wouldn't be possible. Sometimes a friend needed to sacrifice their own personal happiness because their friend needed them. "I enjoy talking to him. He listens to me talk about my day and things. I think it works out for both of us." She shrugged. "I don't think you have to always get something tangible out of a friendship. It's enough that it makes you feel better, isn't it?"

"He's using you, Becca. He's calling you because he needs someone to bail him out of his crappy home life. He doesn't care who he talks to, he's just using you." Kate threw her arms out. "I don't know why you can't see that."

Becca felt the tears pricking her throat again. She swallowed to douse them. "Honestly, Kate, I always feel so good after I talk to him. He's so nice and we have so much in common."

"So a guy uses a few nice words and you're tripping all over yourself to keep him happy. Becca, I need you to grow a spine." They were on their street now, Kate's house in sight. Kate shook her head. "I don't know how to fix you, Becca. I really don't," she said. Then she took off running and didn't stop until she was inside her front door.

Becca was determined to keep her tears inside until she made it through her own front door. She took deep breaths, trying to keep it under control. She didn't know what was wrong with her either. All she knew was that her conversation with Kate had just left her feeling worse than any conversation with Scott ever had.

Chapter 28

The conversations about friendship were still whirling in Becca's head, even though everything had more or less gone back to normal by the night of the winter formal. There were adorable pictures of Becca, Ellie, and Kate taken as they got ready in their dresses. Becca borrowed a floor-length light blue dress that accentuated her thin waist from Kate's older sister. Kate wore a short purple dress with plenty of beadwork which she'd borrowed from Becca's house. Ellie wore a long dark green dress that swept the floor which her own mother had made for her in honor of the occasion.

All three girls delighted in putting on makeup they didn't normally wear, stepping into shoes they'd probably regret wearing by the end of the night, and taking picture after picture for Ellie's mom's camera. When they arrived on campus and stepped out of the car and into the cool night air, they felt like celebrities. In their minds every head turned in their direction, checking out their outfits and marveling at their appearance.

Kate spotted Ernie right away. "There's my date," she practically sang. "I'm off to have fun. Check in with me later?"

Ellie pointed in a different direction. "There's Frank," she said.

Frank was walking in their direction, looking nice in his black shirt with a white tie. "Are you running off, too?" Becca asked, keeping her tone light.

"No, he'll want to say hi to you," Ellie answered.

Frank waved. "Hi, ladies. You two look nice."

"Thanks," Ellie said.

Becca smiled when Ellie's cheeks bloomed with color. She wanted these two to enjoy themselves, she certainly didn't want to be a third wheel. She started to think of a way she could extricate herself from the situation without hurting anyone's feelings.

"We should head in," Frank said, gesturing toward the cafeteria doors. He offered his elbow to Ellie, who shyly looped hers through it. Becca walked beside them, feeling decidedly third-wheel-esque. She figured she would separate once they were inside the doors.

But just inside the door, her eyes found Scott standing beside a gorgeous girl with cinnamon-colored skin and dark hair cascading down the back of her dark blue dress. Jealousy that Becca would've claimed to be above flared up inside her. Scott wasn't touching the girl, he wasn't even looking at her. They were standing next to each other, enough space between them for Becca to slip in sideways if she squeezed, a thought she hated herself for having. She would never do such a thing. That is not how one treats a friend.

Frank followed Becca's eyes. "There's Scott," he said for Ellie's benefit, pointing.

"Oh," Ellie waved. "Who's that girl?"

"She goes to church with him," Frank said.

"Her name is Sarah," Becca said. Her voice was too quiet for the music playing in the cafeteria, even if the volume was turned down because the night was just beginning.

Ellie leaned down, putting her ear near Becca's mouth. "What?"

"Her name is Sarah," Becca said louder.

Ellie stood back up and smiled. Scott and Sarah approached, seeming to notice the group of friends now that Ellie had gone and drawn attention to them. "Hi, I'm Ellie," she offered her hand to the gorgeous newcomer. "You're Sarah, right?"

The girl nodded with a sweet smile on her face. "Nice to meet you," she said.

Ellie handled the rest of the introductions, pointing to each person as she went. "I'm Ellie, this is Frank, and that's Becca."

"Nice to meet all of you." Sarah didn't appear to recognize any of their names. She didn't offer up any I've-heard-so-much-about-yous. Becca wondered if Scott talked about any of them at all outside of school. Had this Sarah heard more about them than they'd heard about Sarah?

"Where's Kate?" Scott asked. "I thought she was meeting all of us here."

Becca shrugged. "She found Ernie." A slow song started up and the DJ turned up the volume. "She'll probably drag him onto the floor now, I'm sure you'll see her out there." Becca didn't want to be trapped here forcing her friends to feel awkward for coupling off for this slow song. She reached up and touched her face. "It's warm in here, actually. I'm going to go get a drink. Be back soon," she turned and walked off toward the picture corridor and the bathroom before anyone could think to stop her.

In the corridor, she leaned her back against the wall and took a deep breath. She had decided to come to this dance tonight. She had decided to come alone. She had known all of her friends were bringing dates and she had made this decision anyway. She was perfectly capable of handling this entire evening with grace and class. She pushed off the wall and reached into her bra, the only acceptable place on this particular outfit to stash money, to pull out the $20 her mother had slipped her. Holding the money, she walked into the room where they took pictures at the last dance. Sure enough, there was the table and the backdrop for photos. This time the backdrop was a pretty blue with white snowflakes, as if that was the perfect depiction of the type of holiday weather they got in the desert.

She stepped up to the table and ordered a $10 package. She

decided she could always get pictures again later with some friends. For now, she was proud of being alone at this dance and she was going to make the best of it.

She was allowed two poses. For one she smiled primly, like her mother would want. For the second one, the photographer encouraged her to do something silly. Becca couldn't think of anything silly. But the thought of trying to come up with something made her giggle with discomfort. He took the photo while she was giggling. She seriously hoped it didn't look ridiculous.

Back on the dance floor the music was continuing at a loud volume, but was no longer slow songs. Becca joined her friends and lost herself in the music. It amazed her how the simple act of letting her inhibitions and self-judgment go during dancing felt so freeing. She didn't find herself thinking about what Kate was up to, whose feet were closest to hers, or if she was making a fool of herself when she was dancing. She focused only on the song and the beat of the music. She tried to match the rhythm with her feet on the dance floor. She danced for her and it was one act that never failed to put a smile on her face.

When the beat slowed to another slow song many songs later, Becca seemed to wake out of her trance. She moved around the throng of bodies until she was in the quiet space at the edge of the floor. As she watched the couples pair off and move to the floor, wrapping their arms around each other in various levels of closeness, she slipped off her shoes and put her stockinged feet on the cold tile.

Frank was only a little bit taller than Ellie, she noticed. She couldn't even see Frank's eyes over the top of Ellie's head. In fact, if it weren't for the fact that the pair was slowly turning, Becca wouldn't be confident that was Frank at all. She smiled when they turned again and she noticed they were dancing pretty close. Frank had his arms on Ellie's waist tight enough that his hands could touch behind her back.

Becca looked away, trying to find Kate. Instead, her eyes fell on what was obviously Scott's back. He was moving slowly on the dance floor, his arms on someone she couldn't see. She told herself to look away. She told her jealousy to take a hike. But still, she found her eyes watching, waiting for the pair to move enough to allow her to see who he was dancing with.

She forced herself to look away and her eyes glazed past the couples along the dark outer edge of the dance floor, near the DJ. These were the couples who were wrapped around each other, locking lips. Their feet would be tangled up together, their hands roaming around each other. In movies and television, there was always a teacher on hand to break up these couples. Becca had noticed many of them actually managed to get away with it here. Whether that was because her school was a little more lax or because the movies played it up like those kinds of things weren't allowed, Becca wasn't sure. She only knew she had no desire to watch them make out on the dance floor.

Like magnets to a fridge, her eyes were drawn back to Scott. Becca was not surprised to see that the girl in his arms was, in fact, his date. Sarah's hips were under Scott's palms. Becca could see that, although they had more distance between them than most of the couples around them, they looked like they were having a genuinely good time. Both of them had smiles on their faces and they looked like they were in the middle of a friendly conversation. This, more than anything else she'd seen tonight, made Becca wish she could swap places with Sarah. She would love to be the one laughing with Scott about some story or another, talking about their lives and their interests. Just like their afternoon phone calls, but add music and dancing. It would be heavenly.

She shook her head and forced herself to look away. Her eyes, again, glazed past the close couples. This time something caught her eye and she looked back at the pairs. That dress. That was Kate.

Becca looked a little more closely, squinting across the darkness and the floor full of dancing bodies. She was pretty sure that was her dress, the one Kate was wearing. The dress might have been worn by two different people, a fact that would irritate Kate if it turned out to be true. Or, perhaps more likely, that was actually Kate dancing in the darkness and making out with some boy. Becca hoped it was Ernie.

Instantly she felt frustrated with herself and the way she automatically doubted Kate. Of course it was Ernie. Who else would it be?

The song ended and a faster one started. Becca stood up and slipped her shoes back on her feet just in time for Frank and Ellie to join her. "Let's get pictures," Ellie said. She pulled on Becca's arm.

"Sure," Becca agreed. She looked up to where she'd found Kate, thankful the faster music had stopped the heavy kissing session. Becca waved in Kate's direction and watched her friend bob her head in acknowledgment before heading her way. "Kate's coming right now."

Ellie waved at someone. "Scott too," she said.

Becca stood in the little room while couples took pictures and then was placed in the middle of the shot with couples all around her for their group photo. Ernie and Kate, Frank and Ellie, Scott and Sarah, and Becca. She tried to smile her best smile. She tried not to think about the fact that she was essentially the spare tire on this bus, the only one without a partner.

At the end of the night, after more awkward dances and more moments of pure bliss on the dance floor, the group filed out the side door of the cafeteria and into the blissfully chilly air. Slowly, the group separated. Kate, who was Becca's ride, moved off into the darkness with Ernie's arm draped over her shoulders. Becca presumed this was to resume the manic kissing they'd be locked in for most of the second half of the dance. Frank's mother picked him up in her truck. Ellie's car came for her shortly after. Finally, Sarah shut the door of a small brown sedan after a handshake from Scott. This left Scott and Becca alone out there, waiting.

Becca flopped to the curb and Scott sat beside her, his thigh resting up against the thin material of her dress. "Did you have fun?" he asked.

"I did. Did you?"

Scott nodded while continuing to stare off into the darkness of the evening.

"Sarah seems really nice," Becca offered.

"She is." Scott turned his head and leaned back on his palms all in one motion. "She's just a friend." His mouth twitched up into a smile that Becca couldn't help but return.

"You said that before," Becca said, looking away to hide the blush creeping up her cheeks.

Car headlights appeared along the back road behind the school, moving in their direction. Likely this was for one of them since no one else appeared to be waiting in this area for a ride. Becca knew the car would have to wind behind the football field and around the parent pickup area before it was in front of them. They didn't have much time, but they had a little.

"Did you really have fun?" Scott asked.

"Yeah, of course. I really do like dancing."

"I wish you hadn't sat out all the slow songs," Scott said. "I feel bad I didn't ask you to dance even once. I should have."

Becca shook her head, emotions warring inside her. "No, I'm good." She wanted to add, I don't need your pity dances or, maybe, don't do me any favors. Instead, she forced herself to smile. "Honestly," she added.

"Becca," Scott said her name in a low voice and then paused. She turned her head to find him staring at her like he was waiting for something.

"What?"

"Will you save me a dance at the next one, no matter who your date is?" he asked.

Becca blinked, unsure of how to answer this. He sounded genuine and serious. He didn't sound at all like he was making fun of her. She nodded, the gesture small. But Scott must have seen it despite the darkness because he nodded in return. "Good."

The car pulled up in front of them. It was a large car, possibly orange in color. A woman was behind the wheel. "That's my Mom," said Scott. "I should go." He stood up, brushed some dirt off his pants, and smiled down at Becca again. "Can I ask you one thing though?"

"Of course."

"If I hadn't taken Sarah to this dance... if I'd asked you instead... would you have gone with me?" he asked.

Becca felt a surge of joy through her entire body. It was like chugging a cup of hot chocolate on a cold day. That burning feeling almost hurt but at the same time, it felt so good. "Were you thinking about asking me?" she asked quietly.

The way Scott was looking at her in that moment was the exact way boys in movies looked at girls. The way that made their hearts flutter and blocked out the rest of the world. When he nodded, the motion slow and precise, Becca felt like her joy was going to explode out of her chest and coat the entire parking lot with little hearts and pieces of confetti. "I thought about it a lot. I'm sorry I chickened out," he said.

The car horn behind him honked, and they both jumped. Scott turned around, holding up a single finger for his mother in the universal signal for "just one second". Then he turned back to Becca, who had taken the interruption as a moment to catch her breath and compose herself.

"I would've liked that very much," she answered. Then she tacked on the part of the line she'd composed when she'd had that second to think of something witty. "You'll have to ask me to the next dance."

Then Scott delivered an even bigger surprise. He leaned toward her with his arms out and wrapped her in a hug. Becca patted him on the back. She didn't have time to do anything else because the hug was over before she fully knew what was happening. Then, he was gone. In the car and out of the parking lot.

But Becca had a memory that would last a lifetime.

Chapter 29

Kate's mother picked up both girls from the dance and brought them directly to her house. Becca had already arranged to spend the night with her friend, expecting to want to unpack the evening and discuss anything that happened. They stepped into Kate's bedroom and shut the door. "Alright, spill," Kate said. "Why do you have a goofy grin on your face?"

"Because I had fun," Becca answered. She took her hair out of the bobby pins that were holding it off of her face and ran her fingers through it. It took a lot of self-control to not moan with pleasure at the feeling of almost pain that sprang up from the release of the strands from the position they'd been in for hours. When she opened her eyes again, Kate was giving her a skeptical squint.

"That's the entire story?" Kate asked.

Becca shrugged. "Yup."

"Alright, whatever you say," Kate said. She reached into her closet and pulled out a long-sleeved shirt. Then she reached into her dresser drawer and pulled out a pair of black sweatpants. "I'm changing. Close your eyes if you don't want a show," she said.

Becca obediently closed her eyes. "Scott did mention that he thought about asking me to the dance," she admitted.

"Open them," Kate said. Becca complied. "That's awesome, Beck. Did he say why he didn't ask?"

Becca shrugged, she didn't want to bring up the grocery store thing again. Nothing new or good was going to come out of that conversation. "It doesn't really matter. What's done is done. I'm happy he said he thought about it at all. He seemed like he might like me, maybe."

Kate frowned and held up a pair of sweatpants practically identical to the ones she was now wearing. "Do you want to wear these?" Becca held out her hand in answer and Kate tossed them at her. Becca pulled a shirt out of the backpack she'd stashed here earlier in the day. She had also packed a pair of pajama pants, but given the option she usually chose to wear Kate's clothes. There's something comforting about wearing clothes that you aren't always in. It almost lets you pretend you are a different person, even if it's only for one night.

"Don't get your hopes up," Kate said, flopping down on her bed. She laid her head back on her pillow and stared up at the ceiling. "I don't want you to get hurt."

Becca lay beside her, adopting a similar stance. She sighed. "It was just nice to feel seen. I don't think he's going to, like, ask me to be his girlfriend or anything."

Kate sighed. "What does that word even mean?"

"What word?"

"Girlfriend," Kate said. "What's the point of that label? Do we want that? I don't even know anymore."

Becca turned on her side and propped her head on her elbow. "Where is this coming from?"

"Ernie."

"Did he say something?" Becca asked. She watched Kate's face for a sign of what she might be feeling. Kate's face, however, was an unreadable mask.

"Not specifically."

Becca reached out and ran her hand lightly down Kate's arm. "Tell me what he said."

"Just that he wasn't looking for a label right now. He said it like it was obvious or like I should've known. Then he said he knew that wasn't a problem." Becca couldn't be sure because Kate's eyes were on the ceiling, but she thought Kate rolled her eyes. "He asked if it was alright with me."

Becca fell silent, just watching Kate's face. She looked for a sign, a flick of eye movement, a smile, anything. But because she could only see the right side of Kate's face, she got nothing. Finally, she probed. "And what did you tell him?"

Kate sighed. "I didn't really know what to say because I hadn't really thought about it." She turned her face to Becca's and her cheek twitched like a smile was trying to fight its way out. "I've spent the night thinking about it since then and I think I might like the label." Her hand came up and rested under her head. "Everyone at school would know we belonged together, that we were an us. I think, maybe, I do want that. Does that make me shallow?"

Becca considered this. She could assume, based on the fact that Kate sounded like this was a conclusion she'd recently reached, that it was not what she told Ernie. Yet Becca had seen Ernie and Kate making out on the dance floor. Did that mean that Ernie thought Kate didn't need the label? She needed to be careful of Kate's feelings here. She didn't want to give her false hope, but she also didn't want to break her heart. "I think it's possible to belong with someone else and have everyone know you are together without having the label," she said. "Feelings and caring for each other are more important than labels, aren't they?"

Kate took a deep breath. "Yeah, I suppose."

"Maybe you should bring this up with Ernie again, talk about it more. Especially if you didn't get a chance to tell him all of this tonight," Becca said.

"We didn't really talk much after that," Kate said. She smiled. "We were a bit busy using our lips for other things." Her eyebrows bounced up and down. "If you know what I mean."

Becca laughed an airy version of her normal laugh that ended quickly. "I thought that was you in the make-out section of the dance floor," she said. "Seems like he was fine showing off how he felt about you in public then, with or without the label." She hoped that made Kate feel better. It would not have made Becca feel better if the situation were reversed. It seemed odd to Becca that Ernie felt the need to specifically say he wasn't looking for a relationship before diving lip-first into Kate.

Becca yawned. "Alright, enough chatter. Can we talk about this tomorrow? I'm exhausted."

Kate closed her eyes. "Fine, but you turn the light off."

Becca got up off the bed, flipped off the light, changed into her pajamas, and dropped onto the floor beside the bed. "Good night," she said.

"Mmm hmmm," Kate answered, already drifting off to sleep.

Chapter 30

Even after a family day on Sunday and an early morning band practice on Monday morning, Becca was still thinking of the relationship conversation when she ran into Ernie before second period Monday morning. "Hey," she said, "can I talk to you for a quick minute?"

He waved at her. "Yeah, of course."

She fell into step beside him and the pair headed toward the gym lockers. "What are you thinking will be in the future for you and Kate?" Becca asked.

Ernie raised his eyebrows at her. "Wow, you don't waste any time on small talk, do you?"

Becca chuckled. "Sorry, short walk."

"Right," Ernie let out a dramatic breath. "Well, she said she didn't really want a label so I didn't plan to label anything. We were just having fun."

"I was afraid of that," Becca said. "What if she did want a label?"

Ernie ran his fingers through his hair and frowned. "So she lied?"

"She reconsidered."

"That's good to know." He looked serious, Becca noted. Then he ran his hand down his face like he could wipe away the stress of this situation.

"Is that a problem?" Becca asked.

"I don't really know." He shrugged. "I thought we were just having fun. This is a lot to think about."

They reached the outside of the locker rooms where they would need to split up to get ready for PE. "I want to think about this a little, but it's good you told me," Ernie said. "You're a good friend."

"I wish people wouldn't say that," Becca said softly, her voice tinged with something more than just annoyance. "It feels like it's a label I don't fit. Or maybe I do, but... it's complicated."

Ernie's smile was a little crooked, she noticed. "Sounds like all labels are," he agreed. "But you are good to Kate, whether she deserves it or not." He pointed at the men's locker room door. "I have to go. I'll think about this whole label thing, I promise."

"That's all I can ask," Becca said. "Thanks."

She just hoped she hadn't made things worse. If she'd pushed too hard, if she'd said the wrong thing, it could all blow up. And she'd be the one to blame.

Chapter 31

By the second cross-light on the walk home on Monday, Frank noticed Becca had begun looking nervously over her shoulder up the street behind them every ten steps or so. He frowned and shook his head. It didn't take a genius to figure out what she might be looking for. There was only one thing that was known for running full speed up this street at them right around this same point of their walk. "Are you looking for Kate?" he asked.

"I just didn't see her after school," Becca answered, checking again for her friend. "I'm not sure where she is."

"She's fine," Frank said, a little harshly.

"Yeah, I know." Becca sighed. "Change the subject."

"Alright." Frank wracked his brain, trying to come up with something. They'd already talked about the dance, Scott's admission after the dance, and a little about Ernie and Kate. He didn't really want more detail about that latter topic. "I'm thinking I might take Ellie out to dinner," he said. He hadn't really been thinking about this, but he knew Becca would love the idea.

He was right. She smiled and, for a moment, forgot about checking for Kate. "That's a really good idea. You two looked like you had a great time at the dance and I'm sure a dinner would be amazing. Where are you thinking you'll take her?"

Frank shrugged. "Somewhere with actual waiters but nothing too expensive."

"Yes, exactly. Maybe something with a dessert menu."

"Because it's not a date unless you have cake?" Frank asked, raising one eyebrow.

"Because it should be an option you can use as an excuse to spend more time together," Becca answered. It was ridiculous that she was pretending to be an expert on this topic. She'd never been out to a restaurant with anyone who wasn't part of her family. She certainly had never sat at a restaurant with a waiter and ordered a slice of cheesecake as an excuse to spend more time with a cute boy.

"Noted," Frank said. "I'll find one reasonably priced restaurant with waiters and dessert." He laughed. "Anything else I should know?"

Becca considered this. She realized she felt absolutely no jealousy when it came to this topic. She wasn't interested in being the one to go out to dinner with Frank, not even a little. She was also extremely happy for Ellie, who she genuinely liked. She smiled at Frank. "I think you two should keep spending time together for as long as it makes you happy to spend time together," she answered.

"That's deep," Frank said. He gave a little laugh. "Does it make you happy to spend time with Kate?" he asked. His voice changed like someone had flipped a switch taking him right to serious.

"What?" Becca laughed. "I honestly thought you were going to ask about Scott."

"I don't have to ask that one," Frank answered. "But Kate, she's a different potato altogether."

"Now she's a potato?"

Frank stopped walking just as they reached the end of Becca's street. He moved his body directly in front of Becca on the sidewalk so that she had to stop too. Then he poked her in the shoulder. "Stop avoiding the question and answer me. Does it make you happy to hang out with Kate, to spend time with Kate? Because, if you really are best friends, shouldn't it make you happy?"

Becca rolled her eyes even as she felt a lump forming in her throat. She tried to move around Frank, literally trying to avoid the question. He threw his right arm out, blocking her. She faced him again and sighed. She knew Kate stressed her out and made things difficult. She knew that sometimes she left Kate's upset, hurt, or otherwise feeling negative. But she also knew that Kate had done so much for her and had been there for her when no one else had. She tried to remember something pleasant and recent, something she could hold on to and think of when she answered Frank so that she wouldn't have to lie. But she couldn't think of anything. That, she decided, was more a reflection of the fact that she was trying to come up with something quickly and not because there wasn't one. She smiled at Frank, trying to put on the air of someone who had thought of something. "Most of the time, yes," she answered. This time, when she pushed his arm aside, he let her.

She stomped off down the street, her feet angrily punishing the pavement for the lie she had just told. Her brain tried desperately to think of an example of a time when it wasn't a lie. Frank followed, hanging his head a little more than usual. Becca was about three houses down the road before she stopped and spun, her face the perfect picture of the AHA moment you'd see on a comic book character. Frank almost laughed at her, but wisely swallowed it down.

"You know, sometimes a friend is the person who makes you feel better when you feel like crap. You don't always have to leave them feeling amazing, but it's enough that you can leave the messy feelings at their doorstep. Kate and I do that for each other," she said. She tossed some hair over her shoulder and rolled her shoulders back. "I'm not saying Kate is perfect, but neither am I." She shrugged her shoulders just once. "But I'm absolutely positive that if I needed her, she would be there. That's what we are for each other."

Frank nodded with his lips pursed. It wasn't an agreement. It was processing. Becca waited him out, prepared to fight for Kate if she had to. She was fully expecting him to come back with something harsh. This felt like the moment he'd been building toward for years, the moment when he would declare that Kate was a terrible person and make some kind of stand. Becca felt anger bubbling inside her. There was no way she would stand for that, she decided. If he wanted to stomp the ground and tell her to choose him or Kate, she would choose Kate. Because anyone who made you choose should lose, that's what she knew.

"Ok," Frank said softly, his voice low, as if the weight of what he had just said was settling in. "I just want you to be careful, that's all."

Becca's shoulders returned to their normal position and she let out the breath she was holding. Frank started walking and when he was past her, she turned and walked with him.

Near her own house, she broke the silence that had engulfed them. "See you later?" she asked, the question more of a water tester than actually a question in need of an answer. Becca felt like something was still weighing on Frank's mind, something he hadn't said. Sure, it could be Ellie or something fun. But that wasn't the impression Becca got. She got the impression this was more about Kate than Ellie.

"Of course," he answered. Then he squinted at her. "One thing though, about your comment earlier."

Here it comes, thought Becca. Here's the lecture. She propped her hand on her hip and widened her eyes, hoping to convey her "give me your best shot" attitude. She looked ready to stand here and fight.

"What if you needed her tonight?" he asked. "You said your friendship is built on the idea that she is absolutely always there for you if you need her, right? Where is she right now? What if you needed her right now?"

"I don't," Becca answered. The premise was laughable. Becca didn't mean they were literally always available in that exact second for the other one. She meant that if something went wrong, Kate would be the one to pick up the pieces. "But if I did she would be around tomorrow to help me with whatever it was," she added.

"Ok," he answered. Again, he looked like there was something he wasn't saying. He turned like he was planning on leaving this conversation like that, heading home.

"No, say whatever it is you were about to say," Becca yelled. "You don't get to walk away with whatever you were just thinking unsaid."

Frank turned around. "I don't have anything to say about this topic, not yet. I just want you to think about it. Because, if I know Kate, there's going to come a time when you need her and she's not there. Hell, there's going to be a time when you need a friend because of something Kate did. You won't feel like you can come to Kate when that happens."

"That's never —" Becca tried to interrupt.

"I hope I'm wrong," Frank said, his voice tight with frustration. "But something's going to happen. It always does. I just want you to be prepared. When the time comes, don't say I didn't warn you. Not because I want to be right. Not because I want you to come to me. But because I know you, you'll eventually get over it and then you'll go running back to Kate. You'll conveniently forget that it was Kate who caused you pain. You give her too many chances. I want to be the voice in your head that tells you it's alright to walk away instead of walking back. That's all I want because you deserve better."

Becca didn't know what to say. She stood there with her mouth hanging open as he shrugged, turned, and walked away. He was wrong, she decided. Kate was her best friend. Kate had been there for her, and Becca knew deep down that she would be there again. But a deep part of her wondered if Frank had a point. What if one day Kate wasn't there when she needed her most? She shook the thought away. She couldn't think about that now. She had to trust that what they had was real.

She supposed the only way to prove that to him would be to

just keep being Kate's friend. When this worst-case scenario he imagined never came true he'd have to admit that he was wrong. Maybe he'd even become friends with Kate. What would it take? She wondered. Would it take a year? If summer rolled around and they were still friends and Kate hadn't let her down, would that be enough to convince Frank?

She shrugged and headed inside.

That night after dinner, she picked up the phone in the hallway and dialed Kate's number. "Hello," Kate's sister answered.

"Hey, it's Becca. Can I talk to Kate?" She still hadn't shaken the little worry that was balled in her gut after this afternoon. Where was Kate?

"Hold on." She heard muffled talking and then the sound of the phone moving around. Becca smiled, Kate was getting on the phone. She imagined her friend would have a great excuse for why she wasn't there this afternoon. Probably something funny.

"Becca?" The voice was not Kate's. It was Kate's mother.

"Yeah."

"Kate is at a friend's house."

"It's a school night," Becca said, hating herself for pointing out something Kate's mother was likely to have already known. "You don't let her have sleepovers on school nights," she added.

"She's supposed to be home in about thirty minutes. You can call back then if you want."

"OK, thanks." Becca hung up the phone and the feeling in her stomach got worse, like someone had tightened a lug nut near her belly button. Whose house was Kate at? Why didn't Becca know about it?

More importantly, was Kate alright or was she going to need a friend?

Chapter 32

Kate still hadn't been home when Becca called before she went to bed last night. Becca took small comfort in the fact that Ms. Tare hadn't sounded worried or upset. She'd sounded tired. She'd told Becca that Kate was going to have to go straight to bed when she did show up. She suggested Becca just "talk to her tomorrow morning".

Becca didn't see Kate before band practice, although she hadn't really expected to. She'd changed clothes after practice as quickly as she ever had, but still, she didn't have enough time to swing by Kate's first period to catch her. So, instead, she'd had her backpack all packed early and been the first person out the door when the bell rang to start second period.

She caught Kate in the quad area. Kate was walking slowly, her eyes staring off into the distance, distracted. Becca immediately linked their elbows together, a move that was normally Kate's to perform. "Good morning sunshine," she greeted. "Where were you yesterday?"

Kate, who had dark circles under her eyes and looked like she was absolutely exhausted, smiled. It was not the normal Kate smile, the one that filled her entire face and made her eyes crinkle. It was soft-spoken and small. The smile of someone who had, inexplicably, changed overnight. Becca pulled back a little. "Are you alright?" Becca asked. "Seriously, where were you?"

"I'm fine," Kate said. She winked, a classic Kate gesture that made Becca feel only a little better. "I was with Ernie."

That shocked Becca enough that she stumble stepped to keep up with Kate, who didn't slow down. She sped up for a few steps to catch back up to Kate's rhythm. "Ernie?" she asked. "I called you pretty late. It was after dinner. Your mom said you weren't home."

"Right." Kate didn't elaborate. She didn't spin around and tell some story about how they were fighting, or how she met his family. Nothing. She just kept walking. In Becca's mind, that was a really bad sign.

Becca pulled her friend to a stop by applying pressure to her elbow. "What happened?" she demanded.

Kate pulled her arm free and rubbed her elbow. "Don't overreact."

"What happened?" Becca repeated, emphasizing each word.

Brandon walked up just then. He either didn't notice or didn't care that the two friends were in the middle of what could be an important discussion. He slid right up next to them, turning their line segment into a triangle. "Morning," he said. He spun his backpack around to the front of his body and started rooting around in the small pocket on the front. "I have something for you, Becca."

"Can it wait?" she asked, annoyance trickling into her normal tone.

"No idea. Probably not, since I was asked to take care of it before lunch." Brandon kept digging around in the pocket but turned his eyes on Kate. "So, you and Ernie huh?" He tapped her with his elbow.

Becca's eyes widened. "What?"

"He lives near Ernie," Kate said as if that was an answer.

"Yeah, so? What does that mean?" Becca turned her angry expression to Brandon. "What does that mean?"

Brandon produced a folded piece of paper from the pocket of his backpack. "Found it," he declared. He handed the paper to Becca, zipped the pouch, and spun the entire backpack around. "See you later," he shouted. He practically jogged off to his next class, a good indication that he had finally picked up on the tone of this particular conversation.

Becca looked down at the paper, which had her name printed on the front. Curiosity got the best of her and she unfolded it. "Eat lunch with me today, please. I have something I want to talk to you about." It was signed "Scott". Becca folded it back up and slid it into the pocket of her jeans. She faced Kate again. "What did he mean?" she asked.

"We have to get changed for PE. We're going to be late," Kate said.

Now Becca knew something big was being kept from her. Kate never cared about being late to anything, especially not PE which was her least favorite class. "Then you better explain yourself quickly because I'm not moving from here until you do." She stomped her feet as if to prove they were going to stay in this exact location.

Kate rolled her eyes. "Brandon lives near Ernie. He probably saw Ernie's mother drive me home last night after she got home from work."

"He's friends with Ernie," Becca challenged. "He may have talked to him after that. You're acting weird. What happened?"

Kate shrugged. "Ernie asked me to be his girlfriend."

Becca softened and let out a breath like a sigh. "Kate, that's awesome."

"I guess. Can we go to class now?"

Becca nodded and followed Kate toward the locker room. But inside she was confused. She decided not to hold back this feeling. "I thought this is what you wanted," she said.

"I did. I do." Kate opened the locker room door and slipped right in, leaving Becca to grab the door and follow.

"But," Becca prompted, feeling like there was more to this story that she wasn't getting.

"But I guess I just realized the label doesn't matter. Not really. It's more important that both of us get what we're looking for out of the relationship, right?" Kate reached her locker and threw her backpack in. She pulled the shirt over her head and threw that in as well. Then, standing in a bra showing more self-confidence than Becca ever would, she took her time digging around in the backpack for the shirt she was supposed to wear for PE.

"I guess." Becca shrugged. She turned to the right, ready to head down the row of lockers to her own space. Then she turned back around, deciding she knew how to ask the question that would be more telling than anything else she was getting from Kate this morning. "Are you happy?" she asked. "With Ernie, are you happy?"

Kate pulled her shirt on and turned to smile at her friend. It was the real smile. The one that crinkled Kate's eyes and changed the shape of her face just slightly. It was Becca's favorite Kate expression. "Right now, yes."

Becca nodded. "If that changes... " she let the thought linger, hoping Kate would pick up the thread.

She didn't disappoint. "... I'll end it."

Becca closed the gap between them and pulled Kate into a hug. When she pulled back, she smiled at her friend. "Then I'm happy for you. Congratulations."

Chapter 33

All the way to the cafeteria Becca considered ways to tell Scott that she really needed to eat with Kate. It wasn't that she didn't want to eat with Scott, because she did. It was more that she had a strange feeling Kate needed her. Kate, of course, wouldn't admit to that. But after the conversation with Frank in which Becca had said that a good friend would always be there for you, she felt obligated to follow through. Surely it was part of being a good friend to recognize when the other person needed you even if they wouldn't admit it.

Becca had just resolved to tell Scott the truth, that Kate was hiding something about her new relationship with Ernie and that Becca needed to spend lunch with her friend to figure out what that was when she turned the corner of the walkway and the cafeteria area came into view. She didn't see Scott right away, which was probably good for her resolve to tell him she wasn't going to be able to eat with him. But she did see Kate and Ernie. His arm was draped across her shoulders in a protective way and they were laughing about something. Kate was carrying a bowl of salad with a plastic lid and Ernie was carrying what appeared to be a burrito in his free hand. Becca watched as Ernie steered Kate toward the tables along the side of the cafeteria. They picked an empty table with another empty table beside it. Becca assumed this was a hint they wanted some privacy.

It was this act that finally gave Becca the green light, though it felt a little too easy. The unspoken permission to eat with Scott clashed with the growing knot in her stomach about leaving Kate alone. She had to admit it: she wanted to spend time with Scott, and that felt like a betrayal to Kate.

Becca walked into the cafeteria and stepped into the line for a sandwich. She ordered the toppings she wanted and stepped toward the pay line. That was the moment when she saw Scott standing in the center of the cafeteria with something in his hands turning in a slow circle. She waved. "Miss," the cashier called. Becca turned around and handed her a ten-dollar bill. She slipped her change into her pocket and hustled over to the table with Scott.

"Hi," she said, dropping onto the bench beside him. The round table could fit six people, but it was blissfully empty today. It was a sunny, cloudless day. This meant that, although the temperature wasn't going to get exceptionally high, it was kind of warm if you stayed in the sun. The perfect weather for high school students to be found eating outside like Kate and Ernie had opted for.

"How was your morning?" Scott asked. "I hope you didn't have other plans for lunch. I just thought it would be nice to eat together."

Becca squinted at him. Was he talking faster than normal? He seemed to be nervous for some reason. That observation made Becca nervous. Her hands shook as she tried to unwrap her sandwich. She glanced at Scott and noticed he was having trouble snapping open the plastic lid on what looked like a chicken and rice bowl with some kind of sauce that would masquerade as Asian sauce in the cafeteria kitchen. "My morning was fine," Becca answered. She managed to get her sandwich unwrapped and took a bite.

Scott, meanwhile, had managed to get the lid off his lunch. It smelled vaguely like teriyaki. "Good," he said. "So I had something I wanted to talk to you about."

Becca smiled and took another bite to cover her nervous

feeling. She tried to give herself a pep talk: Scott is a friend, Scott wouldn't want to bring you into the crowded cafeteria and drop some bad news on you, and Scott isn't out to embarrass you. It mostly worked.

But, on the other side of her argument, Scott also felt like it was important to arrange a meeting with you to tell you he had a date with another girl once. Sure, since then they'd had a nice conversation about how he wanted to ask her to the formal. But they hadn't actually talked about that since the conversation. Maybe, she told herself, he changed his mind and felt like she needed to know that?

This, she decided, was getting her nowhere. "OK, what's up?" she prompted.

"I was thinking about some things," he said. His eyes dropped to the bowl of food he was now pushing around in circles with his fork.

Becca laid her hand on his arm. "You can tell me whatever it is you need to tell me, we're good." He brought his eyes up to hers and she smiled at him. Her heart fluttered a little, but only a little.

"You're so easy to talk to and I really like spending time with you," he said. When he smiled Becca felt her own smile tugging at her tired cheeks. "I like you, Becca."

The fluttering in her chest was much more pronounced now. "I like you, too," she admitted. Now it was her turn to drop her eyes to her food. She also felt that telltale heat creep up her face.

"Becca, would you consider... maybe... being my girlfriend?" Scott asked.

Becca felt like the world stopped spinning for a beat. The entire cafeteria had fallen silent, the world had paused. She felt her heartbeat strong behind her ribs. Nope, she was still alive. This was really happening. She was tempted to pinch herself, to see if this was a dream world. She was afraid that if she did she would wake up and all of this would be over. It if was a dream, shouldn't she at least enjoy it?

She turned to face Scott and smiled. "I would really like that," she answered.

Lunch, somehow, tasted better after that.

When the bell rang, Scott took her wrapper from the sandwich along with his trash and dropped them into the nearest trash can. Becca grabbed his backpack as well as her own and met him near the door, holding out his supplies to him. "Thanks," he said.

"No problem." She offered him a smile.

"Call you tonight?" Scott asked, his voice a little hesitant.

"Of course."

He smiled. "Great. See you later." Then he was gone, off in the direction of his next class period. Becca walked quickly to avoid being late for her next class. It was funny, she mused, how you can have something you've been waiting for happen and yet not feel any different at all. Once you got past that "be my girlfriend" question, lunch had felt exactly the same as it always had.

Maybe, she realized, Kate was exactly right. The label doesn't really matter after all.

Chapter 34

Frank was waiting for Becca in their normal spot after school. She sauntered over with a little skip in her step. "How are you?" he asked. "You have quite the smile on your face."

Becca pulled a slip of paper out of her back pocket, unfolded it, and held it up toward him. "You'd be happy too if you scored a ninety-eight on your history exam," she crowed. History was not her best subject.

Frank laughed. "If you say so." He started walking in the direction of their houses, following their normal route automatically. "Congrats," he added as if it had just occurred to him.

"Thank you." Becca dropped into a fake bow.

At the first intersection, Frank punched the walk signal while Becca scanned the crowds behind them for Kate. She was nervous. Kate had definitely been acting strange this morning. Then she'd left Becca at lunch, granted that had worked out. Remembering her new situation, she turned to Frank. "Oh, I almost forgot to tell you. I have other exciting news," she said.

At the sight of Frank's face, her words died in her mouth. Frank's jaw was clenched and pulsing as if he were grinding his teeth with all his might. Becca had never seen him angry before. Clearly, this was it. "What's wrong?" she asked. She gently laid a hand on his arm.

He jumped under her touch and plastered his fake smile, the one usually reserved for Kate, on his face. The walk signal illuminated and Frank used the opportunity to rush across the street. Becca jogged to keep up.

"Seriously, what's up?" she asked when she had caught him on the far side of the road.

"I'm fine," he said. He flashed her another, fake, smile. "Why wouldn't I be?"

Becca sighed. "I honestly don't know. But you look angry."

"It's nothing. What was your good news?"

Becca didn't feel like talking about it anymore. Whatever was bothering Frank seemed like something she should know about, didn't it? What was the use of having a friend if you couldn't rely on them when you secretly were seething about something? "Did something happen at school?" she asked.

Frank shook his head. Nope, not school.

Becca tried again. "Is everything alright at home?"

This time she saw that twitch in his jaw again, just for a step. Definitely something at home. "Is your Mom alright?"

Frank stopped walking so suddenly that Becca ended up two steps in front of him. She whirled around to face him. "I don't want to talk about this," he said with a sternness in his voice that surprised her. "My Mom and I had a disagreement about my sperm donor of a father. I lost the argument and have to go see him this weekend. I'm not happy about it. It's not a big deal."

Becca didn't know what to say. In the absence of brilliant words, she merely nodded. "Thank you for telling me." She wished she could say something to smooth over the entire situation. But what would she know about dealing with divorced parents? What would she know about the pain of a father who didn't want you deciding to come back around? Everything in her life felt really unimportant and small just then.

She took her cue from Frank and only resumed walking when he did, keeping her silence for as long as he kept his. "This is why I didn't mention it," Frank whispered.

"I wish I knew what to say," Becca said honestly.

"It'll be fine. He'll spend a day with me, pretend like he's done me a great favor, go back to his life, and tell all his friends he's making a difference in my life. I will be able to go back to not seeing him for about three months, then he'll do it all again."

Becca swallowed hard. "You saw him three months ago?" This was news to her. She hadn't heard Frank mention his father more than passing comments about him in the entire time she'd known him. She was surprised by how much that hurt. To learn that someone she considered to be her friend had been keeping something that made him this angry to himself with no one to share it with? How does a friendship recover from that?

Frank, who was now walking a few steps in front of her, turned his head to see her face. Instead, he shook his head. "Shit. Incoming," he whispered.

Becca tuned into the sounds around her and realized she could hear footsteps drawing closer. She didn't even have to ask. Kate. Despite wanting to continue this conversation with Frank, she felt a load of stress drop off her shoulders. Kate was alright. She smiled as Kate pulled even with her. "I missed you today," Becca said.

Kate smacked her on the shoulder, a playful and familiar action. "You didn't even tell me your big news. I had to hear it from Ellie," Kate said.

Frank turned. "Big news?" His voice sounded light again. Becca was confident Kate wouldn't notice anything different in his mannerisms at all. He was back to being the same old Frank everyone knew and loved. Happy-go-lucky, not-a-care-in-the-world Frank.

"Yes," Kate said, looping elbows with Becca. "Scott asked her to be his girlfriend at lunch today," she revealed.

Becca had the presence of mind to offer the smile she should have had for this announcement. She pushed thoughts of Frank's grumpy mood and secret weekends with his father out of her mind. "Yes, I was just going to get around to telling you that story," she said. As soon as the words were out of her mouth she realized it would come across as a secret she'd kept from him, exactly the thing she was upset at him for doing to her. Of course, could a boy asking you to be his girlfriend really be the same as someone being forced to see their father? These two secrets didn't even feel like they were in the same ballpark. Especially considering her secret was less than twenty-four hours old.

"He asked me at lunch. It was really cute, actually." She let herself focus on Kate and melted into telling the story. "He told me that he really liked me."

Kate made the appropriate squealing noise. Becca smiled and relaxed even further into the story. "Then he asked me to be his girlfriend."

"Obviously, you said yes. Right?" Kate asked.

"Yes."

Frank nodded approvingly. "That's awesome, Beck. Congrats."

She looked carefully at his face but didn't see any indication he was bothered or upset by the news. She smiled. "Thank you."

"So, do you feel different?" Kate asked. "You're someone's girlfriend." She dragged out the last word like it was a lyric to a song.

Becca rolled her eyes. "So are you. Do you feel different?" The question reminded her that Kate had certainly been acting different since last night, even if she was acting like herself right now.

Kate pulled her elbow free and shrugged. "I told you, it's just a label."

"Wait," Frank looked confused. "Are you and Ernie dating now too?"

"Since last night," Becca answered for her.

Kate shrugged. "It wasn't a big deal."

Becca noticed all the excitement Kate had obviously had for her situation had melted completely out of Kate's voice. She doubled down on her bet that something was terribly wrong. She promised herself this wasn't the last time they'd discuss it. She had a feeling Kate didn't want to have this conversation with Frank. "Kate, I'm coming to your house when we get there, sound good?" she asked.

Kate smiled. "Of course."

It didn't take Becca long to get Kate talking once they were inside Kate's house, safely ensconced in her bedroom. Becca grabbed a box of cookies on their way into the familiar room. She flipped the tape deck on and dropped in a copy of Reba, hitting play to let the familiar tones prevent any eavesdropping from Kate's sister. Then she flopped down on Kate's floor, facing the ceiling, and waited.

The third song had just started when Kate sniffled and let out a deep breath. Becca propped herself up on her elbows and turned her eyes on her friend. "What's up?" she asked.

Kate didn't answer right away. Becca started to wonder if she was going to. Then, just about the time Becca was prepared to ask her question again, Kate whispered a single word. "No." Then a few tears slipped down her face.

Becca sat up, scooted closer, and wrapped her arm around Kate's shoulders. "You can tell me anything. No judgment."

"We had sex," Kate whispered. "It hurt. A lot. I didn't expect it to hurt. I didn't know... " She sniffled and wiped the back of her hand across the tears on her cheek. "No one ever tells you that it's going to hurt. Not like that. It's fine. I think. I hope. But... " She turned her eyes to Becca, the watery orbs showing something like fear.

Becca's heart skipped, her body stiffening with the weight of the revelation. "Oh my God, Kate... are you serious?" Her voice was thick with disbelief, though deep down, she already knew the answer. This explained the way Kate had been acting. A part of her brain gave a little shock at the realization that she and Kate were living such radically different lives. She had her first boyfriend, in name only, who she hadn't even kissed. Then there was Kate who, apparently, was having sex. "Did he force you?" she asked. That seemed to match with the tears.

Kate shook her head, vehemently. "No, of course not. Would I be dating my rapist? God, you're so dumb sometimes." She wiped at her cheeks again. "I told you, we like each other. This is what you do with people you like, Becks."

"But why are you crying if this is normal?"

Kate sighed. "We didn't use anything like protection."

Becca wanted to shake her, tell her she was being an idiot. How many times had health teachers or parents told them to use protection when and if they had sex? How could Kate have forgotten that?

Then again, if someone offered Becca one hundred dollars to hand them a condom right now, she wouldn't actually know where she could grab one. She supposed you could get them from a store, although she didn't know what aisle. Even then, she'd have to walk to the store because she wasn't old enough to drive. She supposed, for Kate, that had been the problem. In the heat of the moment, there just wasn't one available.

She squeezed her friend's shoulders. "So what happens now?" she asked.

Kate shrugged. "We hope the God my mother believes in recognizes that I would be a terrible parent and decides to give me my next period."

"When was your last one?" Becca asked the question even though she wasn't sure she could answer it about herself if it came to that. It seemed like the kind of thing someone who was having sex should be able to answer, didn't it?

"About three weeks ago. I won't have to wait long, I guess."

Becca couldn't imagine living with that fear for a week. "Maybe we should get you a pregnancy test," she offered. "I don't know how much they are but I have some cash under my bed. I'd help you pay for it."

Kate took a deep breath in, her chest expanded with the force of it. Then she blew it out of her mouth in a loud exhale. Her head dropped to the side, gently bumping Becca's shoulder. "You're the best, you know that?" she said.

Becca smiled. "Not really, but I'm here for you." She tipped her own head until it rested on Kate's. "You just tell me what you need from me and I'll do it. I mean it."

"I know you will, Becks. That's why you're my favorite person in the world."

Chapter 35

When the phone rang after dinner, Becca's Dad was the closest to the handset. Becca, who was attempting to read <u>Heart of Darkness</u> for her English class didn't think anything of it. "Hello," he answered. After a pause, Becca heard him bark "Who is this" into the receiver. That was the moment she felt nervous. She let the book fall into her lap and looked at her father. He was standing in the doorway to the living room, eyebrows raised in her direction. As she watched, he pulled the phone away from his head and covered the mouthpiece. "Rebecca, there is a boy on the phone for you." His eyebrows stayed up near his hairline, waiting for her to say something.

"A boy?" she stammered. Her father was incredibly kind, strong, and loving. He took pride in knowing all of her friends. This look must be for a friend he wasn't as familiar with, which meant it was not Frank. "Is it Scott?" she asked, hopefully.

"Do I know Scott?" he countered.

Becca worried her bottom lip with her teeth while she considered how to proceed here. Technically, Scott was her boyfriend. But, more importantly, she hadn't actually asked if she was allowed to date anyone. It wasn't that she didn't think they'd allow it. It was more that she probably should have told them. "We've been talking on the phone a lot," she said. She pushed herself up off the couch and crossed the room, holding out her hand for the phone. "I'll stay right here, I promise."

He smiled and held the phone out to her. "I want to meet this boy before anything more serious happens," he said. Becca blushed and wrapped her hand around the phone receiver. Her father bent down and kissed her hairline. "Behave," he said before walking into the living room.

Becca put the receiver up to her ear. "Hello."

"Hey, it's Scott. I didn't get you in trouble, did I? I mean, is it alright that I'm calling?"

"It's fine." She looked behind her to the living room. Her father had settled himself in the recliner nearest her. Of course, that was the chair he always sat in. She was absolutely certain this was the seat he chose because it was his favorite and not merely because it was closest to the phone and, therefore, her conversation. Probably. "What's up?" she asked, conscious that she was using a slightly quieter voice.

"You were worried about Kate earlier, did you find her?" he asked.

Becca smiled at the concern in his voice. He really was a nice guy. "Oh, yeah. I found her. She was fine. It turned out... " she stopped herself. This wasn't really her news to tell. She couldn't very well say that her best friend had lost her virginity to her boyfriend. She was smacked again with the realization that she and Kate were really living very different lives. "She was fine. Just news about Ernie and the whole boyfriend label had her acting strange."

"Oh, that's good." His voice sort of caught. "I didn't know it would bother her."

"What?" Becca squinted at the wall, a sad replacement for being able to squint at Scott in confusion.

"About the boyfriend label. I didn't know it would bother Kate if I asked you—"

"Oh, no," Becca interrupted. "No, Ernie asked her to be his girlfriend. There was some drama with that." She rolled her eyes at her own choice of words. She imagined walking to the store tomorrow to buy her best friend a pregnancy test with the cash hidden under her bed. Drama, indeed. "It'll all be fine, I'm sure."

"Oh, got it. Sorry, I guess I tried to make that about me. I'm sorry to hear there was drama. Are they alright? Are they happy?" Scott's voice sounded more normal and relaxed, suddenly.

Becca felt a small pang of guilt for not telling Scott more about Kate's situation, but it wasn't her news to tell. She didn't want to drag him into it. She did appreciate how concerned he sounded. "I think so." She had almost forgotten, again, that she now had a boyfriend herself. Kate's news had come right along and swallowed that up. She smiled. "She did seem happy for our news though," she offered.

"Yeah? That's great. I'm more interested in if it makes you happy though."

That, she decided, was the absolute perfect thing to say. Her smile stretched further across her face. "Yeah, I think it does." She turned and glanced over her shoulder. Her father had the television on now. The volume was a respectable level, clearly meant to communicate that he was not listening to her conversation. "Let's talk about something else. How's everything at your house?" she asked.

"Same as always," Scott answered. Becca thought she detected a note of sadness or something. "My brother hates my parents and thinks they're ruining his life so he's locked himself in his room down the hall. They think he's up to no good so they're banging away on the door. I'm escaping the entire situation by excusing myself to listen to music and talk to my girlfriend on the phone."

Becca winced. "That sounds terrible. Do they fight a lot?"

"My parents and my brother? Yeah, pretty much. It's not a big deal. He's just really dramatic. He'll get over it eventually."

"What music are you listening to?"

She heard some shuffling around and then music filled her ears. Typically, with Kate, the music that supplied the background to Becca's life was country music. With her parents, it was usually popular music from the seventies or classic rock of some kind. This music, although Becca couldn't place it, was angsty and raw in an entirely unique way. She felt her head bobbing without permission.

When the music quieted she spoke up. "What is that?"

"Green Day."

His tone of voice clued Becca into the fact that she should probably know them. She winced. "Right, maybe I just haven't heard that song." Why was she lying? "Honestly, I listen to country music more than anything else."

"Like Garth Brooks?"

"Yeah and some newer stuff too. But I liked that tune. What radio station do you listen to?" she asked, thinking maybe she could try it out and see if there was more to life than country artists.

He rambled off the radio dial of a few stations. Becca nodded along, holding the numbers in her head like a secret.

Behind her, she heard her father clear his throat. "I should probably go," she said. "I wasn't finished with my reading for English class and I think I'm talking too loud for the family room."

"Yeah, alright. I'll talk to you later." She liked that he didn't say it as a question. It was a fact. They would talk later. That made her smile. It made her feel little flutters in her stomach, nerves probably.

"Yeah, talk to you tomorrow. Goodnight."

"Goodnight, beautiful."

The flutters definitely increased. She put the receiver down and crossed back to her book. But the smile on her face left nothing to the imagination. She was sure her father could read her expression more easily than she could get through this awful excuse for a book. She had a boyfriend and she really liked him.

Chapter 36

Becca made time after band the next morning to find Kate. She shrugged her backpack up onto her shoulder and rudely elbowed her way past the gathered students in the corridors directly toward Kate's next class. When she turned the corner she spotted Kate standing with Ellie, laughing about something. Her head was thrown back and her brown hair was cascading behind her, catching the rays of the morning sun. For just a beat, she looked like the heroine from some movie. Becca felt an almost instant sense of relief. She had been dreading finding Kate and admitting she hadn't had time to get the pregnancy test for her yet. She had a plan, but that plan involved more waiting. Waiting was Kate's least favorite thing in the world to do. But in this moment, Kate looked like she didn't have a care in the world.

The guilt slammed into Becca's chest, as real as Kate's fist would be if she had said it out loud. Kate was allowed to look carefree. She was surely putting on an act. No one else would be privileged to protect the secret Becca was guarding. She hurried up to the girls. "Good morning," she greeted. "Kate, I'm going right after school to get that thing you need. I have the cash with me." She patted her pocket where the twenty dollar bill was nestled.

Kate frowned. "You didn't already go?"

"Go where?" Ellie asked, narrowing her eyes "What do you need? Can you just borrow it?"

Kate turned her scowl on Ellie. "No. Never mind. I don't want to talk about it." Her eyes snapped back to Becca's face. "We're not talking about it."

"Sorry I brought it up," Becca said.

Ellie shrugged. Becca was impressed with her ability to shake off the obvious anger of the situation. Clearly, this was a conversation about a serious topic, even if Kate didn't want to admit that. She couldn't imagine being OK with such a big secret being kept from her, if she were in Ellie's shoes. Isn't Ellie curious? "Whatever," Ellie added.

Kate looked like she wanted to say something else. Her narrowed eyes and the pink tinting her cheeks gave Becca the impression that something wasn't going to be pleasant. She braced herself for the tirade.

"Morning girls," a voice called. Kate turned her head away, letting out a breath loaded with anger. Scott, who had just popped out of the classroom behind them, bumped Becca's shoulder with his own. "How are you?" he asked.

The tone was so pleasant and casual. It was a stark contrast to the frustration Becca had been preparing herself for. It threw her off. She shook her head and then smiled up at Scott. "I'm alright, thanks."

Ellie took a step back to widen their circle a bit. "I heard congratulations are in order for you two." She gestured to Becca and Scott. Becca felt her cheeks grow warm. "I'm glad you two found each other."

"Thanks." Becca shuffled her feet just a little, resisting the urge to put distance between herself and Scott. Her mind was flooded with thoughts that she just couldn't shut off. What would happen if her friend was pregnant? Is that really the kind of behavior that comes with a title like "girlfriend"? Would Scott expect her to sleep with him now? She didn't want to imagine herself standing outside her second-period class secretly plotting a plan to get a pregnancy test without anyone finding out while she acted like everything was normal. She looked at Kate again, who was now looking at the ground. There was no way she was ready for whatever consequences came with that kind of life.

"Becca?" Scott said. She shook herself and tuned back into the conversation. Ellie and Scott were both looking at her, confused.

"Sorry, what?"

"Is Scott your first official boyfriend?" Ellie asked, the tone of her voice making it pretty clear this was a repeated question. "I was just wondering."

"Oh," she smiled. "Sorry, I was spacing out. Yes, he is." She shook her head. "Actually, no. That's not true. There was a guy in middle school."

"Chris," Kate offered.

"Right, but it wasn't serious." Becca felt her face redden again. Was she implying that this was serious? Was this serious? They'd had this title for such a short time, for crying out loud. Why all this pressure to label everything? She felt herself getting frustrated.

"Yeah, I get that. Middle school relationships are more about calling each other something different than they are about acting different," Ellie offered. "Seriously, I'm glad you two are together. Congratulations."

The bell rang and Kate, usually the least likely person to care about being late to class, threw her shoulders back. "That's our cue, ladies and gentleman. Off we go." She turned and stalked off into the nearby classroom without another word.

Scott bent toward Becca. She read it for exactly what it was. This was going to be a public kiss. Right here in front of Ellie and anyone else who happened to be watching. He was going to kiss her. Just like that. She didn't have much time to think about it. She only knew that she was in the wrong mindset for something like this, even something as mild as this. She was still thinking about sex and pregnancy tests. With that on her mind, even kisses were too much.

It just wasn't the moment she wanted.

She turned her face just enough that Scott was only able to put his lips on her cheek. "See you later," she said before she could regret the act too much or have to answer any questions. She was off around the nearest corner before Scott could even walk into his classroom right beside them.

Becca's designated seat in this classroom was directly beside Ellie. She dropped into the chair, swinging her backpack onto the floor at her feet. "Everything alright?" Ellie asked.

Becca nodded. "Why?" she whispered, stealing a glance at the teacher to make sure she was fully engrossed in the attendance sheet she was marking and wouldn't catch them talking.

"You seem a little spacey today."

"Yeah." Becca unzipped her backpack and pulled out the binder for this class. "It's just weird, I guess. Everyone keeps asking about this new label like it's a big deal. But on the phone last night everything was exactly the same as it always was." She shrugged and flipped the binder open. "I guess I just don't understand the big deal."

Ellie tapped her lower lip with her eraser. "I guess that makes sense. But, you like Scott right? You didn't just say yes because you wanted the label. So, if it matters to him and it doesn't hurt anything, who really cares?"

Becca felt a little frustration flutter in her chest. How could she explain to Ellie that her biggest concern was sending the wrong message? What if Scott thought, like Ernie apparently did, that being someone's boyfriend meant they were ready to have sex? That wasn't what she wanted. Not at all. "I don't even know what that means right now," Becca said, frustration bubbling in her chest. "It's just a label, right? But what if it's more than that? What if it changes everything? I don't know what he expects. I don't know what *I* expect." Becca tried.

At the front of the room, the teacher moved herself to the podium and the girls fell silent. The class was led through an example and Becca diligently took notes in her notebook. When the teacher turned her back to the class to grab another marker, a piece of paper dropped onto her notebook. It was neatly folded with a little tab sticking out. Becca pulled the tab, freeing the note, before tucking it under her math examples. As the lesson went on she fluttered her notes up to read the paper underneath. It didn't take long to read, since it was so short.

Maybe you should just talk to Scott. He's the only one who would really know what that label means to him.

Becca turned, catching Ellie's gaze and giving a quick, appreciative smile. She understood what Ellie was saying, but it didn't feel that simple. Not yet.

Chapter 37

The lunch room seemed more crowded than usual when Becca sauntered in later that day. Of course, she reasoned, that was probably only because she was actively looking for Kate, which made it seem like the room was positively packed with people who were decidedly not who she was searching for. She had to find Kate. Becca was not at all happy with the way they left things that morning. She wanted to find her friend, smooth things over, and apologize for bringing up the topic with Ellie around.

She stepped into the shortest line, pizza, and grabbed herself a slice. Then, still not having located Kate, she dropped to a table where Frank was already sitting. She kept her eyes fixed on the door. "Are you looking for Scott?" Frank asked. "Because he's in line."

Becca took a bite. "No. Have you seen Kate?"

Frank groaned. The sound was so unexpected that Becca turned and fixated on him. He was holding a burger in one hand and giving her the nastiest look. "No. I haven't seen Kate."

"Why do you look so angry?" she asked.

"Because you are obsessed with her. Live your own life."

Becca blinked rapidly in hopes of fanning back the frustration-induced tears that were suddenly stinging her eyes. Frank didn't yell at her. That's not how they talked to each other. "I am. It's just Kate is going through—"

Frank tossed his burger down onto his tray. The audible slap silenced Becca. Now the tears were really stinging. "Let me guess. She's going through something really hard that I wouldn't understand," he took on an almost sing-song tone as if mocking Becca's voice. "She's always going through something. Most of the time, it's some drama she's completely made up."

"Why would she do that? This isn't made up."

"Why? Because it gets your attention. Because you turn your life into being completely, unapologetically about Kate the second she inserts her drama. You forget that you have other friends. You forget that you have a life. You become completely obsessed with the Kate show. You drop everything for her. It's not healthy and, honestly, I'm done with it." He grabbed his tray and stood up. "If I wanted to eat lunch and talk about nothing but Kate, I'd eat with Kate."

Becca held her hand out. "Wait, please."

Frank froze, glaring down at her. Waiting. Of course, now that she'd successfully stopped him, Becca had no idea what she was going to say. "This isn't like that. Honestly, she's going through something real this time. I just have to help her through this. It could... " she paused, gulping back the fears about how she would support her pregnant friend if it came to that. Would she have to babysit? "It could take a while depending on the situation," she lamely finished.

Frank shook his head. "Tell me what's going on," he said. His tone was no softer at all. The anger was still fresh, shocking.

"I can't. It's not my place."

"Because she's making it up," Frank insisted.

"No."

"What proof do you have? You don't have to tell me, but really think about it. What is the proof that this story Kate has concocted is true?"

Becca shook her head. "I shouldn't have to ask for proof. I wouldn't ask you for proof if you told me something scary and awful."

Frank frowned at her. "Becca, one of these days you're going to realize that Kate isn't like everyone else. You can't keep treating her like she is."

Becca opened her mouth to answer without really knowing what she would say in response. Then she felt a hand on her shoulder. "Hey, are you guys alright?" Scott asked. He dropped onto the bench beside Becca, his leg warm against hers. His hand moved from her shoulder to her back. "What's going on? You two are getting sort of loud," he said quieter, clearly speaking to just Becca this time.

"Sorry, I just feel strongly about this topic," Frank said. He offered a completely fake smile to Scott. "I've got lunch detention. Whatever," Frank muttered, his words sharp and bitter. He grabbed his tray and stormed off without a glance back, leaving Becca to stare at the empty space where their argument had just been.

After the door closed behind him and she felt those tears threatening to fall, she slowly moved her eyes back toward the table. In their sweeping motion, they registered a familiar face four tables away. She froze and turned her gaze back there. Kate, sitting at a table surrounded by older girls Becca didn't recognize. "What is she doing there?" she whispered.

"Who?" Scott asked, trying to follow Becca's eyes.

Becca ignored him. Instead, she stared hard at Kate willing her friend's eyes to find hers. She didn't have to wait long because Kate was looking around the room. Their eyes met and Becca jerked her chin a little clearly meaning to communicate "Come here."

Kate shook her head, just a little. The motion was barely an answer. But her eyes stayed fixed on Becca. Becca held up her hands, palms clasped together. The signal for "please". It was an emergency gesture they'd made up. Their houses were across the street and both bedrooms faced the shared road. In the years that they'd known each other, they'd developed a lot of signals. If one of the two of them used this sign, it meant emergency. It meant come here. Now. Kate used it the most, usually when her parents were fighting and she needed someone to help her ignore it. Once she used it when she was home alone and terrified there was some kind of burglar. Becca didn't recall ever using it.

She watched her best friend, waiting for the immediate reaction she knew she would give if the roles were reversed. She expected to see Kate stand up, apologize to her table, and cross the cafeteria.

Instead, Kate shook her head again and turned her attention back to her table of girls.

Chapter 38

After school, Becca ignored her normal routine and headed immediately for the row of classes she knew held Kate's last-period class. She wasn't going to wait by the auditorium, hoping Kate would show up. She wasn't going to let Kate ignore her. Not this time.

She rounded the corner just in time to see Kate heading down the main corridor, toward the front of the school. Becca picked up speed, jogging through crowds of kids. Her voice became a practically constant hum of "excuse me".

"Kate," she shouted. "Stop."

She half expected Kate to keep going after the disastrous display at lunch. Instead, she did as requested. She stopped in the middle of the flow of kids, spun around, planted her hand on her hip, and glared at Becca.

Becca pulled to a stop in front of her. "What happened at lunch today?" Becca asked. She swallowed her urge to ask if everything was fine. That would be a stupid question. Things were far from fine.

"Give me some space," Kate said. Her voice was louder than it needed to be for how close they were standing. It echoed through the corridor. A few kids snickered, casting curious glances. Thankfully, everyone kept moving.

"What?" Becca practically coughed out the word.

"We don't have to spend every single second together, Beck. God." She rolled her eyes dramatically. "Get your own life." Kate turned on her heel and resumed her march toward the front of the school.

Becca blinked back her shock. She took a beat to convince herself that Kate was acting out of fear. She rolled her shoulders back and followed her. "I'm not letting you run off alone," she said to Kate's back. "You need a friend right now whether you like it or not."

They reached the end of the corridor and Becca noticed Frank standing in the exact spot he was always in. She didn't go to him. She made a decision, at that moment, to stay behind Kate. Part of her hoped he would drop into a sort of line behind them, following them toward their houses. But she wouldn't let herself turn around and check.

Kate continued to stomp her feet louder than usual. She wasn't turning around and she wasn't speaking to Becca. Becca chose to take this as a good sign. She wasn't yelling and she was still heading toward their normal route.

They crossed the first street this way: Kate stomping down the route, Becca following behind, and Frank trailing the two of them shaking his head. All three walked faster than normal, keeping pace with Kate's angry stomping.

When Kate crossed the street and drew closer to the red light ahead, she stepped off the sidewalk and crossed her arms. She was the picture of impatience. Becca drew even with her. "Can we talk about this?" Becca asked.

"Look," Kate started, "I'm not trying to be a bitch here." Her voice was a little softer, a little closer to normal. "We're just growing apart. You're totally immature and I'm not." She shrugged her shoulders. "I'm growing up faster than you are and that's OK. Maybe it's just time we stopped relying so much on each other. You can find new friends who are more like you. Then you won't have to listen to me talk about my sex life." Kate's eyes flitted toward Frank, who was drawing closer. "You have plenty of immature friends you can turn to right now, you don't need me."

Becca wasn't sure what hurt worse. Kate's repetition of the "immature" insult, her insinuation that Becca was annoyed with Kate sharing her fears, or the fact that Frank was hearing all this and would likely hurl his "I told you so" bomb right in her direction. There was no hope of stopping the tears this time. Becca felt them rolling down her cheeks. "Are you serious right now?" she managed to ask.

"Becca, stop crying." Kate laid a hand on her shoulder. "It's only proving my point anyway."

Becca recoiled from the comment.

Kate dropped her hand. "That came out wrong. I'm just saying, I've sort of outgrown crying over things people say. They're just words." She waved her hand between them. "Whatever. I'm not trying to upset you. I'm sorry you're upset." She smiled. "I'm not going to always call you and check in with you, you're not my Mom. Stop freaking out if you don't hear from me or whatever."

"I wasn't trying to—"

"You try too hard," Kate snapped, interrupting. "You call me all the time, you wait for me outside classes, you want me to sit with you at lunch, you talk about my personal business to other people." She stopped her list with a shake of her head. "It's like you think you're my boyfriend and you can't handle that I have someone else right now."

Becca took an actual step back as if she had been pushed by the words. "I wasn't... " she trailed off, not sure what to say in defense of herself. She had done every single one of those things. She just didn't think they were a problem until that exact second. Having them all listed together made her sound desperate and needy. "I'm sorry," she whispered.

"Don't be sorry," Kate said. "Just give me some space." As if that was the answer to everything, Kate resumed her walking. Becca let her go.

Frank, who had been close enough to hear the entire exchange, didn't say a word. He stood next to Becca, watching her and waiting for some clue as to what he should do. Becca held up her hand. "Don't you dare say anything," she warned. "I don't want to hear you attack her right now and I don't want to hear you say you told me this would happen." She sniffed and wiped her tears on her forearms.

"I wasn't going to say anything. Do you want to keep walking?" He tipped his head toward the route. Kate was already across the street and the light had turned red again, meaning they would be a good distance behind her.

Becca nodded and followed the path in silence. Frank let her set the pace. He also let her choose whether they talked or not. Becca chose silence for most of the route. It wasn't until they were halfway down her street that she took a deep breath and spoke on the end of her sigh. "She's not wrong you know."

"How do you figure?"

"I do all those things she said I do. I expect her to call me and check in like I'm her mother."

"You're not trying to be her mother, Becca. You're trying to be her friend and she's clearly pushing you away."

Becca shook her head. "When was the last time I expected you to call me?" she asked.

Frank shrugged. "It's not the same."

"Which is kind of her point. Actually, it was your point at lunch today too. I just didn't want to see it. You said I was obsessed." Becca ran her hand down her face. "I don't know, maybe I am."

They reached the point of the street where they would normally split apart. "You gonna be alright?" Frank asked.

Becca nodded. "Yup. I'm not going to call her. I'm going to give her space. I'm going to go home and over-analyze every wrong thing I've ever done. Then I'm going to try and lose myself in a mountain of homework. Then I'm going to eat a bunch of chocolate while I think about how immature I am." She sighed. "I'll be fine."

She turned and walked off into her house. She let the dogs in and got them their treats, grabbed herself a box of chocolate graham crackers, and sat down at the table with her homework stack. She cracked open the math book and opened the box of crackers. The phone rang. She turned and looked at it. For a beat, she considered ignoring it. It was probably just Scott. At the moment, she didn't want to rehash the whole Kate saga. But, then again, it could be Kate. Maybe she was calling to apologize.

Becca crossed the room and snatched the phone before it could finish ringing and trigger the answering machine. "Hello."

"There's no formula for friendship, you know." It was Frank. Frank almost never called her.

"What?"

"Friendship is messy, it's not one-size-fits-all. You may not expect me to call you but I recognize when you need me to and I do it."

"Is that why you're calling me? Because I needed to hear from you?"

"Today? Yes. Just like you'd call me if I needed it. I don't have all the answers, Becca. I don't know what Kate needs right now. You might be right, she might need you. It just doesn't seem like she ever worries about what you need. That's all I was trying to say at lunch. There's nothing wrong with caring about your friends the way you do. I just wish it was balanced. That's all."

Becca didn't know what to say so they sat in silence for a beat. "Hey, how was the weekend with your Dad? I know you were worried, did it go alright?" Becca mentally berated herself for the stupidity of the question. How do you just come out and ask something like that? There had to be a better way to broach this subject. Maybe he didn't want to talk about it. Maybe —

"It was fine." Frank didn't sound upset.

"Yeah? What did you guys do?"

Frank sighed. "Nothing, really. Just sat around. We talked a little but nothing big. It was pretty boring, just like the last time I saw him. He never knows what to say to me."

Becca pushed her lips together to keep herself from admitting she didn't know what to say to that. It wouldn't help anything for her to admit that right now.

"Whatever," Frank said. "At least he showed up and made an effort I guess."

"I guess," Becca agreed. "Thanks for calling, seriously. I think I needed that."

"You're welcome. Talk to you later."

Becca heard the click of his line hanging up. She copied the movement, putting the receiver back down on her end. Balance. That was an interesting concept. One, she decided, she'd need to think about a little more.

Chapter 39

After dinner that night, Becca convinced her Dad to let her walk to the grocery store. It wasn't difficult. Her Dad had a weakness for chocolate ice cream. Becca simply waited for the right moment to drop the hint about the sweet treat. Then she offered to grab some from the store. It wasn't too hot, and the store was nearby, so the ice cream would survive the trip. He pretended to think about it for a while, but eventually relented. Becca made sure her own cash was safely folded into her pocket even as she accepted extra from her Dad for the ice cream. Her plan was to grab that pregnancy test for Kate. Even if they weren't speaking, she could help her friend get the answers.

At the store, she grabbed the ice cream first. Then she headed for the aisle with the pregnancy tests, scanning for anyone she knew, just in case. Just before she turned down the aisle, she spotted Frank's mom pushing her cart toward her. Becca stopped and waved.

"Becca, sweetie, I haven't seen you much lately. How are you?"

"I'm good. We've been busy with school and stuff. Sorry I haven't been by. How are you? How's work?"

"Work is good. Thanks for asking." Frank's mother had this way of smiling that made her look years younger. Her eyes got brighter and for a second you could almost imagine she wasn't old enough to have a teenager. "I'm actually glad I caught you. I just wanted to thank you for always being there for Frank. I am so glad he has a friend to lean on when things get a little too real for him. It's not at all fair what his father puts him through and he's getting too old to want to talk to me about it." She shook her head. "Anyway, I'm not bad mouthing him or whatever. I'm just really glad Frank has someone." She laid her hand on Becca's shoulder and smiled again. "So thank you."

"Right, yeah, of course." Becca narrowed her eyes a little in confusion. "But his Dad, things are ..." she trailed off, hoping Frank's mother would fill in whatever gap she was talking about. Becca tried to remember what Frank had said about his father. He's not in the picture but he came for a weekend. Frank said it was fine. He said it was boring.

"Things are the same as they always are, even when I wish they were different. Checks that bounce or show up late, phone calls that are snippy or argumentative, and then not showing up when you're supposed to."

Not showing up? Becca's chest felt the weight of that one. "He didn't show up last weekend?" she asked, already dreading the answer.

"He sure did not and now he's not answering the phone at his place. So I can only hope that everything is all right with him." Mrs. Armstrong shook her head and rolled her shoulders back. "But we'll get through it. We always do. I'm just glad Frank has you to vent about these things to. Thank you, sweetie." She started moving her cart again, clearly eager to get on with her shopping, or get away from this conversation. "Come by and visit us."

"Yeah, I will," Becca promised. "Bye."

She wanted to stop right there in the aisle and drop to the ground. Frank had lied. He said his dad showed up—didn't he even joke that it was the *least* he could do? That line echoed now with hollow pain. Oh God. Becca felt like she could cry just thinking about that. Frank must be so hurt. He knew it was the *least* his father could do and his father couldn't even be bothered to do that. She had to check on Frank.

Becca paid for the ice cream and rushed out of the grocery store. She speed-walked all the way home, dropped the ice cream with her Dad, and grabbed the phone. She dialed Frank's number but there was no answer. She groaned. Why didn't he have an answering machine?

"Come have some of this," her Dad hollered, holding out the tub of ice cream.

"Yeah, I will. I'm trying to call Frank. He has a homework assignment I need to help him on," she said. She tries again. Still no answer. She could just go to his house, except he probably wouldn't be home. She tried again. This time, Mrs. Armstrong answered. "Hi, it's Becca. I was just remembering something I wanted to ask Frank. Is he home?"

"Sorry, he's not. He had some band thing today. Wait, aren't you in the band? He's not lying to me, is he?"

"No, of course not," Becca answered. Actually, she had no idea. "He's not in my squad." True. "So he might have something today." False. Well, unlikely at least. As far as Becca knew, there was nothing scheduled today for anyone. But she was not telling Frank's mother that until she knew what was going on. It was possible Frank was meeting with his band friends just to hang out. Technically, that qualified as a band thing but it's not one that would be on the schedule. "Tell him to just call me after, OK?" Becca asked. "Please."

"Yeah, of course."

"Thanks. Bye." Becca held down the hang up button and then reached for her address book. This was a phone number she didn't have memorized. She flipped through the book until she found Brandon's name and dialed the seven digits.

"Hello?"

"Hi, I'm looking for Brandon. This is Becca from school. Is

he home?"

There was a rustling on the other end. Then a voice. "Hello?"

"Brandon?"

"Yeah, who's this?" He sounded guarded. Whoever that was who answered the phone didn't bother to tell Brandon anymore than they told Becca about what they were doing with this phone exchange. "It's Becca, from school."

"Right. Hey, how are you? What's up?" Instantly, he sounded more relaxed.

"I'm actually looking for Frank. Do you know if he's got some band thing today or something?" she asked. "I know it's weird that I don't know and it's not an emergency. I'm just curious."

Brandon sighed. "Um, I have no idea. There wasn't anything on the schedule and I don't remember any of the other brass saying anything about getting together. But it's possible. Why, what's up?"

"I just ran into his mom and she said he was at a band thing. I think I accidentally made her suspicious because I didn't know what band thing. I just wanted to give him a heads up that he might get a lot of questions when he does get home," Becca explained. "Sorry, it's not your problem. I'll figure it out."

"Becca, wait. Don't hang up. I'll ask my brother."

"Why would —" Becca stopped talking. There was a rustling on the other end making her think Brandon wasn't listening anyway. There was no point in finishing her question yet. She heard muffled talking. She strained her ears, trying to listen. She got nothing. Then the rustling started again.

"Becca, you there?"

"I'm here. Why would your brother know anything?" she asked.

"Oh, he graduated last year. Played the trombone too. He had the number for the squad leader. You want to call or you want me to?"

Becca thought it was sweet he would offer to call for her but this wasn't Brandon's problem. "I'll call," she said. She wrote the number down and disconnected the call. Again, she didn't bother to hang up, just pushed the button and then dialed the new number.

"Hello." A voice she did not recognize answered the phone. She could recall what Frank's squad leader looks like but she could not think of his voice. Actually, she realized, it's possible she'd never heard him speak before.

She swallowed her nerves. "Hi. My name is Becca. I'm a freshman in the band and I'm looking for my friend, Frank. He's also a freshman. He plays the trombone." Her sentences were all clipped and awkward. She wished he'd break in and save her from continuing. "Have you, maybe, seen him or scheduled something?"

There was a laugh from the other end of the phone, a small one. The kind Becca associated with being made fun of. Definitely a laughing-at-her sort of chuckle. It made her blush. "Hey, kid, I didn't schedule a thing. But my son is here with some other guys from the band. Let me see if any of them is who you're looking for."

The blush deepens. This, Becca thought, was why her mother was always trying to get her to use proper phone etiquette. If she had led with asking for the squad leader she would've already known this was his father. Stupid mistake.

"Is there a Frank in here?" the man bellowed.

There was a lot of shuffling before Becca heard a voice that made her smile. "Hello?" Frank's voice rang with confusion.

"Hey, it's Becca. I just wanted to give you a heads up that I called your house and your mother asked about a band thing and I think I made her suspicious." Now that she had him on the phone, her words tumbled out like a flood. "I didn't mean to make her suspicious. I didn't know you were at a band thing and then she realized that I'm in band but I'm not at a band thing so she asked if I thought you were lying to her. Obviously you're not and I stood up for you but I wanted you to know that she might question you." She heard Frank trying to say something but she felt like she just couldn't stop. "Also she told me the truth about your Dad's visit and

I'm so sorry I wasn't the person you thought you could tell. I don't really want to get into that right now because I know you're with the guys from the band and you probably don't want to talk about it but that's why I was calling your house to talk to you and obviously you're not there. Anyway, I just wanted to warn you about your Mom being suspicious and to tell you to call me later because we have other stuff to talk about." Becca finally stopped talking and took a deep breath.

Frank took this as his chance to jump in. "That was a lot of information," he said. His voice was barely a whisper. "I'm going to leave here in a minute and I'll head to your house. Be there in fifteen or so."

He didn't wait for agreement. Becca just heard the silence that comes from being hung up on. She finally replaced the receiver in the cradle and sat back. Suddenly she felt stupid for calling all these people just to pull Frank from his life. He was with friends. Maybe even friends he feels comfortable confiding in. Maybe those guys all knew about his Dad not showing up last weekend. Maybe her and Frank were growing apart. Maybe he was tired of the kid sister hanging around all the time expecting to be in on everything. It made sense.

She got up off the floor and headed to the kitchen. She had fifteen minutes until she had to say all of this to Frank and let him off the hook for being friends with her. She had time to open her ice cream and eat quite a bit of it. She wondered where her Dad had gotten off too but didn't feel like answering the questions that would come with finding him.

From the table she heard a knock at the front door. She heard her Dad call out "Come in." She heard the front door open ad Frank greet her parents.

"I'm in the kitchen," Becca called.

Frank appeared in the doorway. "Hey," he said.

"Hi. Want some ice cream? Grab a spoon."

"Yeah, alright." Frank made his way across the kitchen and

opened the right drawer on the first try. He'd only been here a few times but his memory was practically perfect. He dropped down into the seat beside Becca. "So, about what you said on the phone," he started. "I did lie to you about my Dad."

"I know. I ran into your Mom at the grocery store and she told me. I'm sorry I wasn't there for you."

"What?" Frank dug his spoon into the ice cream, freeing a large chunk.

"When your Dad didn't show up. I'm sorry I wasn't there."

Frank brought the ice cream to his mouth and swallowed before saying anything. "You would've been, if I told you."

"Why didn't you tell me?" Becca asked, keeping her eyes focused on the table.

"I think I wanted to pretend it didn't happen that way. I wanted to pretend it happened the way I told you."

Becca's eyes snapped up to Frank's face. "That's really sad, actually."

"I know. I don't want to be your sad friend, Beck. I don't like being that. I don't need people to feel sorry for me. That's why I didn't tell you."

"I don't feel sorry for you." The words flew out too fast. Maybe she did, a little—but mostly, she was furious. At his dad. At herself. At all of it. "I think it's stupid that he didn't show up. He's a jerk."

A single chuckle escaped out of Frank. "Yeah, he is. But I'm really sorry I didn't tell you the truth. It put you in a bad spot when you ran into my mom and that's not fair."

Becca shook her head. "No, it's fine. I get it." She took a scoop of ice cream, let it melt, and swallowed. Then she dug deep down inside and found the courage to say what needed to come next. "Are we still friends?" She shook her head. "That's not what I mean. Obviously we're friends. What I mean is, am I still someone you want to be friends with? I feel like, with everything going on in my life, I spend too much time relying on you to be there for me.

You always give me advice for dealing with Kate. But now, when something happens in your life…"

Frank cut her off with a wave of his hand. "Stop. Don't do that to yourself. I didn't let you in. This one is on me. Do I think you have a toxic friendship situation with Kate? Absolutely. But don't for one second think that you're like that with me. I would drop your ass so fast if you were."

He winked, letting Becca know it was OK to laugh. "You're my friend, Becks, and I wouldn't have it any other way." He reached for the ice cream container. "But I'm finishing this. I have sorrows to drown."

Becca laughed. "I was full anyway," she said.

Frank threw his head back and laughed.

Chapter 40

After dessert was finished and Frank had gone home, Becca curled up in the chair nearest the front window with a book. "What are you reading?" her father asked.

Becca held up the small paperback with the bright colors. "A crazy fantasy sort of story about shapeshifters."

"Not for school, I take it?"

Becca laughed. "Not for school."

"Is your homework done?"

She nodded, although technically there was a project she could be working on for Science. She had a few days until it was due and fully planned to spend time on it this weekend. Right this second she wanted to lose herself in the fictional world of shapeshifters with way bigger problems than the ones she was dealing with. She spun the recliner so her back was to the television and opened the book. Within ten pages she was completely immersed.

When her father laid his hand on her arm, the warmth radiating through the fabric above her elbow, she jumped. "Sorry, didn't mean to scare you. Kate's here." He took his hand away from her to point toward the front door.

Becca spun her chair, already pushing herself off the cushion. Her eyes fell on Kate, sheepishly staring at the floor. "What are you doing here?" she asked. Her voice was a knife blade of accusation.

Kate flinched. "I deserve that. Can we talk?" Her eyes flitted up to Becca's father, still standing beside Becca's chair. "Alone, maybe?"

Becca was at war with herself. There was a part of her that wanted Kate to hurt. The things Kate had said this afternoon still stung, they were fresh in her mind. But there was another part of her, the part that had been rescued from isolation in this new neighborhood by Kate's outgoing ways. That part of her wanted to help in any way that she could. That part—the part that still felt like she owed Kate for rescuing her once—won again. Just this once more.

Becca crossed the living room and headed toward the hallway that led to the solace of her bedroom. She didn't say a word. If Kate really wanted to talk, she would follow her. Becca opened her door, dropped onto her bed, and turned her eyes to the door. Kate entered, shut the door behind her, and leaned on the wood. "I'm sorry," she said. "I was angry and hurt and I said things I shouldn't have said." There was a hitch in her voice, like she may have been on the edge of tears.

Becca blinked slowly, deliberately not saying a word. She hoped Kate would say more. She was hurt too much by those words to erase them because of one lackluster apology.

Kate sighed. "There's not much I can say, is there?"

Becca shook her head.

"Right. It's not an excuse," she took a step away from the bedroom door, "just an explanation. Ernie has been super weird since we had sex. He's like... different, I guess. He's not talking to me as much and he's sort of distant. I'm not sure what's going on and I'm freaking out."

"How is that my problem?" Becca asked. The truth was she felt bad for Kate. But, as Kate pointed out, this wasn't her business. This was exactly the kind of thing Kate yelled at her for caring about. She wasn't supposed to be feeling the pull to get involved in this drama right now. She was supposed to stay focused on her own life. This wasn't her problem.

"It's not. It's just... " Kate frowned. "I need someone to care."

Becca closed her eyes and clenched her jaw. She took a few calming breaths through her nose and then spoke without opening her eyes. "You told me I needed to stop caring about you and worry about myself." Her eyes popped open. "I have to get my own life, which will be much harder to do if you don't quit asking me to be a part of yours."

Kate nodded. "I deserve that." She took another step closer to the bed where Becca still sat with her arms crossed over her chest. "I was angry. Haven't you ever said something in anger that you regret?"

"Yes, I have. But you didn't just say one little thing and move on. This was big, Kate. You ignored me at lunch and you screamed at me this afternoon. This was not one little thing."

"Can't you just get over it? I need you." Kate took another step. She was only one small step away from being close enough to sit on the bed beside Becca. "Did you get that test for me?"

Becca's eyes widened. "Are you serious right now?"

Kate took the last step and perched on the bed. "It's no big deal. I just wanted you to know that I'm not mad you didn't get it. I don't actually even need it anymore. I... um... got my period this afternoon." She reached for Becca's leg. Becca pulled it away. "Maybe that's why I was so upset, actually. You can't really blame me for what I said while I was hormonal, can you?"

Becca shook her head. "I can and I do."

"Oh my God, Beck." Kate's voice echoed around the room, her anger obvious and shocking. She jumped off the bed, swinging her arms. "So, what?" she yelled. "This is just the end of our friendship?" She ran a hand down her face. "Years of friendship and you just abandon me after one little scare. It's not my fault that my first time having sex with someone was so miserable. Now Ernie's not talking to me and things are weird. I don't have anyone else I can tell about all this stuff and the one person I did tell decides this is a good time to leave me on my own." Kate's voice dropped as if she was talking privately to herself. She spun in slow circles. "I can't believe this is how this ends. I don't have anyone who will stay by my side when I'm trying to figure out what happens with my first real boyfriend. This is the kind of thing you'll remember for your entire life and now I don't have anyone to talk to about it."

"Kate—" Becca shook her head, confused by the rambling.

"What?" Kate stopped her spinning and put her hands on her hips.

"What are you talking about?"

Kate threw her arms up. "I'm talking about you cutting off our friendship and how in the world I'm expected to pull myself together right now when I'm completely alone."

Becca moved to the edge of the bed and let her feet drop to the floor. "I didn't say our friendship was over. You told me to get my own life. That was your decision."

"I changed my mind," Kate said.

"Then give me the space to make up mine."

"So, you don't want to forgive me? How does that play out?" Kate accused, frowning.

"I don't know." Becca stood up, facing down her friend. "I just need time."

Kate bit her lower lip before nodding. "Alright, I can give you that. I'm sorry." Kate turned around and headed back toward the closed bedroom door, moving much faster than she did when she came into the room. "I'll try again tomorrow. Maybe you'll accept my apology then."

"Kate," Becca said. "I'm glad you're not pregnant."

"Me too," Kate said. "Can you imagine me trying to take care of a kid?" She shook her body in an exaggerated shiver. "That would be a disaster."

Chapter 41

The walk to school the next morning was lonely. Becca left before Kate, giving herself enough time to get to the early band rehearsal. Frank never showed up. When Becca was almost at the final crosswalk, she caught a flash of someone up ahead turning into the school that looked like it might be him. Either he left earlier than he knew she would or he walked a different route. Either way, this felt intentional. The loneliness hit hard, a deep hollow that she hadn't felt in a while. Was this what Kate felt last night? Maybe. But that didn't make it all okay. Forgiveness could wait.

Band rehearsal allowed Becca to get her mind off of everything happening with her friends. She was focused on rolling her feet, counting her steps, hitting her marks, and keeping her instrument playing music. As she changed into her school outfit after the demanding practice, she realized her mood was greatly improved. Music, apparently, was something that could lift Becca out of even the darkest cave. She grabbed her backpack, tossed her morning clothes into her locker, and rushed out to class.

In the main center of the campus under the open air, Scott was standing with a group of other students. She considered rushing right by but then he raised a hand and waved at her. Her eyes caught on his blue ones and she realized, as her heart fluttered, that she actually wanted to stop and say hello. He left his group of friends and met her halfway. "Are you OK?" he asked. "I tried to call you last night and your Dad said you were with Kate. I told him not to disturb you but I was a little worried."

"Yeah, it's fine. She's going through some stuff with Ernie and she just needed my support. I think we'll be fine."

Scott reached out and brushed her upper arm. "But you're doing OK?"

"Me?" Becca shrugged. "I'm fine. Ernie and Kate might not be though. She's really worried."

His eyebrows pulled together. "That's too bad." He reached out and gently slid his hand into hers. "How can I help you? Do you need anything?"

Becca smiled. She liked that Scott was focused on her, not Kate. It felt like he saw her strength, her ability to handle things—but also that he cared enough to ask. It also reminded her of what Frank said about true friends. Scott was asking how he could support her because she was the person he cared about in all this. It made her feel warm and accepted. "Honestly, I'm fine. I think I'm going to need to try giving a little space to Kate. We spend too much time together and we need some boundaries, I think."

"Walk to you to class?" Scott asked, bumping her shoulder with his own.

"That would be great."

Together, they walked toward Becca's first period. She let the first few steps pass in silence. Then she let her mind wander to the idea of labels, of Ernie abusing the fact that Kate was his girlfriend. She thought about how Ernie had pushed Kate to use his language in his way and had taken that as a way to push her to do things she may now regret. "Do you think we have a different relationship now that we're officially boyfriend and girlfriend?" she asked.

At first, Scott didn't react. Becca started to wonder if he had heard her. Had she kept the question in her head instead of speaking it out loud? She considered asking it again. Then Scott drew a slow breath in through his nose. "Not really. But I think that's because what we had before was so special. I like talking to you. I don't think I've ever spent as much time on the phone as I have since I met you." He laughed lightly. "But the boyfriend-girlfriend thing is just a label. If it bothers you... " He let his voice sort of trail off like the idea wasn't something he wanted to give words to.

"No, I'm not saying it bothers me. I guess I just wondered if there was something wrong with what we had before."

"You mean the friendship?"

Becca nodded. That is exactly what she meant. The friendship that let her be on the phone with him all the time without the expectations. Was that so wrong? Why did she have to push herself to do things she wasn't comfortable doing? Was she uncomfortable with Scott... or just afraid of where things might lead? He hadn't pushed. Not really. But the fear was still there. The fear, she supposed, was that he would want more.

They arrived outside her first period and pulled to a stop. Scott moved so he was face-to-face with Becca. "Hey, seriously, we're still friends and we still have a good relationship. I have no problem with what we were before. But I also like being able to hold hands with you like this and tell people you're my girlfriend. What you want matters. Talk to me."

"I think seeing what happened with Ernie and Kate just... shook me," she said. "It's not about you, really. I just need to figure out what I want." Scott's eyes dropped to the ground in what she assumed was sadness. "I'm sorry if that's upsetting."

"No, it's fine. Just promise that you'll think about it and let me know what you decide."

She smiled. "I promise."

"Alright. I need to get to class." Scott squeezed her hand, which he was still holding between them. "I'll talk to you later."

She watched Scott disappear down the hall. For the first time, she realized no one could answer this for her. And that was terrifying.

Chapter 42

Becca decided there was no way she was letting Frank ignore her this afternoon. He'd been absent from lunch, which was fine because it gave her a chance to sit with Scott. They'd laughed, eaten, and pointedly refused to talk about the status of their relationship. Or maybe, Becca mused, that last one was just her. She raised her hand three minutes before class was scheduled to end. "I really need to use the restroom," she said.

The teacher turned around and faced the clock. When he looked back at her it was with an exasperated sigh. "You can wait three minutes," he said.

She crossed her legs, bouncing them a little. "It's an emergency." Becca knew this was a long shot. But if she could convince him to let her leave early she could be sure to catch Frank outside his own classroom. She was hoping the teacher's memory extended back far enough for him to remember she had never asked to leave his class for any reason.

Another sigh escaped his lips. "Fine. But this is the one emergency you're getting and don't think I'll forget."

"Thank you." Becca grabbed everything she owned as quickly as she could and dashed out of the door. She was two rows away from Frank's classroom and, judging by how long that interaction took, she had two minutes to get there. She rounded the corner and stepped up to the classroom just as the bell rang.

Frank was not the first person out of the door. A few kids shuffled by, not paying any attention to Becca. She saw him, talking and laughing with someone she didn't know. She could tell the moment he noticed her standing there. His laugh caught in his throat and he tossed a dangerous glare in her direction. "I'll talk to you tomorrow," he said to the girl walking with him. "What's up?" he asked. The words sounded casual, normal. But coupled with his guarded expression, Becca got the impression they actually meant the exact opposite of casual.

"I just wanted to walk home with you and I was afraid you'd try to ditch me again," she explained. She held up her hands. "I could use a friend and I promise it's not for anything Kate-related."

Frank nodded. "Alright, let's start walking." He flashed her one of his classic smiles, the one that always made her think everything in the world was perfect for Frank. Then he started walking. Becca joined him, matching his pace. "So what are we talking about?" he asked.

"Scott." Frank nodded as if he had been expecting exactly that. "But not really. It's more about me, I think. My parents never wanted me to date, which you know. Technically, they don't even know I have a boyfriend."

"You hate lying to your parents," Frank pointed out.

"Right. Plus, what does 'boyfriend' even mean when you're our age?" They hit the crosswalk while the green light was flashing, meaning they never even had to slow their steps. Becca smiled at their luck. "I talk to Scott practically every night on the phone, but I did that when we were just friends. I eat lunch with him, but I eat lunch with you and we're just friends. I guess I'm just looking for guidance from someone I can trust whose opinion matters to me."

Frank nodded and they walked a few more steps in silence. Becca wanted to rush him but she also knew that Frank needed thinking time. It was part of the reason she valued his judgment. He never rushed to decisions. So she continued walking beside him in silence, letting him have his brain moment.

They jogged across the street and then, once they reached the safety of the other side, he finally answered. "It really sounds to me like you've already made up your mind and you're just worried you'll hurt Scott's feelings when you tell him that."

Becca took a moment to consider this. Had she truly already made up her mind?

"Is there a reason why you thought you had to be someone's 'girlfriend'?" Frank asked.

"Isn't that what you're supposed to do?" Becca shrugged. "Movies, books, TV shows... they all make it seem like that is the ultimate end goal. I guess I just thought it would feel different or be different once I could be called that. I thought I'd feel like I reached the summit of the mountain."

"So you're frustrated because the label didn't change anything?"

Becca shrugged. "No, actually. I'm frustrated because I'm not sure if it feels like this to Scott. What if he thinks the label gives him the right to push me to start doing other stuff I'm not comfortable with?" Of course, her mind was on Ernie and Kate. She was still of the opinion that Kate had made a huge mistake by taking her relationship to the next level. She couldn't imagine putting herself through a pregnancy scare and the stress that Kate seemed to be under the last few days. All of that had proven to her she was absolutely not ready to be in a sexual relationship.

"First of all, I don't think Scott is the kind of guy to force anyone to do anything," Frank said. "I feel like that's important to point out."

"Right, I don't either. Not really. But what if he has expectations for what a 'girlfriend' should be doing?" She considered that attempt at a kiss outside class the other day. She felt terrible for how she handled that. Yet, if she was honest, it wasn't something she felt ready for.

"Again, it sounds like you've already made your choice. What are you afraid of? Why can't you just admit you don't want a boyfriend and break up with him?"

Becca pulled on a strand of her hair that had come loose, tugging it back toward the ponytail. It gave her something to do with her hands. "What if he doesn't want to go back to being friends? What if I lose him completely?"

Frank turned toward her and frowned. "That's the risk, kiddo." He bumped her shoulder. "But if staying in this is making you feel wrong, that's a bigger risk."

"Is it just me or does growing up truly suck sometimes?" Becca asked.

Frank laughed and Becca was relieved to hear that it was his real laugh and not the fake one he usually reserved for Kate. She had worried, briefly, that the stress she put their relationship through lately would be the end of their friendship. That laugh signaled that she was wrong about that. She decided she would add it to the list of things she'd been wrong about this year, which was growing exponentially.

When they pulled up near her house, Frank surprised her by leaning on the fence. "Can we talk about that thing we're not supposed to talk about?" he asked, tipping his head toward Kate's house.

"Sure." Becca drew out the word with her hesitancy.

"I overstepped the other day and I need to apologize. I'm not good at that. I was wrong. It's your life and you should be the one to decide how you live it." He held up a finger as if trying to pause an interruption he expected to spew from Becca's mouth. "That includes choosing who to be friends with and how that works for you."

Becca waited until his pause finger dropped back to his side. "Thank you for saying that." She let a smile flit across her face. "But I think maybe you were right, even if I didn't want to see it then. "Kate makes me doubt myself. Like I'm never enough, no matter what I do. I've been doing a lot of thinking and that's not how a friend should make you feel. Regardless of whether I can explain what is wrong with Kate and me, that's the basics." She sighed. "I think I'm going to start giving her more space."

Frank pushed himself off the fence. "As long as you don't blame me for that, we're good."

"I don't blame you." A little laugh bubbled out of her. "I'll talk to you later. I have a phone call I think I need to make."

Chapter 43

After letting the dogs into the house and getting them a snack, Becca went straight for the phone on the wall. She picked up the receiver and then realized she didn't know the number. Usually, Scott called her. She put the receiver back, crossed to her backpack, and took out her paperback. She paged to the bookmark and flipped it over. There, scrawled in Scott's handwriting, was his number. She repeated it to herself a few times before putting the bookmark back and going back to the phone. Her stomach churned as she dialed the number. She wasn't sure what scared her more—that Scott would be upset, or that he'd be perfectly fine.

"Hello," a voice that was not Scott's answered.

"Is Scott there?"

There was a shuffling noise in the background. Becca hoped it was whoever this was moving to hand the phone to Scott. She waited. "Is this the plain girl from school?" The voice asked.

Becca blinked a few times, shocked. "Um... this is Becca. I'm Scott's..." she hesitated to use the label, "... friend."

"Right. What do you want him for?" Again the shuffling noise came through the receiver.

"Is Scott there?" she asked, frustration tinting her voice.

"He's here. Tell me why I should let you talk to him."

Becca pulled the receiver away and glared at it as if it had some hidden information about what was happening in this strange situation. "Who is this?" she asked.

"You called me, plain girl. I don't have to identify myself."

For some reason, the use of the obnoxious, condescending nickname triggered something in her memory this time. "You're his brother, aren't you? Put Scott on."

"Alright, fine. I was just trying to have a little fun with you. Calm down."

Becca exhaled, the tension in her shoulders starting to fade. Then she heard the click telling her he had hung up. "Hello?" she tried. The dial tone was her only answer.

She slammed the receiver down and stared at it, anger seething through her. That was the most frustrating conversation she had ever been a part of. The phone rang and Becca continued to stare at it. She considered letting it ring through to the answering machine. She counted as it rang once, twice, three times. She reached out and grabbed it before it could ring for a fourth time and trigger the answering machine. "Hello," she said, her voice clipped with frustration.

"I am so sorry," Scott said. He sounded it, she noted. "My brother is a jerk. I'm so sorry. He was standing just out of my reach. I knew it was you but he wouldn't give me the phone. Seriously, I'm sorry. Are you alright? Are you mad?" His voice came out all in a rush and Becca felt herself releasing her anger with each pleading apology.

"I'm fine. Is that what it's like to have siblings?" she asked.

Scott chuckled. "I don't know about all siblings. That's what it's like with my jerk of a brother. He's always making my life impossible. He does things just to piss me off."

"Where is he right now?"

"I don't know. I'm in my bedroom and I locked the door. He's running around the house somewhere, probably doing something to get back at me for returning your call." He sighed. "It's fine. He does this kind of stuff all the time. I'm, unfortunately, used to it."

"You're making me glad I'm an only child. I take back any time I've ever wished for a sibling."

Scott laughed. "Thanks for calling, even though it didn't work out the way you wanted."

"Right. I actually called you to talk about that conversation we had earlier. The one about labels."

She could hear rustling in the background and music started up. "Good, yeah. Let's talk about that."

"I just…" She gulped up some courage for the conversation and willed herself to be strong. "I'm not sure that I really want to have the label. I don't think I'm really ready to be someone's girlfriend." She gulped again, this time feeling like she was swallowing a mouth full of regret. "I know I should've said something sooner. But I thought it was what I was supposed to want." Becca forced herself to stop talking. She took a deep breath and held it, listening for noises coming through the phone. She tried to guess what he might be thinking or feeling. She closed her eyes, hoping that would heighten her other senses even more.

"Well…" Scott said, drawing out the word. Becca let out her breath but kept her eyes closed, sure that whatever he was about to utter would hurt. "I've been thinking about it all afternoon." Becca heard a flopping sound and imagined Scott dropping into a comfy chair. "I think you're right."

"You do?" She hadn't expected that. She expected more of a fight, more pushback. She expected him to be hurt or upset.

"Yeah," he continued. "I think we are really good friends. I don't want to jeopardize that by using some label you're not comfortable with. The bottom line is, this doesn't work unless we're both happy with it."

Becca realized she was smiling at the phone but that Scott couldn't see that. "Thank you," she said. "It means a lot that you'd be willing to sacrifice the label you wanted just because I'm not happy with it."

"It's just a word, Becca. It doesn't matter."

That, she realized, was the most mature answer to this question. Really, he'd made this easy and she'd be grateful for that for a long time.

Chapter 44

"I don't get it," Kate said. She planted her hand on her hip and shook her head. "So you broke up?"

Becca had done her best to explain the situation to Ellie this morning while they were standing outside her math class. Kate had sauntered up while they were discussing it and caught most of the conversation. Becca had wanted to shut down the conversation as soon as she'd seen Kate, but it felt rude. So she'd pressed on. Now, seeing the condescending glare she was getting from Kate, she regretted her choice to push on with the explanation.

"It sounds like they're just ditching labels," Ellie explained. "Is that right?"

"Yeah. We are better as friends than we are as a couple, basically," Becca said. "It's not a big deal."

Ellie nodded. "Plus, they're staying friends." She smiled at Becca. "I'm really proud of you for having the guts to talk about it with him, actually."

"I was really worried about it," she sighed. "I'm so glad he was understanding."

Kate put her hand on Becca's shoulder. Becca hoped this was the sign a warm moment was coming. Maybe Kate would tell her she understood, or that she made the right choice, or that she was proud...

"That just proves you made a huge mistake," Kate said softly. "You found the one understanding guy on the whole entire campus who was willing to put your needs first and listen to you when you talked and you broke up with him." She shook her head. "He is never going to take you back. You blew that one."

"Kate, you're not listening," Ellie tried.

Becca pushed Kate's hand off her shoulder. Ellie froze, her eyes wide. Becca was never physical. She never laid a hand on Kate before. Suddenly, this moment felt big. Becca didn't care. She took a step toward Kate and stuck her finger in her former best friend's face. "You are being awful. I have no idea why you feel like you need to be mean to me this morning, but I don't need this. I'm happy with my decision and I'm not going to let you or anyone else make me feel badly about it." Then Becca turned on her heel and walked into her math class, leaving Ellie to decide if it was worth it to comfort a suddenly angry Kate.

At lunch, Becca spotted Kate sitting with a group of friends. Kate waved, wearing the smile that told Becca she was ready to move past the argument this morning. Becca was shocked to find she was the one who didn't want to. She shook her head side to side and made her way to sit with Frank and Scott.

Frank, who was laughing at that exact moment, widened his eyes at Becca. "What was that?" he asked, bobbing his head in Kate's direction.

"Nothing," Becca shrugged. "She sort of crossed a line this morning and I don't think I want to let that go so quickly."

"Fair enough," Frank said. Then, because he was Frank and could be counted on to recognize when things needed to be dropped, he changed the subject. For the rest of lunch they talked about movies, books, music, or anything that wasn't Kate.

Chapter 45

Kate didn't call or try to come over for two weeks. Becca spent a lot of time alone, enjoying things she'd always enjoyed. She also spent time talking to Scott and Frank, playing basketball, and taking walks. She stopped worrying so much about what Kate was up to or what Kate would think if she were watching. She stopped thinking about Kate altogether.

So when Kate showed up at her house two weeks after the argument outside of Math class, Becca was startled to see her. "What are you doing here?" she asked.

"I'm not apologizing," Kate said. "Aren't you going to let me in?"

Becca, instead, stepped outside and pulled the front door shut behind her back. "Let's talk out here," she said. She wasn't how this conversation was going to go. This way they could be way from the ears of her parents, just in case.

"Fine." Kate marched across the yard and dropped into the grass. "I'm not apologizing," she repeated.

Becca crossed her arms over her chest. "I got that. So why are you here?"

"Are we really just throwing away this whole friendship because I think you made a mistake breaking up with the only guy you'll probably get?"

Becca couldn't help it, she laughed out loud. "You don't hear yourself, do you? That was the absolute rudest thing you could have said to me about this topic."

"Oh my God," Kate said, rolling her eyes. "It's not rude. It's accurate."

"Why, exactly, would I want to be friends with someone who thinks that about me? Someone who thinks I'm not worth being around and wants to make sure I know she feels that way?"

"Because I've been here for you since the day you moved in. Frank didn't walk over here and make friends with you that first summer. He didn't make sure everyone treated you nicely when you started at our school. He didn't talk to boys for you to give you a chance to be someone's girlfriend." Kate shook her head. "I did all those things. You'd be no one without me."

Becca couldn't believe the anger coming off Kate right now. She couldn't believe that any past versions of herself had heard this kind of venom and missed it. Kate was angry but that wasn't an excuse for any of the things she was saying right now. Deep down, Becca knew that she probably would've forgiven Kate a year ago. Heck, she probably would've forgiven Kate two months ago.

But right now, she didn't have it in her. Suddenly, Becca couldn't think of a single thing she needed Kate for.

"You know what," she said, "you might be right. I might be nothing without you."

Kate opened her mouth as if she was going to speak. Becca stopped her by getting to the words first. "But I guess we'll find out."

Kate snapped her mouth shut, shock written on her face. "I've had two weeks without you to remember what it's like to not be torn down all the time by the person who is supposed to be my best friend. I think we're done here. Thank you for everything you've done for me and I wish you the best." Before she could change her mind or start to feel guilty, Becca turned and headed back for the front door.

"Are you serious?" Kate called.

Becca kept walking. Her hand reached out and grabbed the doorknob. "OK, fine. I'll apologize for speaking my mind. It hurt you feeling sand I shouldn't have said anything."

"That's your apology?" Becca asked. As apologies went, that was awful.

Kate just shrugged.

"No hard feelings," Becca said. "It was good you showed your true colors."

Even as Kate hopped up off the ground and made her way over to the house, Becca spun the doorknob and crossed the threshold. Before she closed the door, she offered Kate a smile. "I wish you the best, Kate. Really, I do. Bye."

She shut the door and leaned her head on the wood. Behind her, someone cleared their throat. Becca turned to find her mother standing behind her. Mom smiled. "That sounded pretty final. Do you need to talk about it?"

Becca shook her head. But something in her face must have shown how hard this was. Mom opened her arms and Becca ran into them, letting her Mom hug out all the pain and keep her from opening that door again.

This was the right choice and she had to stick to it.

Epilogue

Well, this is it. The last day of my freshman year of high school is over. I've officially survived. Actually, I suppose I did more than just survive. I ended the year with a report card full of A's, which was a relief because Spanish didn't seem to be moving in that direction! I had an actual C in Spanish at midterms, so thank goodness for crash studying before final exams.

I found marching band is a lot of fun and I've met a lot of really great people there. Ellie is one of them. She's so great. I hope I keep being friends with Ellie next year, although I don't think I'll see her much over the summer. My parents work all summer and Ellie doesn't exactly live close by. I can't drive yet and neither can she. So I guess we'll have to wait for school to start up again.

Frank is also in marching band so I see him all the time, too. He's still a great friend of mine. Of course, we don't see each other much outside of school. I know he and Ellie went on a few little dates and they like each other. It'll be fun to see if that keeps up. They're both great people. I just hope they make each other happy if they're going to be together.

As for Kate, we're done. I did a lot of thinking about our friendship this year. As the year wrapped up, I paid more attention to how Kate acted with people. She's openly rude to anyone who she thinks is a waste of her time, usually including me. I've noticed she's really nice to the older students or kids who play a sport or something. I guess Kate just needs her friends to have a high social status and, honestly, that's not a competition I care about entering. She can find herself popular friends. I'm fine with that.

I am worried about this summer if I'm being honest. For as long as I've lived here, Kate and I have kept each other occupied in the summers. She lives right across the street and we can always see each other. We listen to music, watch movies, or bike around the neighborhood. I guess I just haven't figured out whether this will be the first summer where I have to do all those things alone.

There's also Scott, that was interesting this year. He was my first boyfriend. We "dated" for almost one month. Really we missed that marker by two days, but who's counting? That's such a stupid term for it: "dating". We never actually went on any dates. We never really did anything different than we did before we were "dating". Or after, I suppose. We still talk a lot — mostly about school, family, music, math. He's really smart. I like him, sure, but I'm not in a rush to be anyone's girlfriend again.For now, I'm happy with my friends.

So, all in all, it's been an interesting freshman year. I went to my first high school dance, I had my first boyfriend, I got in my first epic fight with a friend, and I learned to walk away from relationships that make me feel uncomfortable whether they are friendships or "dating".

Sometimes I still get nostalgic for what Kate and I had when we were alone. You know? Those moments when she seemed like she needed my advice. The moments where she was friendly, caring, or all those other adjectives you use to describe the person you think of as your best friend. But then I remember the bad moments. The times when she screamed at me, belittled me, or made fun of me. The times when she intentionally hurt me just to make herself seem cool. Then I can stop myself from calling her to apologize for being so aloof. Aloof is good for me right now. Aloof is what I need to be.

Anyway, that's my life as it stands right now. Can you believe I'm going to be a sophomore next year? Maybe that will be the year when I understand why everyone cares about being someone's girlfriend. Maybe it'll be the year when I make a new best friend.

I might not know who I'm becoming yet — but I know who I'm not.

And that's a pretty good start.
        Whatever happens, I'll be ready!

Closing

I said in the beginning that this was a work of fiction and that's still true. But, like so many of you, I had a toxic friend like Kate in my life. If you have one, don't let them become your inner voice. Find who you are. Be true to yourself.

I'm rooting for you.

All my love,
Tabatha

About the Author

Tabatha Shipley is an author, avid reader, and book addict from Arizona. She has an amazing husband and two remarkable children who are growing up entirely too quickly in this wild world. She can often be found on social media raving about whatever book she is most recently obsessed with. Find her to join in on the obsession and add to her TBR with your favorite titles.

For more information visit https://tabathashipleybooks.com/